_rielle Mullarkey was born in Oxford of Irish _rents. Before starting her writing career she worked _sub-editor on various women's weeklies, including _ _, *Take a Break* and *Chat*. She has published short _stories in *Woman's Realm*, *Woman's Own* and *That's Life*, and her first novel *Hush, Hush* was published by TownHouse in Ireland.

A TALE OF TWO SISTERS

GABRIELLE MULLARKEY

POCKET BOOKS

TOWNHOUSE

First published in Great Britain and Ireland by Pocket/TownHouse, 2001
An imprint of Simon & Schuster UK Ltd, and TownHouse and
CountryHouse Ltd, Dublin

Simon & Schuster UK is a Viacom company

1 3 5 7 9 10 8 6 4 2

Simon & Schuster UK Ltd
Africa House
64-78 Kingsway
London WC2B 6AH

www.simonsays.co.uk

Simon & Schuster Australia
Sydney

TownHouse and CountryHouse Ltd
Trinity House, Charleston Road
Ranelagh, Dublin 6, Ireland

A CIP catalogue record for this book is available from the British Library

ISBN 1-903650-03-8

Typeset by SX Composing DTP, Rayleigh, Essex
Printed and bound in Great Britain by
Omnia Books Ltd. Glasgow

For Jim

Chapter One

At twenty-eight and a bit, Katie Gibson chucked in her job and went to university. She'd worked in the same London health-food shop since doing A-levels. For this next phase of her life, she chose a small university in rural Sussex. She'd always wanted to study history, but it took a catalyst to spur her into action.

The catalyst was a shattered relationship. She went to university not only to learn but also to lie low and lick her wounds, reasonably confident that she wouldn't fancy eighteen- to twenty-one-year-old men.

For the first two terms, she knocked around with another mature student, Virginie. Virginie was a French schoolteacher, doing a bilingual MA. She was scornful of everything she found on campus – the library, the lecturers, the stale scones in the caff. But most of all she was scornful of a mature student called Jack Gold.

Everyone knew Jack Gold by sight. Most days, he wore a suit to the library or his lectures, just as if he were going to the bank where he'd once worked. Virginie had all the lowdown on her fellow-students. Apparently, at twenty-eight, Jack Gold had thrown up the bank to take a degree in accountancy. How totally, incredibly boring, pointed out Virginie scornfully.

Katie gave half an ear to Virginie's scorn while feasting on Jack Gold from afar. She loved his heart-shaped face, his dark-blond hair rising from his forehead in a peak, his aquiline nose and Nordic blue eyes. He looked a lot like Ralph Fiennes. The merest glimpse of him in the bar, caff or refectory was enough to provoke Virginie's scorn and Katie's blatant stares. 'Here we are,' Virginie would declare, 'two intelligent late-twenty-something women who've knocked around a bit and have something to say for ourselves, but men our own age, the Jack Golds of this world, would rather run around with silly, giggling teenagers.'

Katie would nod in violent agreement. Jack Gold was often seen in the company of blonde, fresh-faced undergraduates. But she found herself making excuses for him. He was entitled to enjoy the company of blithe spirits; girls (women?) not yet jaundiced by the 'life's a bitch' axiom. Plus, it would take a brave man, whatever his age, to approach Virginie and risk her withering scorn.

At the start of her second year, Katie went along to the mature-student buffet evening in the refectory. She hadn't attended the previous year's, but she was at a loose end. Virginie had long since returned to France.

Katie knew most attendees of the buffet, so she

circulated politely, then took a loaded plate and glass of wine, and sat in a corner, people-watching.

Somehow, she didn't see Jack Gold approach. She'd never expected him to be at the buffet. 'Oh my God,' she gasped, choking on cheap wine as he materialised in front of her, suit-clad, as ever.

He stared down at her. 'It's you,' he said abruptly.

'Looks like it,' she laughed shakily.

'I'm Jack.'

'I kn—. I mean, I'm Katie!' Juggling a wine glass and half-eaten onion tartlet, she turned the simple act of shaking hands into a complicated Masonic ritual.

They stared off in opposite directions for a bit. 'Well,' said Jack Gold at length. 'Nice to meet you. I'll see you around.'

'Expect so,' she cringed, as he sidled away. That was obviously his attempt at polite circulation, and she'd blown it.

By the time she found the courage to scan the room, there was no sign of him. Maybe he'd just popped in and found it as boring as he'd anticipated. Katie drained her wine, finished her tartlet, and prepared to depart. Suddenly, she wanted to be alone. She wanted to analyse her crass handling of the one chance she'd had to impress a bloke she more than quite fancied.

As she went to get her coat from the pile stacked on a chair, he swooped back to her side. 'May I walk you back to your digs?' he asked.

'Um, God!' she twittered. 'I live in halls, so it's just a quick trot across campus.'

'Even so, it's not well-lit, is it? I assure you,' he added formally, 'you're perfectly safe with me.

Anyway, everyone will see us leave together so I'd be prime suspect if anything befell you.'

'Well, thank you.' It was one of those terrifying yet exciting situations not felt since her break-up with Stephen. She had nothing interesting to say to Jack, but she was already toying with asking him in for coffee. Would he interpret that as a come-on? Had he picked her as an easy conquest because she wasn't as good-looking or bubbly as the younger students?

Trying to conquer her nerves preoccupied her on the short walk back to the hall. By the time they arrived, she and Jack hadn't exchanged a single word.

'Er, coffee?' she offered aggressively, afraid of sounding coy.

'Love some, thanks.'

Her tiny room was a mess. She was in the middle of an essay. She went to the sink to rinse mugs while Jack moved about behind her, looking at things. What things? she wondered uneasily. Her standard Monet poster? Her dog-eared textbooks?

'You don't have any family photos on display,' he said, joining her at the sink.

'Well, no. It's just . . . I don't feel the need. We're not mushy about each other.'

'Know what you mean. I can get just about get on with my dad as long as we don't expect too much of each other.'

'And your mum?'

'She died when I was sixteen. Cancer.'

'Sorry.'

Jack folded his arms. 'Brothers and sisters?'

Her heart curled into a ball. 'One of each. You?'

'Only child. Lucky old me.'

'Yes, you are.' She took a deep breath. 'When I think of my family, I always see my sister at the centre. And I just don't get on with her, never have done.'

'Why?'

She laughed nervously. 'Well, it's complicated. You'd need siblings to understand.' He looked sulky and crestfallen, so she added hastily, 'No, no, I didn't mean to sound patronising. Thing is, my sister and I never got on, growing up. Then she went and stole my last boyfriend off me, and that was the end of even pretending to get on as far as I was concerned.'

The words hung in the air as the kettle boiled. She rushed to switch it off, hardly able to believe what she'd just said – blurted out! – to a stranger – a man!

Her mum knew the Steve Sheridan saga, as did her younger brother, Simon. But the only person Katie had ever discussed it with in depth was her oldest friend, Nikki. Now she'd gone and blurted it to the best-looking bloke on campus. Jack Gold would think she was neurotic, paranoid – and not up to much as a girlfriend, if she couldn't hang on to a boyfriend in the bosom of her own family.

Jack cleared his throat. 'I see Monet is the poster of choice this year,' he observed.

His clumsy tactfulness only made things worse. Katie felt an overwhelming need to explain. 'Look, it's no big deal any more. I was going out with this bloke for about a year, before I came here. I always found family life a bit stifling, so I left home at eighteen and got a flat that came with my job. I did pop back to my mum's for weekend visits, and one Sunday I brought my boyfriend Steve for lunch. He wanted to come and I thought, why not? I'd kept him under wraps, but I suppose I was kind of flattered he wanted to meet the family.' She paused, building up to the next bit. 'My kid sister happened to be there for Sunday lunch, too. I knew she would be, but I never thought . . .' She stared at the kettle. 'Anyway, fireworks exploded the minute she and Steve clapped eyes on each another. The upshot was, he rang me the following week to say they were an item.' She puffed out her cheeks and spooned coffee into mugs.

'Who do you blame, him or your sister?'

'I like to apportion blame equally,' she replied through gritted teeth. 'I'm an equal opportunities blamer.'

Jack looked solemn. 'It was one of those things.'

'Says who? Bottom line – you don't steal your sister's boyfriend.'

'But he wanted to be stolen.'

'Now you're making fun of me,' she said angrily and, to her horror and surprise, she burst into tears.

Jack stood rooted to the spot, presumably by shock. Katie mopped up her tears with a tea-towel. 'Sorry,' she mumbled.

'Don't be. I put my size twelves in it, as usual. I should go.'

'I'm cross with myself, not you,' she sniffed, half to herself. 'I thought I'd got over this blubbing stage. So much for moving on. And just for the record, it wasn't a case of them being meant for each other, 'cos she chucked him two weeks after they got together. Once she'd wrested him off me, she lost interest in him. She'd made her point. Flick wants, so Flick takes, just to prove she can.'

'To get one over you?'

'God, yes. She doesn't really want anything I have, she just can't bear to see me have it. When we were kids, she'd wait and see what ice lolly I got out of the chiller cabinet. If it was the last one of its kind, she'd develop an overwhelming urge to have it instead.'

'Aren't all kids like that?'

'I suppose they are.' It wasn't, she realised, a good analogy. It didn't give him a proper insight into her sister.

'Did you have it out with her about Steve?'

'No. I just ignore her when our paths have to cross. I always thought throwing a strop would play into her hands, give her too much satisfaction. Anyway, it's demeaning, handbags at ten paces over a man who isn't worth it.'

'Maybe I'm better off as an "only",' said Jack.

Katie smiled wanly. He was no help or comfort at all, just an embarrassed witness to her humiliation. She wondered if she should demean herself still further, and beg him to keep a lid on her juicy tale of family betrayal.

'So,' he said, hugging his elbows as he leant against the sink. 'Do you go home much at weekends now?'

'About twice a term. When I've overdosed on crap food and need a nutritional boost.'

'What about inviting me some time?'

She stared at him. 'You serious?'

'Yeah, why not? Unless you're scared of encountering the creature from the black lagoon.'

She knew he meant Flick. 'She's got her own flat in London, Hampstead no less. She pops over to Mum in Balham, but I always manage to arrange my visits around hers.'

7

'What does your mum think of that? Sisters at war.'

'She knows the score,' replied Katie, suddenly feeling hard. And powerful. She looked at Jack. His handsome face was deadpan. He was still standing there awkwardly with his arms folded. She was warming to the idea of taking him home for lunch, turning up at 23 Alderney Road with a gorgeous man in tow. It'd be good for her self-esteem. And he'd *asked* to come. Wasn't it a sort of date?

She was due to ring her mum anyway. She'd find out if the coming Sunday was a Flick-free zone. Even then, she couldn't trust Flick not to turn up, once *she* rang Mum and discovered Katie was bringing a male guest to lunch. The curiosity might kill her.

It was best not to analyse it. It was better to speak now, before the silence got any longer and Jack made his excuses to leave without drinking coffee.

'You could come this weekend,' she said, blotting the last of her tears on the tea-towel. 'Once I've checked Mum has nothing else planned.'

He smiled at her. 'If you like, we could just let on we know each other vaguely as mature students. Leave it open-ended what we are to each other. Say you felt sorry for me living in digs and I pestered you for an invite at the buffet tonight. You can play up my lack of family to explain my pushy request for a free lunch.'

'Open-ended. Right.'

'Then you won't get the third degree from your mum about "whatever happened to that sex god you brought home for lunch?"'

'Sex god. OK.' She was so busy planning Sunday in her head that she wasn't paying close attention.

'When you've phoned your mum, give me a ring at my digs,' he said. 'If I don't answer, someone will shout up the stairs to get me, or take a message.'

'OK,' she said, feeling breathless and reckless. 'God, I haven't made you coffee yet. Milk and sugar?'

'It's all right. I've got to catch the last bus. They don't run late past my place. If you've got a scrap of paper, I'll write down my address and phone number.'

To her disappointment, she didn't see Jack again until their rendezvous at the railway station for the trip to London.

She had phoned her mum, Tess, and manipulated her cleverly into revealing that this Sunday she was all on her tod. Katie had then offered her services as a lunch companion, adding casually that she might bring 'another starving student who's on the scrounge. He doesn't eat red meat'. She was pleased with the casual deployment of 'he' in the sentence. Now Tess knew what to expect, but also knew Katie well enough to realise that she didn't bring boyfriends home for lunch.

Not any more.

After that, Katie had phoned Jack's digs to confirm the arrangement, but been forced to leave a message with a surly housemate. She'd decided that if she didn't see him at the station, as directed in her phone message, she'd go to Balham without him.

She hadn't seen him around college since the night of the buffet. She'd been stuck in the library, trying frantically to finish her essay. She assumed he was busy, too. In fact, she wondered if the arrangement had been a figment of her imagination, until she saw

Jack standing on the station platform that Sunday afternoon. She was feeling pretty nervous by then, suffering gymnastics of the colon that came perilously close to what her friend Nikki called 'liquid bum syndrome'. Wouldn't that be just great, sitting opposite Jack all the way to London with clenched buttocks and a gurgling tum?

He was wearing another immaculate suit and carrying a bunch of yellow roses. 'For your mum,' he explained straight off, in case she got the wrong end of the stick. 'Mothers expect flowers, don't they?'

'You tell me,' replied Katie suspiciously, as he held the train door open for her. 'How many invitations to Sunday lunch have you wangled? Not just here, but when you worked at the bank?'

'Who told you I worked in a bank?' he asked, on guard.

Blushing, she told him about Virginie's hot gossip link.

'Good old Jackboot Ginny. Never knew why you hung around with her.'

'She wasn't that bad. Why are men so scared of forceful women?'

Settling into her seat, she realised two things. He hadn't provided the merest sliver of info on his own lovelife, past or present. And he must have *noticed* her hanging around with Virginie.

The train journey passed in silence, Katie reading a course book and Jack doing a broadsheet crossword. The silence wasn't cosy. Katie reckoned he must be entertaining second and third thoughts, like her.

As the train slid towards London, she began to panic. She and Jack knew so little about each other.

Why was she bringing a complete stranger to lunch? She still didn't know how she'd react if Flick turned up, assuming Tess had volunteered the news about Jack during their weekly phone chat.

When Katie brought Steve to lunch, Flick had been a long-standing invitee. She hadn't put in a special appearance just to check him out – just to see if Katie cared enough about him to make him worth taking.

Steve Sheridan. Katie would've walked through hellfire for him. He was her first proper boyfriend, unless you counted (and she didn't) Roger Livesey when she was twenty. Twenty! A disgraceful age to acquire your first boyfriend, even one as duff as Roger.

She'd been a late starter, shyness compounded by low self-esteem as she grew up comparing herself to Flick. Between Roger and Steve there was Dave, a plasterer, who thought daily washing was for 'poofters' but saw nothing wooftery in concealing his manly sweat with bucketloads of cheap aftershave. And Tony, the wholesale nut-seller opposite the health shop, who was kind but vague, uncommitted and frankly (though Katie hated to be shallow), pig-ugly.

Steve Sheridan had been *the one* – the walking, talking, twinkly-eyed proof that Katie could pull a more-than-half-decent bloke and achieve this feat without the aid of careful lighting, an illusion created by alcohol or the supplementary attraction of a rich daddy.

All through their teens, Flick had collected boys the way Tess collected milk-bottle tops for *Blue Peter* appeals. And just like the bottle tops, Flick's boy-

11

friends increased in number but ended up discarded, one languidly handsome dark youth indistinguishable from another. Flick usually went for the dark look to complement her own dark beauty. She made an exception for Steve. Steve Sheridan was the blond, blue-eyed antithesis to Flick's surfeit of darkly brooding admirers. She must have been experimenting with accessories when she nicked Steve Sheridan to hang off her arm.

'Why do you wear suits around campus?' Katie asked abruptly, desperate to think about something else.

'Because I bought them for working at the bank. No point stewing them in mothballs for three years. I've only got three,' he added defensively.

'OK,' she muttered, thoughts drifting back to Flick.

It was a muggy May day, the first bees circulating drowsily. Tess welcomed them briskly, announcing she'd serve a ham salad on the patio overlooking the back garden of her end-of-terrace house. She took Jack by the hand and looked him up and down, head cocked to one side. 'You remind me of my father,' she said. 'He was a handsome, strapping chap, too. I hope you've an appetite to match.'

Katie saw Jack relax. Her mother was the perfect hostess, interested but never nosy, attentive but not overwhelming. She wasn't very different as a mother. She didn't get involved or take sides. Which sounded like a dream, until you were in desperate need of mother-comfort.

'So you two have known each other how long?' smiled Tess, pouring wine.

Jack looked at Katie. 'It must be five months, is it

now, Katie?' he asked lightly. 'I had to get in the queue. All the blokes are after Katie at college.'

Katie threw him a warning look. Tess had never known her to be fighting off men with a stick. So much for leaving things open-ended.

'And where do your parents live, Jack?' asked Tess.

'Dad's a widower, retired from working on the railways. He misses Mum, of course. Well, you have to cope with the same situation, Mrs Gibson.'

Katie threw down her salad fork in alarm. Tess said quickly, 'Oh, I'm not widowed, Jack. I'm surprised Katie didn't tell you. I'm divorced. I was raised a Catholic, so being a widow would be more respectable, but there you are. Another slice of ham?'

'Sorry,' said Jack. 'I just assumed . . .'

'Not at all.' Tess cocked an ear. Katie froze.

'Ah, I think I hear Flick,' said Tess, gaze sliding away after a quick glance at Katie. 'She said she might drop by after all. I'd better set another place.'

As Tess rose and bustled off, Katie hardly dared look round.

'You OK?' Jack asked.

'Yes,' she hissed, all her faculties trained on her sister's approach, straining to catch the tell-tale clop of high heels on gravel at the side of the house. Like cloven hooves. Her chest constricted. The garden colours swam before her eyes.

It was all suddenly clear to her. Tess had innocently mentioned that Katie was bringing a man to lunch. Flick, having bagged Steve Sheridan, was going for the double.

The heels grew louder. They rounded the side of the house and emerged on to the patio. 'Hello all!'

announced a tinkly voice. 'This seat taken? You must be Jack. I'm Flick.'

Her real name was Pippa, but she'd been known as Flick since her early teens, after their brother Simon noticed she kept flicking her long hair about.

Now she slipped into the empty chair opposite Jack, smile painted wide, a vision in a wisp of a gauzy dress. Its leaf-green shade matched her huge green eyes. Two years younger than Katie, she was elfin, stunning, with long, shining, chestnut-brown hair and a button nose.

Men – especially in most recent, painful memory, Steve – saw her as fragile, a little birdy that had tumbled from the nest and needed a new home. Men forgot, as Katie never did, that orchids bloomed in the desert, fragile but stubborn, outliving even tough old cacti.

'Thought I'd drop by, seeing as Mum had company,' Flick claimed, beaming at Jack.

'Nice to meet you,' he said.

Katie gritted her teeth and actually spoke to her sister. 'Fancy you just dropping by, when Hampstead's the other side of London.'

'I was up this way anyway, visiting Dolly from school,' replied Flick to the air in front of her, rather than to Katie. She darted a conspiratorial, mercurial, definitely flirtatious smile at Jack, while crumbling a bread roll between delicate hands. 'Thought about coming over on my bike, but gave it a miss.'

'You cycle?' asked Jack, too enthusiastically for Katie's liking. 'I imagine you need nerves of steel, weaving in and out of London traffic. And then there's the pollution.'

Flick tossed back her long hair. 'Usually I only cycle to work, as it's so close to my flat. Caught the tube out here. I normally wear one of those yashmak thingies when I'm on the bike. You know, like Princess Di in the operating theatre.' She batted her long eyelashes in a Di impression that emphasised her own coyness and big-eyed beauty.

Katie watched with horrible fascination as a blob of salad cream fell unnoticed on Jack's shirt-front. Tess returned with cutlery and a plate for Flick. She noticed Jack's shirt at once and and dabbed at him with a paper napkin. She asked mildly, 'Isn't Gold a Jewish name?'

'Yes, my grandfather was a Jewish immigrant,' replied Jack. 'He eventually dropped the "stein" from the end of "Gold".'

'Was he a tailor, dear?' asked Tess.

'Mum!' protested Katie. 'That's like asking if your Irish ancestors were all navvies.'

'It's all right, Katie,' said Jack soothingly. He smiled charmingly at Tess. 'My grandad worked in a plastics factory, actually. He married a woman called Beryl, who came from solid English yeoman stock. I don't think he was ever religious, probably to his family's disappointment. But they were mostly dead anyway, killed in pogroms in Lithuania and Russia.'

'That's awful,' crooned Flick, green eyes radiating sympathy. 'We've had a bit of that in our family. Persecution, I mean. Mum's parents were Irish Catholics and Dad's were Scottish and belonged to this idealistic, low-kirk sect that everyone kept pelting with stones. I really despise intolerance.' Flick, flick,

flick. Her eyelashes batted like frantic humming-birds. Jack gaped slightly.

'We know all about your love of your fellow man,' seethed Katie, with a rare flash of bitchy wit.

Flick smiled. She curled a slice of wafer-thin ham into a pink rosette and speared it with a fork.

'I've forgotten the mustard,' murmured Tess, casting nervous glances between her daughters. It was clear she wanted to escape the thickening atmosphere. 'Back in a tick.'

'Being Jewish is inherited through the distaff side, isn't it?' Katie asked Jack. 'I mean, your granny would have to be Jewish to make you Jewish, Jack. Right?'

'Er . . .'

'How very nearly almost interesting,' observed Flick, rolling her eyes at Jack with another con-spiratorial little smile.

Katie felt her blood rise to a slow boil. Gritting her teeth, she continued to look doggedly at Jack, hoping to hold his attention. Out of the corner of her eye, she had Flick's every predatory movement covered.

Jack was now gazing openly at Flick. Flick! She went for the simultaneous hair-toss and eyelash-bat. Katie blinked. No man had ever resisted the double-flick combination.

Jack was now staring at Flick with that rabbit-trapped-in-car-headlights look.

Flick clearly scented triumph. A smile played on her full lips. She twirled a bracelet on her wrist, allowing Jack to admire her fine bones.

Suddenly, out of the blue, he leapt up, lunged forward and swatted Flick's shoulder with his napkin. In the process, he knocked her glass of wine into her lap.

'What the bloody hell?' shrieked Flick.

'Sorry,' panted Jack. 'I've been watching a sleepy wasp crawl up your dress for the last few minutes. Had to wait before I took aim. I think it's gone for good now. Sorry about the wine. Can you dry-clean your dress? I'd be happy to pay.'

Flick blushed and tossed her hair. 'Don't worry.'

'I thought for a minute there you were flicking it away yourself. Then I realised those were just, um, your natural hand movements.'

The look on Flick's face made Katie smile broadly and bitchily. Oh, how glad she was that she'd brought Jack Gold to lunch!

'How are we getting on here?' asked Tess, puffing back, suspiciously on cue with the jar of mustard. 'Everyone eat up now, none of it going to waste. I've a raspberry pavlova in the fridge for afters.'

'Thank you, Mum,' said Flick in a faintly strangled voice. 'But I ate a whole eclair at Dolly's. I've had quite enough here already.'

Katie didn't dare look up and seek out Jack with her own conspiratorial smile – one of triumph. That would have sullied her wicked pleasure in the moment.

But on the train journey back to Sussex, she could no longer contain her curiosity. 'Was there really a wasp crawling up Flick's dress?'

He snorted. 'If there had been, she'd have thought it was trying to profess undying love.'

Katie laughed, then grew sombre. 'She's beautiful, though, you've got to admit.'

'Gorgeous,' he agreed. 'Intelligent with it. What does she do?'

'Fashion buyer for a department store. Her monthly expense account is more than I've ever earned in a year.'

'She's got the lot then.'

Katie slumped down in her seat.

'Shame she's not my type,' he added.

'Why?' asked Katie aggressively. 'Too much competition for you? Ugly birds try harder?'

'While I concede the potential validity of both points,' he replied after a pause, 'the fact is, I don't like phoney women with tinkly laughs and designer affectations. Your sister's got too many layers a bloke would have to peel away to find the real person, and all the time a bloke was trying, she'd be pulling his strings, putting herself centre-stage. She's an attention-seeking neurotic, a mind-fucker, if you'll pardon the lingo. I couldn't be bothered with all that. She did the doe-eyed girly bit with me to – what would the Yanks call it? – seek validation, trying to reassure herself she's irresistible to every bloke she meets. Deep down, that girl doesn't like herself.'

'Whew,' said Katie, sitting up on her seat. 'Thank you, Doctor Freud.'

'You did ask,' he reminded her. 'I'm sure you had your reasons.'

She looked out of the window.

Jack leant forward. 'Can we go out together some time next week? Cinema, pub, you choose.'

'Er . . .' Thrown for a loop, Katie blushed. 'The Drama Society are doing *Ghosts* on Saturday.'

'What's that when it's at home?'

'A play by Ibsen. Lots of family strife with a bit of syphilis thrown in. You'll love it,' she added with a

18

giggle, amused at his appalled look.

'You art-degree types are degenerate. Anything on with a feelgood factor?'

'Nothing for grown-ups,' said Katie, thinking jealously of his blonde admirers around campus. 'I mean, I know some of your other female friends would be up for *My Little Pony, the Movie*.'

'What female friends?'

'Oh, for God's sake. All those adoring girlies who dangle off your arm. Plenty with tinkly laughs that I've noticed.'

'I'm shocked, and you're a sad case, Katherine Gibson. Haven't you noticed that girls outnumber blokes four to one at our place? I can hardly avoid having female friends.'

Katie suddenly felt very embarrassed. 'I never thought about it.'

He looked at her. 'Why do you think I applied to go there in the first place?'

With the help of Jack and unfeasibly short essay deadlines, Katie began to bury the memory of Steve Sheridan. Of course, she still thought of him from time to time, but that wasn't the same as fixating unhealthily on images of him and Flick being knee-capped, garrotted, killed by falling anvils. Her life filled up with Jack and left little time for blubbing into tea-towels.

Ironically, Steve had been a student when she met him. He'd ambled into the health-food shop one afternoon, his yellow hair a startled dandelion clock above his studenty Goth black jacket, transfixing her with his melodious Welsh accent and his sheepish apology for a pocketful of small change, which led on to a discussion about student poverty, Steve painting a picture of Dickensian garrets and consumptive PhD students down to their last candle-stump, and Katie just wanting to cook him hot broth and stave off his inevitable entry to the workhouse.

In fact, he later admitted to living with his auntie, who had a nice little semi in New Cross, close to the university library at Goldsmith's where he did most of the research for his PhD (the history of intellectual ideas in eighteenth-century English literature. Katie was suitably awed).

He never moved in with her, but her tiny flat became his accepted bolt-hole from auntie. More than once, Katie returned from the cash-and-carry to find him shivering on her doorstep in a downpour, chin buried in his jacket collar (he possessed neither over-coat nor umbrella), pathetically grateful for her return. When she let him in, he'd scamper around the flat, reacquainting himself with its shabby warmth and textures, like a cat returning to base.

Looking back, Katie realised that Steve's greatest gift had been to need her. Not just her flat as a bolt-hole or her body as a release-valve – even she, inexperienced with men, would have seen through that – but *her*; a straightforward woman who didn't play games, or tease, or throw mood switches to keep a man on his toes.

And she had needed him. He gave her self-esteem, confidence, a decent sex-life and the thrill that came from knowing she was as capable as Flick of attracting a good-looking boyfriend in her own right. For that alone, she'd always be grateful to Steve.

Except it was now impossible to separate that warm glow of nostalgic well-being from the impact of his treacherous transfer of affections as soon as he set eyes on Flick.

It wasn't as if she'd primed him before that fateful Sunday lunch, whetting his appetite for an encounter with the bitch-queen from hell. She'd only ever mentioned Flick in passing, lest she let slip her true loathing and suspicion of her kid sister. That would've piqued his interest straightaway, investing Flick with a tantalising air of mystery.

In the end, it didn't make any difference. Steve hadn't needed prior rumour and report to find Flick fascinating.

Noise disturbed Katie as she hovered between sleep and reluctant wakefulness. She burrowed back into sleep, only to bump her head on triple-glazed glass. Then she did wake up. She wasn't in bed. She was on flight 106 from Stansted to Rhodes, on holiday with Jack. Their first holiday since they'd moved in together ten months earlier, straight after graduation.

'What's the racket?' she yawned.

'Air-rage incident in progress, I think.'

He fidgeted with his seat buckle and her heart sank. 'Leave it to the cabin crew, Jack.'

'They might need help to sort it out.'

'Says you and whose army?' demanded Katie on a wave of irritation. She was surprised by how many she had felt since becoming part of her first cohabiting relationship.

Jack raised his eyebrows to her, then leant back in his seat, wearing a deadpan expression. His Fu

Manchu face, Nikki called it. Inscrutable and ever so slightly shifty, especially when challenged to defend his corner.

Katie sensed his irritation at being stopped in his intervening tracks. Assertiveness towards him came to her in fits and starts, and then only when she was bone-weary and snappy, but it was always followed by guilt. Jack, by virtue of his looks, confidence and other women's interest in him, still held the relationship cards. Even getting a flat together had been his idea, Katie falling rapturously into agreement.

She knew Jack as well as she was going to know him, she suspected. He'd joined a blue-chip accountancy firm after graduating, while she ran the gift shop of a monastic abbey in leafy Kent. It was funny how she'd ended up back in retail, but she loved her new job.

Jack seemed to thrive on his. Although his father, Freddy, was an old-style socialist, Jack mingled comfortably with the alumni of public schools. He played squash twice a week with his colleague Milo, a loud-voiced, baby-faced man in pink braces who'd once offered Katie a 'bagged pheasant'.

Jack was ambitious. He believed in knowing the right people and using your contacts. They'd had their first row when he admitted to admiring Mrs Thatcher. But political differences hadn't stopped Katie moving in with him. She was besotted with Jack, enslaved for ever by his declaration of love, which came after the second time they made love.

'I'm going to sort it out,' he suddenly decided, as the rumpus at the back of the plane grew louder. He unbuckled his seat-belt with slow deliberation, daring her (she felt) to make one more attempt at stopping him. 'Oh God, Jack, no,' she obliged, for the sake of form.

'Back in a tick.' Almost cheerful in the knowledge he'd flouted her twittering objections (or was that her paranoia?), he set off purposefully, drawing murmurs of appreciation from other passengers. The men probably saw him as clean-limbed and heroic, maybe handy in a martial art. The women saw him as a dish.

A hint of pride underlay Katie's irritation and embarrassment. So he wasn't someone who tried to blend in with the fixtures and fittings, like her. So he was prepared to stand up and be counted. Good. She only wished he wasn't so public-spirited, because have-a-go heroes often ended up with a punch on the jaw, or worse.

'Come on, pal, you've had enough,' she heard Jack point out to someone.

'Fuck off!' roared a male voice in response. Unsurprisingly, it sounded drunk.

'Look,' said Jack calmly, 'you can't carry on like this at thirty thousand feet, and I—'

'It's only fifteen thousand, smart-arse. We're levelling off for descent.'

'Leave it, Gordon,' pleaded a female voice, inevitably.

'Why should I leave it? Who is this smarmy-chopped git shoving his two-pennyworth in? Fuck off, mate, if you don't want more trouble than you can handle.'

'And how much is that?' challenged Jack, still reasonable, but ever so slightly patronising. Presumably, he had the full measure of Gordon.

Katie looked up in relief as a steward, at last alerted by the row's escalation, went hurrying to intervene. 'Gentlemen, please,' he began.

'Fuck off!'

'Gordon!'

There was a scuffle, a thin, theatrical scream, then silence. Katie sat up, filled with dread. Now what? God, they imposed prison sentences for air-rage, didn't they? If Jack had decked Gordon, *he'd* be seen as the aggressor. Or maybe Gordon had decked the steward and provoked Jack into making a citizen's arrest. In which case, he'd sit on Gordon until they landed and then happily spend hours hanging around a police station, giving his witness statement through an interpreter. Weariness bubbled up in Katie. This was her holiday, too.

'All done and dusted.' Jack flopped back into his seat.

Katie stared at him. 'What happened?'

'Gordon threw a punch at the steward, missed him, then vomited with a vengeance. He'll get what's coming to him when we land.'

As he spoke, a burly, drooping man was led up the aisle, trailed by a quivering, big-haired woman in white stilettos. 'It's Mrs Gordon I feel sorry for,' murmured kind-hearted Katie.

'Well, don't,' said Jack shortly. 'They're the type who give Brits abroad a bad name. Middle-aged whisky louts instead of teenage lager louts.'

Katie chewed her lip. 'I wish you wouldn't get involved.'

He squeezed her hand and leant across her to check their descent. 'Pity we can't see anything, landing in the wee hours like this. You all right there? Blood still circulating below waist-level?'

'Yes, thank you.'

'Thatta girl.'

He was manipulative. He'd wound her round his little finger when they first met, exploiting her naivety with men and her habit of wearing her heart on her sleeve. But he was manipulative in the nicest possible way. She loved Jack. She'd surprised herself recently by wanting to marry him.

Nikki reckoned he might even pop the question on this holiday. 'You've been living together all these months with no aggro. You've both got jobs. The next step will be buying a place together, so you might as well get married at the same time. That's deffo what *he'll* be thinking.'

It was hardly a romantic way to go about things, Katie felt. But that, said Nikki, was the way the male mind worked. Blokes proposed when the time was right, not when the moon was full. And did it matter, if she loved him anyway?

The plane bumped to the ground, 4am local time. Katie waited at the thronged carousel while Jack searched for a trolley. She folded her hands pensively in front of her creased linen dress. She'd painted her nails coral-pink for the trip. Two were already chipped, and she hadn't started biting yet.

Jack returned. 'Not a trolley to be had.'

'Oh well, we'll manage.'

In the end, it was academic. Forty minutes later, they were the only ones still at the carousel, upon which revolved a battered push-chair. Katie's suitcase stood at her side. There was no sign of Jack's new holdall. He was struggling, Katie knew, to contain his frustration within philosophical ennui.

'Look sharp,' murmured Katie. 'Here comes a Helos Tours rep. She'll sort things out.'

'Your faith is touching,' snorted Jack, as a blonde in a blue beret approached. 'Probably doesn't speak a word of the lingo. Probably thinks Mount Olympus is an instruction.'

'Shush! Just charm her.'

On that at least, Katie could rely. Jack's good looks and coolly informed manner enraged the likes of Gordon, but awed more impressionable men and wowed women every time. He gazed levelly at the rep, whose tremulous name-tag bore the name Mandy. 'We have a slight problem here, Mandy,' he told her. 'My luggage has failed to materialise. We're booked in the name of Gold.' He pointed at her blue clipboard. 'J Gold and K Gibson.'

Mandy laughed nervously. 'Oh gosh, yes, you're my missing two for the bus to Dimaklion. Hotel Apollo, sea view but not bothered about a balcony?'

'My luggage?' repeated Jack politely.

'Well, um, you're sure it wasn't hand-luggage you left on the plane?' hazarded Mandy.

Katie tensed.

Jack's face adopted the Fu Manchu look. He looked from Mandy's name-tag to her heap of blonde hair, as if he suspected a vacancy for a vital organ at its core.

'Of course he's sure,' said Katie quickly. He wasn't one for losing his temper, but she knew when he was tipping over from forbearance of idiocy to a dark, brooding sulk that could last days. She'd be the main loser.

Patting her pink raffia shoulder-bag she said cheerfully, 'Lucky the passports and essentials are in here.' Then she slipped her hand into his and gave it an appealing squeeze.

Jack hesitated. He squeezed her hand back briefly, dropped it, but said more affably to Mandy, 'Tell you what. I'll stay here to see if my bag turns up. Katie can go ahead to the hotel, and I'll follow in a taxi. Helos will pay the taxi fare, I presume?'

'Well . . .' dithered Mandy.

Jack gave her The Smile. Katie called it his Killer Smile. It transformed his deadpan features. She'd been dazzled by it once, before she realised it was the smile he used to end a conversation or confuse the enemy.

In Mandy's case, both. She blinked and adjusted her beret. 'Of course, Mr Gold.'

As a walkie-talkie crackled at Mandy's hip, Katie picked up her suitcase by its retractable handle. 'Which coach number?'

'Forty-nine, Mrs Golding. I'll wait here with your husband.'

'He's not my— Oh, OK then.' She touched Jack's arm. 'See you soon. Chin up.' She wanted to add, 'Be gentle with her,' meaning Mandy. If Mandy's search and location powers proved unfit to the task, Jack would take no prisoners.

Katie headed for the sliding doors. Outside, the heat stuck to her like syrup while the merest hint of pink stained a distant horizon. She found the right coach and flopped gratefully into a seat.

At the hotel, ensconced in their twin-bedded room, she didn't bother going to bed. Instead, she stood on the scrap of a balcony and watched the sun come up in a rich melange of citrus colours.

It made her feel thirsty. Jack had packed two bottles of spring water in her suitcase, despite her objections they'd quickly turn stale in a room without a fridge. But now, even stale water was better than nothing. She unpacked a bottle and glugged down half its tepid contents before immersing the bottle in a sinkful of cold water. Then she forced herself to gaze in the mirror above the sink.

She couldn't help it. The first thing she always did on scrutinising herself was compare herself to Flick, far more beauteous flesh of the same flesh. Were there any likenesses at all? Well, for a start, she was too hefty to be elfin. Size 12 on non-period days might have been fine if you didn't have a size 8–10 sister. She was now thirty-one, bobbed brown hair streaked blonde. By her own assessment, she had small features spoilt by an outsize hooter. She was short of stature and pear-shaped in the hip department. Definitely the blend-in type.

She was also plagued by the occasional worry that Jack had chosen her as his foil – just as the school knockout might choose a fat, spotty best friend to make herself look even better. Was Jack's preference for her over, say, a woman like Flick, simply a sign of his own egotistical insecurity? Except Katie knew she wasn't fat, spotty or ugly – just middle of the road. While Jack was roaring down the fast lane, and Flick was hot-rodding nearby in an open-top convertible.

Sighing, she peered at an ominous formation on her outsize hooter. It looked like a blackhead.

By the time she'd squeezed it and had a quick wash, it was a quarter to seven. Breakfast in the hotel was

28

served from seven until ten. The water had sharpened her appetite. She was ravenous and couldn't wait for Jack.

She ran down the marble staircase in her flowery flip-flops and selected a table out by the pool, even though a cool breeze was lifting the tablecloths. She seemed to be the only guest up at that hour.

Alone in the brisk, warming air of a Greek morning, her spirits lifted. Waiting for someone to serve her, she leant back in her white rattan chair, tilting her sun-starved skin towards the creeping arrival of a hot day.

'Ahoy there, early riser,' said a voice nearby. 'Mind if I join you?' She jerked upright, but, without waiting for her response, a white-blond man slipped into the chair opposite. 'Up catching worms, are we?' he grinned. His green-blue eyes crinkled at the corners and he had a Brummie accent.

Still getting her brain in gear for a reply, Katie glanced bashfully at the plastic sunflowers sprouting between her big toes.

'Girl friend sleeping off the flight?' he probed.

Even Katie, slow on the uptake in these matters, knew he was fishing for her availability. She felt flustered. 'Um, no.'

'Not here on your own?' he gasped, with fake admiration for her intrepidness.

Watching an ant investigate the petals on her flip-flops, she replied, 'I'm here with my boyfriend, actually. He'll be along in a bit.'

'Oh, right.' He looked heroically crestfallen. 'Just my luck. The good ones are always taken.'

Katie blushed.

'Well, see you around.' He winked at her, pushed back the chair and loped off, whistling. Katie watched him go, wrong-footed by his early-morning chirpiness and his quick retreat once he'd marked her down as a waste of time. On his way back into the hotel, he grabbed a croissant off a passing waiter. And nearly collided with Jack, who was standing on the edge of the poolside terrace, looking across at Katie.

She waved to him over-heartily, blushing again, this time with irrational guilt that he'd obviously witnessed the whole scene. He came and sat down at the table. To her chagrin, instead of grunting, 'You're my woman and don't you forget it,' he said evenly, 'No sign of my bloody luggage. They've given me a form to fill in. Looks like our first trip will be shopping for replacement clothes.'

She nodded, now annoyed with him for not alluding to the Brummie, thus making her feel she deserved her irrational guilt. But as Jack buttonholed a waiter, she experienced a sense of detachment, a fleeting pleasure at being on holiday under a blue sky, far away from problems and niggles.

She lifted the ant carefully off a painted toenail and set it down on a crack in the concrete, watching it burrow downwards to some cool, dark domain. She felt the sun on her shoulders and thought of Jack's tendency to burn. She looked across at him as he buttered a slice of toast.

She loved the whole package of him, even his cool, unexcitable restraint, and his tendency to withdraw and brood. There were parts of him he wouldn't or couldn't let her reach, but everyone had a right to that. She had the true extent of her Flick-neurosis boxed off from his view. She hoped.

'Jack, that bloke who was here a minute ago. I didn't encourage him.'

'I know that, Katie. His type prey on attractive women on holiday. They're even deadlier than local romeos.'

Katie preened a bit. So he thought she was attractive enough to be chatted up. A bit of possessive jealousy would've been nice, but still . . .

'You seem to be bleeding from that scab on your nose,' he added dryly, and leant across to dab gently at her squeezed spot.

Her élan evaporated. The Brummie obviously wasn't fussy who he tried it on with. She had to ask herself yet again: was a gorgeous boyfriend a help or a hindrance to a woman's self-esteem?

Chapter Two

After breakfast, Jack showered and redressed reluctantly in the same clothes. Then they caught the bus into Lindos to buy him new gear and toiletries. Strap-hanging in the crowded aisle, Katie felt relieved he wasn't sulking about his mishap. The beauty of the place had a serene influence, she was sure. When the bus lurched within sight of the Lindos acropolis, perched on a hilltop, they both gazed silently at its sun-bleached skeleton. Below it, the sea sparkled a deep cerulean blue, its shoreline frilled with white cubed houses.

'Makes you think,' murmured Jack. 'About life, the universe and everything.'

'Mmm,' she agreed.

Their philosophical reverie was cut short by the bus screeching to a halt and everyone trying to squeeze out of the narrow exit at once.

Clothes-shopping with Jack was a new experience and more straightforward than Katie had anticipated. He had firm, unfussy requirements. He bought a six-pack of underpants, a couple of designer T-shirts, two pairs of bermudas and a pair of canvas deck shoes. 'Bit of a dent on the old plastic,' he grimaced, as the carrier bags mounted up. 'I'll get one hell of a Visa bill when this holiday's a distant memory.'

'Oh, Jack, don't hurry us back into boring old reality. And we're not going to stint on spending money because of this. I still want to work my way through the cocktail menu at the hotel.'

'OK,' he said affably. 'Don't get your sarong in a twist. Fancy something overpriced and alcoholic for elevenses?'

As they meandered through backstreets in search of a café, Katie's eye was caught by a splash of colour. A Hawaiian shirt billowed from a pole above a vendor's stall. It was one of a kind, and so *not* Jack, she decided to get it for him; give his good taste a day off.

They found a café and ordered hazelnut-flavoured lattes laced with rum. Jack, who had a well-bred disdain for novelty beverages, sipped his cautiously. Katie gulped hers down, intent on backtracking to the shirt stall.

Announcing she was off to the loo, she left the table and snuck out. Back at the stall, she bought the shirt without even checking its size. She ran back to the café, getting a stitch, and as she wasn't the sort of girl who could keep a minor-league secret, she dropped the carrier bag in his lap and said breathlessly, 'Go on, open it, it's an extra for your wardrobe.'

Jack unfolded the shirt and gazed in silence at scarlet parrots perched on emerald branches against a turquoise sky. For one awful moment, Katie thought he was going to take serious offence. Then a slow but spontaneous smile spread across his face. 'Book him, Danno!' He stood up and kissed her cheek. 'It's great. I'd never have the nerve to buy this for myself. My exes had to teach me how to shop for clothes in the first place. Um, I'll wear it tonight,' he added, realising the reference to ex-girlfriends was a faux pas.

Katie sat down and paddled her spoon in latte foam at the bottom of her cup. She knew she should be way past twinges of jealousy, but she couldn't help it.

In spite of early protestations to the contrary, Jack had eventually admitted to romantic involvement with quite a few of his blonde 'friends' at university. Before that, working at the bank, he'd nearly got engaged to a high-flyer called Julie. And Katie knew there must be less significant others he'd completely glossed over.

She'd have preferred it if Jack had evolved in splendid isolation, like a windblown fern clinging to a rock, with no formative assistance, sartorial or otherwise, from girlfriends. 'You've certainly got the cheekbones for a colourful shirt,' she mumbled, looking into her cup.

He was watching her carefully. 'No time like the present to show them off.'

To her amazement, he stood up, slipped his sweaty T-shirt over his head and pulled on the Hawaiian shirt, all in a few deft movements that brought oohs and ahs of shock, relief and appreciation from other tables. He did a twirl to a scattering of applause.

The shirt fitted perfectly, the jibing colours coming together and setting off his own colouring. If he'd been a woman, Katie would have been jealous.

Instead, she marvelled at him and said, 'Jack, you're being very, very . . . '

'Impulsive?' he suggested dryly.

'Well, it's just . . . doing a striptease and modelling in public aren't your thing.'

'I have hidden depths.'

His admission of this, however glib, gladdened her heart. Maybe he was about to start opening up to her. She willed herself to forget about the ex-girlfriends and smiled at him. 'Let's have two more coffees-with-rum,' she suggested. 'We might get them on the house.'

Back at the hotel, they had lunch, then Jack suggested a siesta. Katie tried it for a while, lying folded into him in the spoon position. But soon they were stuck together by a midday heat that kept her peevishly awake.

She gently uncurled Jack's arm from her waist, left him asleep in the now-crumpled Hawaiian shirt, and decided to walk around the hotel garden. This was a parched square of grass, a few stunted palms offering inadequate protection from the heat. It was unseasonably hot for late April. She took her short constitutional, thinking about writing postcards and buying souvenirs to take back as presents.

Nikki was easy, she just wanted booze. Nikki and her husband Doug hadn't been abroad since having two kids. Nikki was jealous of all holidaymakers. The only holiday news that cheered her up was a hurricane in the Caribbean.

Tess was harder. She had taste. She couldn't be fobbed off with ouzo or pickled figs, and she'd run a mile from tacky Grecian statues posing as garden

ornaments. Musing over her shopping responsibilities, Katie wandered into the cool of the morgue-
like bar. And found herself accosted by the Brummie.

'We meet again,' he told her. He was perched on a
bar-stool, tanned legs wrapped round its metal struts.
'The name's Keith. Boyfriend gone awol again?'

'He's taking a siesta.'

She could have done without Keith. But as she'd
walked into the bar, and as she now fancied a citron
pressé after the dizzying heat outside, she had no
option but to slip onto the adjoining stool. To have
scuttled off to a corner would have looked rude.
'Your name a trade secret?' asked Keith, blue-green
eyes crinkling winsomely.

'It's Katie.' They shook hands and she ordered her
drink from the bored barman.

'You can't sleep in daytime either?' he asked.

'I think I'm still perky after the flight. We had a bit
of excitement, losing half our luggage.'

'Really? That happened to me on a skiing trip a
couple of years ago. It was a disaster, 'cos I'd put my
skis in the hold. The whole holiday was just—'

Katie drifted off, nodding at intervals. Keith was
boring, but he was harmless. He wasn't going to try it
on, with her boyfriend asleep upstairs, though, this
was the second time she'd materialised with a
boyfriend-otherwise-engaged tale. He might think it a
cover story.

'What's your line of work, Katie?'

'Oh. Er, I work in a gift shop, in an abbey run by
monks. We sell fudge, pottery and religious knick-
knacks.' Brother Martin, who was head of marketing,
would have blanched to hear her describe the abbey's

range of religious artifacts thus.

'And what does Mr Sleepy-head do?' asked Keith, with a hint of mocking smile. Or maybe she was imagining it.

'He's an accountant.' She blushed. To be polite, she asked, 'And you, Keith?'

'Freelance photographer. Mostly do people getting spliced on the beach.'

'Oh,' she realised. 'You *live* here.'

He gave her his card. Absently, she pocketed it.

'You're not wearing an engagement ring,' said Keith. 'So no wedding plans in the offing with the sleepy accountant?'

'We're just good friends.' She cringed.

'Parents still alive?' asked Keith.

'Yes.' God, this was almost like her getting-to-know-each-other conversations with Jack.

'Mine too. Not that I ever got on with the old man. When I upped sticks to come out here, he said . . . '

Katie reckoned she'd found the weak spot in Keith's chat-up routine. You had to be a good listener.

She allowed her mind to drift back to her own father. He'd left when she was eight, but she couldn't honestly say she'd ever missed him. Not really. Not in a way she could have subsequently used as a get-out clause if she'd gone off the rails. Going by her own experience, Katie didn't hold with that 'I went bad 'cos I come from a broken home, your honour' line, although she knew there were distinctions between homes broken up and homes lightly fractured. Hers fell into the second category. Don Gibson hadn't been enough of a presence at home to make his permanent absence painfully noticeable. He'd always been a hands-off father, dedicated to work or his off-duty golf, booming away somewhere overhead, occasionally lowering his cheek for a sloppy goodnight kiss.

In the week following his departure from 23 Alderney Road, Katie had avoided the aftermath (or more specifically, Tess) by hiding under her bed, communing with the dust bunnies. It was there that six-year-old Flick had found her. She couldn't wait to show Katie their dad's christening entry in her new, powder-pink autograph book with the heart-shaped clasp. Don had drawn a deft little Betty Boop, all bashful stance and huge eyes, and written underneath, *To the fairest of them all, my Pippa.*

Only their mother could have known that Don was about to cut loose. It was Tess who'd issued his marching orders. He'd been having an affair for a year when she rumbled it and threw him out. Apparently, he'd worked late once too often (the Gibson children had never been privy to the sordid details that led to discovery), and Tess was nobody's fool.

The other woman was called Tanya. Soon after her father's departure, Katie had eavesdropped on Tess telling one of her friends, in a rare outburst of confiding emotion, 'I expect she's got legs up to her armpits and pencil shavings for brains.'

After which, the Gibson children had christened Tanya among themselves Legs Up To Her Armpits Tanya. No one in the family had met her. Not even Tess, as far as the children knew. A few details did filter as far as the junior Gibsons, who were always on the lookout for crumbs of news at family get-togethers and visits from Tess's friends. It seemed that Tanya was younger than Tess, naturally. And she was

American, so, just like those scary women in *Dynasty* and *Dallas*, trashy behaviour was second nature to her. Don Gibson had eventually married Legs Up To Her Armpits Tanya and moved to the States with her.

Flick still had that autograph book. At the time, Katie had been chagrined by her lack of foresight compared to her sister. Flick had gained an image to fall back on, a bit of daddy-love to sustain her on nostalgia trips.

Katie had come across the autograph book at Tess's only last month, turning out cupboards in her hunt for the pink raffia bag. She'd found both bag and book in her old room – the bedroom she'd shared with Flick, growing up.

It had been ironic to see their cast-off possessions jumbled up in cupboards. Once upon a time, they'd fought bitterly over every inch of bedroom space, ending up either side of a peace line running down the centre of the room, between their beds. This had been Katie's idea and she'd soon regretted it. Too late, she realised the wardrobe was on her side, but the coveted dressing-table on Flick's. Every time she put a comb or perfume bottle on the dressing-table, Flick threw it back on her bed. Katie retaliated by clearing the wardrobe of Flick's clothes and chucking them on *her* bed.

Tess then proposed the obvious compromise of allocating shared use of certain areas and items. That didn't work, either. Flick claimed she had more clothes, so needed the lion's share of wardrobe space. Periodically, she shoved Katie's clothes into the back of the wardrobe and spread out her own hangers, to 'air' the fabrics. Katie hated to think how much of her adolescence she'd spent moving coat hangers about and judging the distance between them. Inevitably, there'd been coat-hanger fights. Looking back, it was all so pathetic, the very stuff that childhood feuds are made of. Except theirs had grown up with them.

Katie had leapt at the chance to leave home at eighteen and move a few miles down the road, into the tiny flat over the health-food shop.

She sipped her citron pressé and realised it was a long time since she'd said anything to Keith. He'd finally come to the end of his ramble and was sipping his beer, giving off slightly offended vibes at her lack of conversational input. She rallied and said tentatively, 'So, Keith, is this your lull before it gets busy in high summer?'

Standing foolishly on the edge of the bar, Jack couldn't believe she still hadn't spotted him. Especially in the daft shirt he'd worn to please her. She was, it seemed, too busy giving every scrap of her attention to that peroxide dickhead he'd seen at breakfast. A wave of ugly emotion rolled through him, belying his calm stance and rather superior expression (had anyone bothered to look).

He wasn't used to being jealous. It wasn't the ugliness of the emotion that disturbed him. It was its power over him – and the power it gave Katie.

Until he met Katie, he'd been used to women fighting over him. Not literally, of course, but jockeying discreetly for pole position in his affections. Jack wasn't vain, but he knew his own worth. He'd been attracted to Katie because her mixture of beauty and artlessness had made him feel rested and secure. He'd known she wasn't going to flirt with every presentable man who crossed her path, just to test the power of her beauty. Not like her worldly sister, who was too pert for Jack's taste. So what was the story with this bloke? Jack mentally scratched his head.

A thought made him cold. She might be perfectly aware he was hovering in the shadows like a lemon. She might be *trying* to make him jealous. If so, she wanted something off him. She might not be as artless as he'd presumed. Milo was always reminding him that women never came straight out with anything. They went all round the houses to drop obscure hints about something, then threw their eyes up to the sky when you still didn't get it, and said, 'Honestly, there's no getting through to you!'

So what could Katie want? Was it all about taking their relationship 'to the next level'? Since hitting thirty the previous year, he'd developed an unsettling feeling that he'd reached a plateau instead of crossing a threshold. He'd hated all the 'past-it' ribbing at work, though he'd given as good as he got, pouring humorous scorn on the callow twenty-somethings in the office, trying to pretend he didn't envy them.

But the next level, the mark of a grown-up post-30 life was – well, everyone knew what it was. Katie knew, too. She was testing him. He chewed his lip, smoothed down the creases in his Hawaiian shirt, and moved towards the bar.

'Be seeing you,' said Keith, slipping off his stool. 'And remember, if you need my services as wedding snapper . . .' He tapped his nose and grinned. Then he looked past her, straightened up, and loped off at a fair old lick.

Sighing with relief, Katie drained the last of her drink, only to hear Jack's voice at her elbow. 'So this is where you get to when I'm flat out? Canoodling with Romeo again.'

'You mean Keith?' she squeaked in panic, and turned to see Jack's dark blue eyes regarding her with an expression she couldn't fathom. She bit her tongue too late. She'd no idea what Jack had seen before he crept up on her. But she'd just revealed that she and Keith were on first-name terms.

'He was a bit of a nuisance, but he's gone now,' she twittered.

'I suppose he doesn't wear a medallion in case it rusts in the heat,' grunted Jack, claiming the adjoining stool.

Katie looked at him in surprise and confusion. Above the florid parrots, he looked very dark and brooding indeed.

'He was here when I came in for a drink,' she gabbled. 'It would've been rude to ignore him.'

'Katie,' he said urgently, tapping a beer mat with his fingers. 'Katie, you know I love you?'

She gulped. 'Y–yes. I love you too, Jack.'

She tried to act nonchalant, and knocked her glass over with her elbow. Luckily, it was empty. Jack was showing some of his hidden depths. And it unnerved her.

'I was thinking,' he went on, stroking her wrist. 'As we love each other, might it not be a good idea, do you think, all things considered, if we, I mean . . .' He took a deep breath and blurted, 'You and me get married.'

Her mouth fell open unattractively. Yes! shrieked an inner voice. Yes, yes, yes!

A warm, golden glow spread through her. But hold on. This was Jack being impulsive, going all caveman because he'd seen Keith chatting her up *twice*.

She entwined her fingers with his, and looked down into her lap. 'Yes, I'll marry you, Jack,' she said shyly. 'Nothing would make me happier. If you're sure it's not just – not just you getting carried away by the holiday mood. You might go cold on the idea, back in rainy, grey old London.' She waited for his comeback, but there was silence above her. 'I mean,' she said, 'it's just a thought. Holiday fever. The romance of the setting.' She risked looking up.

To her amazement, he looked a little punch-drunk, too. 'Hang on, hang on,' he muttered. 'Just got to check something. Before that other stuff, you said yes, didn't you? It was in there somewhere?'

She nodded fiercely. 'Yes. And I was also poi—'

'Barman,' called Jack, flushing a dark red. 'Bottle of champagne, please, for me and the future missus.' He pulled a shell-shocked Katie into his arms. 'I asked and you said yes! Barman, two glasses, please.'

His elation made her dizzy with happiness. She forgot her train of thought. If Keith had returned at that moment, she'd have kissed him.

The barman, not moved to offer congratulations, uncorked the champagne and poured it.

'To Mr and Mrs Gold,' announced Jack solemnly, clinking his fizzing glass against hers.

'Mr and Mrs Gibson-Gold?' suggested a light-headed Katie, not caring either way.

'Whatever,' said Jack.

She sipped the champagne and bubbles shot up her nose. She spluttered and began to giggle.

Jack clapped her on the back and began to laugh, too. The barman looked at them kindly.

Mrs K Gold. Katie Gold. Katherine A Gold. Like a lovestruck teenager defacing her exercise books, Katie practised her future signature on beer mats and serviettes, after shyly checking that Jack wasn't looking.

The rest of their week passed in a honeymoon stupor of smiling idiotically at each other, nursing a secret the whole world wanted to know. They walked hand-in-hand on beaches. They made love a lot. They were given a wide berth by normal, grumpy people. Jack even bought Keith a drink in the bar.

They didn't discuss practicalities until the penultimate day, when they were forced to come off cloud nine and go souvenir-shopping. As they traipsed around Lindos, thoughts of family and friends to the fore, their mood grew reflective.

'Registry office or church?' asked Jack, watching her closely. 'It's your shout. I'll go along with it if you want a traditional do.'

Katie smiled to herself. Jack didn't fancy a big church do, and it was false martyrdom on his part, because he knew she didn't either. 'I'd prefer the registry office,' she replied. 'As long as Mum's OK about it. I was sort of born Catholic.'

'As an atheist, I don't mind perjuring my non-existent soul by taking my vows before a non-existent God. But there's Dad and his "opium of the people" objection. He won't cross a church threshold.'

She thought for a moment. 'We'll cross that bridge when we come to it. Have we been in this shop yet?'

After more traipsing, Katie bought handmade lace hankies for Tess, and thought about wedding guests. 'S'pose I'll have to invite Flick, to avoid family meltdown. But I'm not asking Dad. Anyway, he's so hopeless at keeping in touch, he probably thinks I've been married, divorced and remarried by now.'

Jack peered at her. 'Is he that bad?'

'Yep.' Katie fingered the price tag on a pair of Ray-Bans.

Soon after moving to the States with Legs Up to Her Armpits, Don's letters and presents became sporadic, petering out altogether when his twin daughters came along.

'You think Freddy will be pleased about us?' Katie asked, watching Jack shop in a desultory way for his father.

'He'll be pleased I'm marrying a woman he can stand the sight of. He's been fretting that Milo has a loud-voiced, horsey sister.'

'He's met Milo?'

'God, no. But he gets the gist of where I work. I've already sold out to the enemy, so bolting on you and marrying its sister would be par for the course.'

Katie pounced on a bottle of ouzo for Nikki. Doug preferred a nice after-dinner brandy. That left their little ones, Max and Sarah.

Jack bought some local firewater for Freddy and offered to help her shop for Nikki's kids. 'You don't have to buy ethnic prezzies for little people,' explained Katie. 'I mean, look, here's the cutest little handbag with lots of zipped pockets for hiding things. Sarah will love it.'

'It's dayglo pink vinyl,' pointed out Jack.

'Trust me on little girls, Jack,' she said confidently, checking for 'non-toxic' on the labelling.

'I trust you,' he replied, with mock solemnity.

But suddenly she felt a chill pass over the day. He trusted her, but did he still believe her? Believe *in* her? Did he harbour even the slightest doubt about the Stairs Incident, which had happened at their flat-warming ten months earlier?

She knew the answer already. He'd proposed to her, as Nikki had predicted.

But still . . . The Stairs Incident was subtly different from the Steve Sheridan episode. Flick's deception with Steve had been there for all to see. The Stairs Incident had come down to her word against Flick's. Sometimes, she wondered where Flick's lies would lead. And who they'd hurt the most.

Garden Close in Crystal Palace didn't look its best on a squally April evening. But one thought preoccupied Katie as Jack carried her suitcase up three flights of narrow, twisty stairs. Who would she ring first with her news? Nikki? Her mum? Mutual friends from university?

The 'penthouse suite', as her brother Simon called their flat, was a one-bedroomed flat at the top of a three-storey terraced house. Katie could still recall her excitement and confusion when gorgeous Jack first suggested they pool resources after graduation and share a flat.

They'd been drinking coffee in his digs. Katie, struck with her usual wonder that Jack should want her in any permanent capacity, had shuffled her feet, looked at the carpet and murmured, 'So, in effect, I'd be your lodger?'

'Hardly,' said Jack, in a tone that made her look up. His arms were folded defensively. 'Unless that's what you want. Maybe I've been horribly previous, assuming you'd go for cohabitee status. Have I grossly offended you or anything?'

It had taken at least half an hour to tease out the crossed wires. No, she wasn't insulted. Yes, she did want to be more than a lodger.

The flat had served them well up to now. It was near the station for Jack's fifteen-minute journey to Victoria. Katie caught a bus at the end of the road that took her vaguely in the direction of Pridwell Abbey on the Kent border. She still had a twenty-minute walk when she got off, but that was her favourite part of the day; strolling ever deeper into lush green belt, birdsong overhead, the old stone of the abbey waiting to greet her.

They also had a car – well, Jack had a car – kept in a lock-up in the adjoining street. Katie rarely drove it. She was nervous inching it through gridlocked streets, wary of hitting a slaloming cyclist. She knew that if she did she'd end up apologising profusely and ruining any chance of an insurance claim.

The front door of the flat cranked open against a slope of junk mail. More was stacked neatly on the coffee table, put there by elderly, garrulous Mrs Domenica from the flat downstairs. They'd left her a key so she could pop up to water their straggly plants and sort the mail.

Jack started binning mail. Katie put the kettle on, realised there was no milk in the fridge, and began to load the washing-machine. Her head felt tight, as if she'd been wearing her old school hat with its constricting elasticated crown. She recognised the onset of post-holiday-itis, already activated by the lack of milk for a cuppa.

'I'll go out for essentials,' called Jack, as if reading her mind. 'I'll just play the phone messages. Then I'll ring Dad.'

Beep: 'Greetings, Jacko,' boomed a voice that reached Katie in the kitchen. Milo.

She waited until he'd finished booming. Then she wandered into the living-room to hear the next message.

Beep: 'Welcome back, sun-worshippers. Hope you got skin cancer. No, but seriously . . . .' This was Nikki, with her gallows humour at the expense of the envied charterjet-set. 'Come and visit me, palely loitering in my hovel. But only if you're bringing booze!'

Beep: 'Listen, I hate talking into these things,' complained Tess, talking very slowly and clearly. 'Now, I want you both to come to lunch this Sunday, the twentieth. Everyone's coming, but I can't say more, I'm obviously sworn to secrecy. I've said too much already! You're back by the twentieth, aren't you? Now I hope you haven't got me anything, especially if it's a ceramic dish, because it'll only end up in the bathroom holding bits of stuck-together soap. Don't forget, the twentieth. This horrible thing is going to beep in a minute and cut me off, so I'll go. Bye! Oh, I hope you had a nice ho—' The machine gave a long, chastising beep and cut her off.

'Lunch this Sunday, eh?' said Jack speculatively. 'By everyone coming, I assume she means Flick and Si, plus surprise special guests by the sound of things. Do you think she means your dad?'

Katie went numb. 'Jack, you're not serious!'

'I don't mean they're getting back together. But maybe they've buried the hatchet and he happens to be over from the States, so he's coming to lunch with Tanya and the girls. Your mum did sound flustered, in an upbeat kind of way.'

'You think? I can never tell on an answerphone. Someone could be ringing with sincere condolences and sound ecstatic.'

'Are you thinking what I'm thinking?' pressed Jack.

'I'm not sure,' demurred Katie, having spent most of her relationship with Jack trying to unlock the inner man.

'I'm thinking your whole family's assembling as if by magic, for our convenience. Whether or not your dad turns up, it's the perfect occasion to make our announcement. They'll end up holding lunch in our honour. Imagine the look on your sister's face.'

'Jack!' she said in astonishment. 'That's worthy of my mental machinations. So when will we tell Freddy?'

Jack gave a mock groan. 'God, I'd forgotten about him. I suppose . . .' he hesitated. 'I suppose you could come with me next weekend to visit him. You turning up should be reason enough to alert him.'

Katie looked hurt. 'I would go with you more often, but I don't like to . . . encroach.'

Sixty-three-year-old Freddy Gold was a retired railway-worker in poor health. A few years earlier, he'd sold his house and moved in with a widow called Suzette, nine years his junior.

Jack's Saturday afternoon visits usually took place when Suzette was out, by tacit agreement between all parties. Katie was reluctant to tag along, in case she diluted quality time between father and son. On the few occasions she had accompanied Jack, Freddy had spent the first twenty minutes talking *sotto voce*, ear cocked for Suzette's footfall or key in the lock, in case she popped back unexpectedly. Katie imagined she must be very scary indeed.

'Look,' said Jack. 'We'll play Freddy by ear. Think about this Sunday, though. We could make a big entrance. I'm thinking of wearing my parrot shirt.' He gave her the Killer Smile, which, frankly, she could have done without. 'Right,' he said, conversation ended to his satisfaction. 'I'll go and get that milk.'

'Jack, wait, I've just remembered. We forgot to buy a present for Mrs Domenica. Poor Mrs D. And after she looked after the flat for the week. Buy her something extra nice when you're out.'

Jack lingered in the doorway. '*You're* extra-nice, Katie Gibson,' he said, and smiled the smile she preferred, his slow, spontaneous smile.

As soon as he'd left, Katie did a little victory dance. Jack was happy. He was happy because they were getting married. And that gave her the biggest pleasure of all.

Maybe he was right about Sunday. This was their chance to make an entrance, her big chance to outshine Flick. First, she'd found Jack. Now she was keeping him, with nothing more restrictive than the cobwebby reins of true love. God, Flick would die! If only.

But she could still spill the beans to Nikki, before Sunday came round. And start talking engagement rings with Jack. How brilliant if she could turn up on Sunday actually wearing a diamond solitaire. It would be hard to organise in the next four days, with work to slog through. But a girl could dream.

Chapter Three

Katie went straight to Nikki's from work the following Friday, clutching her gifts from Greece. Nikki and Doug Bissett lived with their two children in a small Streatham townhouse. Before her whirlwind romance, marriage, and plunge into full-time motherhood, Nikki had been a trainee manager with M&S. Doug was an IT manager.

As Katie walked up the path of number 9, Doug came flying out, not bothering to shut the door behind him. 'It's a madhouse,' he told Katie darkly.

She nodded understandingly. She was a bit shy of Doug. He wasn't good-looking, but he was imposing – a big, bluff man with the mashed nose and cauliflower ears of a seasoned rugby player. He looked as if he didn't suffer fools gladly, until he smiled. He had a lopsided, snaggle-toothed smile which softened the craggy planes of his face. Katie always felt gauche in his presence. Now she waited nervously as he hovered to say something. He sniffed under his arms. 'Does this jumper smell all right to you?'

She inhaled from a safe distance. It smelt, vaguely, of puked-up baby food. 'Seems OK.'

'Right then.' He gave her a what-can-you-expect-of-the-wife's-best-friend? look, alleviated by the snaggle-toothed smile. 'I'm off then.'

'Rugby match?' she asked, for the sake of politeness.

'Pub darts,' he replied, a shade defensively. 'She said you were coming round. Don't want to be under your feet.'

Katie arranged her features to look grateful. Unless her radar was damaged, all was not well in the garden of marital bliss. This, Nikki had often hinted, was the inevitable consequence of reproducing. Children were the death-knell of sex, a social life, economic stability, and finding a cleanish jumper to go out in. Prompted to elaborate, Nikki would get savagely maudlin about lovestruck fools who rushed into marriage without, say, a ten-year engagement.

Katie paused to wonder if this was the best moment to break her news. She put a hand up to her face. For the last few days she'd felt a tell-tale tingle there, as if glow-worms were massed under her skin. Nikki might even guess her news just by looking at her.

She pushed open the front door Doug had left ajar. Nikki's head snaked round the kitchen door at the end of the hallway. 'Thank Christ, intelligent life at last. Come in and tell me about the holiday. What a fucking day.'

'Language, Mum,' warned five-year-old Max, scooting past on his way up the stairs. He was a sturdily attractive miniature of Doug. He shot Katie a look to signal his disapproval of Nikki. That was like Doug, too.

Nikki led the way into the rummage sale of her front room. She was long of hair and broad of bottom. She favoured carnival-coloured clothes from junk shops, set off with costume jewellery. Today she wore purple velvet pantaloons and a cerise cropped top that showed a freckled spare tyre. Her disc earrings were as big as satellite dishes, dangling amid Cher-like black hair.

She reminded Katie of an earth mother crossed with an operatic diva. She'd have looked the part at Greenham Common, but she'd have pissed off the other women with her lack of esprit de corps and her insistence that chocolate was more important than a nuclear-free world. Her manner was theatrical, bordering at times on hysterical. Katie could never understand why someone so large and vibrant had crammed her life into four narrow walls and resigned herself to blooming unseen. Content, though, Nikki certainly wasn't. It was all too obvious as she flopped into a chair, just missing a disgruntled cat. Katie turned her attention to one-and-a-half-year-old Sarah, lolling against the sofa cushions. Holding her bottle with both hands, Sarah had tipped it up to drain it, a vein throbbing on top of her downy, alien-sized head. She swivelled her head elegantly, moving the bottle in sync, to fix Katie with a contemplative, old man's gaze.

Katie bent down to tickle her under her bib. Sarah beamed joyfully. Her light-blue eyes sparkled with trusting love. Katie felt a bit choked up. She was ambiguous about having kids and tested her ambiguity regularly on Nikki's two. Max, she found scary. He was over-fond of the 'why?' question and dismissive of anyone who didn't meet his exacting intellectual standards. Sarah was beautiful and mystical and looked a bundle of fluffy-towel-wrapped gorgeousness, until she started screaming or burping up her dinner. Katie now wondered if the pink dayglo handbag was appropriate. Sarah's little hands were more at the clutching than the exploring stage.

'At least Doug can do a runner from all this,' grizzled Nikki. 'I'm stuck in my leg-irons, shuffling from sink to cooker to bottom-wiping. I can't go on, Katie. I can't!'

'I know,' said Katie soothingly.

She'd first encountered Nikki's outbursts at school. She'd averaged one every couple of months, upping to every couple of weeks as O-levels loomed. 'I can't do these sodding O-levels, I can't!' Nikki had wept in the common room. 'I'll top myself first, or run away and become a statistic. They'll fish my body out of the canal and identify me by my dental records. I hope my bloody parents will be satisfied then.'

Even Katie, used to the Maria Callas bit by then, had been sufficiently moved to offer the Holy Grail – sharing her furtively compiled and jealously guarded revision notes.

Nikki's hysteria had been based on the late discovery that her own lesson notes were thin and sketchy. She'd bunked off classes that bored her and handed in homework on the basis of whether or not she liked a teacher. Katie had never managed to convince her that, in the long run, she was the one who'd suffer. Your average state-school teacher wasn't paid enough to give a toss.

The revision-note crisis was the only time Katie had

felt a flicker of suspicion at Nikki's motives for being her best friend. After all, Nikki could have had her pick of best friends. Her rubber-ball personality and customised uniform had guaranteed her popularity, buffering it against the sneers of Flick, two classes below, even when she dubbed Nikki 'My dorky sister's hippo-bummed mate'.

Katie had been known at school as a plodding, reliable worker; someone to copy work from if you had missed a day. She'd begun to wonder if Nikki had been using her all along, to get her hands on the revision notes.

Two things had saved their relationship at this fragile stage. First, even with eleventh-hour help, Nikki had had the good manners to get lower O-level grades than Katie. Second, Nikki had been humbly, slobberingly grateful for receiving eleventh-hour help in the first place.

Now Katie looked around Nikki's tip of a front room, while Nikki frowned from the depths of her armchair. Katie wondered what help she could offer this time. 'I'll make us coffee,' she suggested at last. Nikki snorted her thanks.

En route to the kitchen, Katie picked up a tray of dirty crockery from the scarred pine dining-table. In the kitchen, her heart sank. The sink was full of greying water as greasy saucepans bobbed about in their own scum. Sighing, she rolled up her sleeves and decided a hand with the washing-up might be more useful and appreciated than gifts from Greece. Besides, she'd have to wash the stuff in the sink before she could rinse out mugs for coffee.

Clanging pots and pans brought Max to

investigate. He moved aside the potato-peeler on the draining-board, to uncover the dish-scrubbing brush. 'You gonna wash all them things?' he asked in awe.

'Those things,' corrected Katie automatically. Then she caught his eye, winked and began to sing *It's such a perfect day*, using the brush as a microphone. It was as much to keep up her skivvying spirits as to entertain him.

Nikki appeared on the doorway with Sarah on her hip. 'Where's that coffee?'

'There's gratitude for you.' Katie wiped her hands on a stained tea-towel and nodded back towards the front room. 'I'll bring it through. Then I'll hand out my Red Cross parcels.'

Nikki grinned wonkily. 'Thanks for coming round, Katie. Christ knows, I need someone human to talk to.'

Katie waggled a warning eyebrow in Max's direction. It looked as if the news about Jack would have to wait. There was only one thing more nauseating than an angel of mercy who washed up, made coffee and doled out presents, and that was an angel of mercy getting her reward here on earth, in the shape of Jack Gold.

Back in the front room, Katie handed out her goodies. A 3-D wooden puzzle for Max (Jack's idea) that turned into the Lindos acropolis. 'Thanks, Auntie Katie. I'll do it now on my table.' He went pounding up the stairs to his room.

Sarah received her handbag solemnly and began chewing it, dribbling with contented coos.

For Nikki, besides the wine, she'd bought a peasanty blouse in soft, bright cotton.

Nikki held it up, then looked tearfully away. 'Sorry. It's just too bloody nice for slobbing round the house or supermarket, and it's not as if I go anywhere else.'

'You will.'

'When? Assuming we ever pay off enough debt to afford a week further afield than Clacton, Doug will be long gone. With someone whose tits don't hit the ground running.'

Katie sat down next to her. She kneaded Nikki's hand between her own two. 'Look, you've said yourself that a couple of kids put the squeeze on even the best marriage.'

'I want to go back to work. I don't care if I'm earning just to pay a childminder. At least I'd be part of the human race again. Doug thinks that's bonkers.'

Katie spotted the cankered rose in the garden of marital bliss. 'Well, heavens to murgatroyd, Nik, a girl's gotta do what a girl's gotta do. Would Doug prefer it if you went ga-ga with frustration, at home all day?'

Nikki snorted. 'He'd just say, join the club. Only he'd be talking about sex.'

Katie was at a loss. She had no intention of slagging off Doug with 'Tsk, bloody men' comments, in case Nikki reverted to love's young dream in the coming days, and decided to be offended at any aspersions cast on her Doug. 'I don't know what to say,' she admitted.

Nikki eyed her friend's tan jealously. 'How's Jack?'

'Jack? How's *Jack*?' Katie sucked her teeth, blushed and giggled foolishly. 'Suffice to say, you were right about him on this holiday.'

Nikki sat up, suddenly alert. 'Right about what?

What's happened? Come on, spill.'

Suppressed far longer than expected, Katie's news burst forth. 'He's asked me to marry him.'

'Honest to God? That's brilliant, Katie, really brilliant! He's a lucky sod to get you.'

Katie felt tears threatening. Tears of love for Nikki. Who else would've seen Jack as the main beneficiary of their union?

'How did he do it? Where?' asked Nikki. 'I'd say he's a romantic swine when he wants to be, like Doug of yesteryear. Ooh, I can just imagine.' Nikki came over all dreamy and unnecessary. 'Waves lapping at your feet, Jack kneeling in the midnight surf with a rose between his gnashers.'

'Er . . .' Katie wanted to lay claim to romantic circumstances. She knew Doug had proposed on a ferris wheel that got stuck and left him and Nikki suspended above a moonlit London, staring destiny in the face. Which *was* romantic when you thought about it. She gave Nikki all the details, excluding any mention of Keith. She was reluctant to give house room to the idea that Keith might have been the catalyst.

'Just don't have kids,' advised Nikki brutally. 'Carry my image before you at all times as a dire warning.'

'Still, you wouldn't be without them.' Katie smiled at Sarah, who chose that moment to open her mouth, screw up her face and start bawling. She looked like Mr Magoo. Katie's smile faded.

'Way past her bedtime,' said Nikki, rising slowly from her chair. She picked up her sobbing bundle of daughter, who quietened at once into hiccupping sniffles.

Katie rose too, feeling surplus to requirements in the presence of such maternal competence.

Nikki rubbed Sarah's back. 'I never asked, but I assume you said yes to this proposal?'

'Well, after weighing up the pros and cons,' began Katie sarcastically. 'Of course I said yes. Supposing he didn't ask again?'

'Hmm,' pondered Nikki. 'I see shades of over-gratitude here. Please try to remember, you're lovely-looking, highly intelligent, and probably far kinder and more tolerant than Mr Mean and Moody deserves.'

'Mr Mean and Moody?' echoed Katie, bridling.

'Oh, he's a good bloke, is Jack. I'm just saying, he knows what he's got in you. Don't go selling yourself short. You used to distrust anyone who liked you for yourself on the grounds there must be something wrong with them. You felt like that about me when we first hooked up.'

'I did not!'

'Then you looked for the hidden agenda. Maybe I was just after your clearly labelled diagram of a pig's heart or the Aswan dam.' She smiled mischievously over Sarah's head. 'I never set out to use you, but thank God you were there. Like Jack, I realised long ago what I had in you. The best bloody friend I was ever likely to find.'

Kate laughed shakily. 'Stop. I'm filling up here.'

'Told your mum the big news yet?'

'She's holding a family lunch this Sunday. Thought we'd grab the limelight then.'

'God, in front of Flick?'

'With a bit of luck.'

59

'I bet she'll congratulate you sweetly and fool everyone present. Especially the blokes. She's the sort of woman only other women can see through.'

'But our sixth sense is no good to us. Men just think we're jealous bitches.'

'Not all men. Good old Jack took up cudgels on your behalf and sloshed her with wine, didn't he? Can't say fairer than that.'

'I know,' said Katie, and she glowed at the memory.

Katie wasn't long home when the phone rang. What with worrying about Nikki's marriage and poor Max and Sarah ending up in a broken home (not a lightly fractured one), she eyed the phone warily. She suspected it was Freddy. He was probably calling because Jack *still* hadn't phoned him since returning from Rhodes. Conveniently for Jack, he was out playing squash with Milo. Biting her lip, Katie picked up the phone. 'Hello.'

'That you, Katie?' quavered Freddy. 'Our Jack not there?'

'He'll be back soon,' promised Katie.

'I thought you must be back from Greece by now. Then I thought, maybe not, seeing as Jack hasn't phoned. I just wanted to confirm, like, that he's coming round tomorrow week.'

'As far as I know, he is.' Katie silently cursed the absent Jack. She'd asked him twice already this week if he'd remembered to call Freddy. Each time, she'd got a dark frown, the thin-lipped treatment and the edgy mutter, 'All in my own good time.'

'I'll be coming too next Saturday, Freddy,' she decided gaily, making up for Jack's neglect by offering him two visitors for the price of one. Well, it was what she and Jack had vaguely discussed. Besides, it was only good manners to announce their engagement jointly.

There was a lot of wheezing down the phone. Katie tensed, expecting a coughing fit. 'Well,' said Freddy, recovering, 'that'll be nice, lovey. You and me against Portillo.'

'Looking forward to it,' promised Katie. Her bond with Freddy was based mostly on their private joke at Jack's expense, his nickname 'Portillo'. This was a sardonic reference to the Tory ex-minister whose Spanish father was a socialist. Lamenting his son's political beliefs, Freddy's other favourite expression was, 'I'd be spinning in my grave if I were dead.'

'Jack's been up to his tonsils at work since we got back. He'll ring you as soon as he gets in tonight.'

'No need now, love. I just needed confirmation about next Saturday.' His voice dropped. 'Suzette likes to know how many I'll be having for company before she makes her arrangements to scoot off.'

'Of course. But Jack will phone you anyway. He's been trying to make time for a proper chat, not a conversation snatched on the hoof.'

'Whatever, love. Bye, then.'

'Bye, Freddy.' Jack was going to call Freddy when he got in, come hell or high water. She surprised herself with her vehemence.

The politics of Freddy Gold and Jack's moody ambivalence towards him had given Katie rich food for thought as to how or why Jack had joined the enemy camp. Was Jack's little Englandism an act of rebellion against paternal brainwashing? Or was it to distance himself as far as possible from his working-class father, whose hacking cough was a legacy of freezing winter mornings working on the railways and who found himself, in retirement, a grace-and-favour tenant in the house of a younger, bossy woman?

Like Mary in the Bible, Katie was forced to store up all these things and ponder them in her heart. Jack refused to psychoanalyse his relationship with his father, and got a dangerously sullen look on his face whenever Katie had a go. The key questions she wanted answers to were: 'Is Freddy a kept man? Why did he sell the family home when your mum died? Where's the dosh gone?' Nothing had ever been said, but she got the impression the money from the house sale wasn't sitting in the bank, building up a nice head of interest.

Frankly, it was a worry. Jack had proposed to her, yet he'd stopped short of revealing those hidden depths he'd claimed to have. At least, where his remnant of a family was concerned.

She made herself a sandwich. Was Jack still holding back because he doubted her word over the Stairs Incident? She cut a wedge of cheese unevenly. There never would have *been* a Stairs Incident, if Tess hadn't dragooned her and Jack into holding that flat-warming party. Nibbling cheese, Katie allowed her mind to drift. Every moment of that flat-warming was branded on her brain. She only hoped there'd come a time when the details were hard to recall.

'Everyone should have a flat-warming,' declared Tess, pouring tea for Jack and Katie in the dining-room of 23 Alderney Road. 'I don't mind ringing round to invite everyone,' she offered, knowing the state of play between her daughters. 'And I could bring a few homemade snacks if you two lay on crisps and things. What do you think?' She glanced at Katie, whose chin had sunk lower and lower onto the dining-table.

'It's a good idea, Mrs G,' said Jack robustly. He squeezed Katie's hand under the table. 'It'll make the place feel more like home. What about next Sunday. Say, eight for eight-thirty?'

'That's fine,' said Tess. 'We'll be out of your hair by ten, Katie.'

'Why are you making me out to be anti-social?' mumbled Katie.

'Because you don't look too ecstatic, dear. That's why I'm offering to lighten the load with my nibbles.'

'I'll invite the Bissetts,' said Katie desperately. God, how could she avoid Flick in the bijou confines of the new flat? Suddenly, it didn't seem like her first proper home any more. It seemed like a poky hovel awaiting Flick's judgment on its pokiness. *She* had a two-bedroomed flat in Hampstead, all big and airy (so Katie had heard. Wild horses, let alone an invitation, wouldn't have dragged her over the threshold).

Tess burrowed about in the dresser drawer for an A4 pad and started a guest list. 'Flick, Simon, if he's down from university that weekend. Freddy, Suzanne—'

'Suzette. I don't think they'll come,' said Jack quickly. 'Too far from Hendon on public transport on a Sunday.'

Katie was about to ask why he couldn't scoot over to Hendon and collect them in his car. But she checked herself in time. She was beginning to realise that Jack was stubbornly reticent about a lot of things to do with his father.

'Shame, dear,' said Tess. 'I won't put Nikki and Doug down either, in case they can't get a babysitter.'

Tess's caution had proved horribly prescient. The Bissetts cried off because Sarah had colic. This raised Katie's paranoid suspicions straight away. Was colic an excuse to avoid Flick? Nikki couldn't stand her, either. And didn't colic just afflict horses?

Briefly, Katie had indulged a last-gasp fantasy that Flick would be too busy socialising elsewhere to grace such an insignificant event as a flat-warming hosted by herself and Jack. But no such luck.

She came, saw and conquered. At Katie's expense.

Katie should have spotted what was coming. Flick brewed her storm all through the chitchat. She sat on the new sofa, picture-pretty in a tiny pink suit, one kitten-heeled pink shoe dangling off her high-twitching foot. Katie knew her sister was bored stiff, and still didn't read the danger signals.

Flick had come to the flat out of curiosity, but was soon irked at not being the centre of attention. After accidentally-on-purpose treading a cheese straw into the carpet, she dived into her diamanté handbag and pouted, 'Mind if I smoke?'

'Yes,' said Katie.

'There's an alcove out by the stairwell,' said Jack mildly. 'If you wouldn't mind. I didn't know you smoked, Flick.'

She produced a tiny gold lighter. 'Now and then. Menthol cigs, good for the nerves. I've had a crap week at work.' She stood up and shimmied elegantly out of the room.

Katie felt the tension flow out of her joints. Maybe Flick had only been twitching and scowling all afternoon because she craved a fag, her latest designer habit.

That should have been that.

It would have been, if Milo, ten minutes later, hadn't buzzed the intercom and boomed from the porch downstairs, 'Jacko, boyo! Even though I wasn't invited, I've brought a crate of knock-off beer to christen your flat. Gonna let me in?'

'Come up, mate.' Jack pressed the buzzer to admit him.

Simon Gibson chose that moment to wave a bottle of sparkling wine at Jack, fizzing it up dangerously under the cork. 'I've run out of patience with this, Jack. Harder to open than a mediaeval chastity-belt. I think your corkscrew's packed up under the strain.'

'Rubbish,' said Jack, rising to grasp the bottle. He nodded at Katie. 'Would you mind meeting Milo at the top of the stairs, just in case he's got a hernia after staggering up three flights?'

Katie left the flat and headed obediently for the stairwell. Flick was standing on the top step. The other eight led down to a small platform before the second flight of nine steps began. Flick was staring broodingly into space, a curl of smoke drifting above her sheeny chestnut head. She turned at Katie's approach.

'Milo's coming up,' muttered Katie.

Her face expressionless, Flick threw down her smouldering cigarette and ground it underfoot. Her narrow pink heels wobbled on the top stair. Her ankle turned as she tried to clear the step and wriggle her suit over her hips at the same time. She winced, blushed and flicked.

'All right?' mumbled Katie. She could hear Milo's footsteps labouring upwards from the lobby below.

'Bog off, big-nose,' said Flick.

'Don't mind if I do, tar-breath!'

Katie wasn't prepared for Flick's sudden attempt to lunge past her. She tried to move aside. Instead, she bumped into Flick. Her sister flailed, uttered a high theatrical scream, and fell backwards.

At least, that was how it must have happened. Katie had been turning away from Flick. She only caught the end of Flick's backflip (with full tummy-tuck, degree of difficulty 9.5, she later told Jack) as she pitched elegantly into space, and fell smack into the fall-breaking bulk of Milo.

'Bloody hell!' he yelled, instinctively dropping his crate of beer to catch her. The crash of breaking bottles brought the others running from the flat. 'Christ!' barked Milo, heaving himself and Flick upright. 'That was a close one. Lucky for you I'm a big boy.'

Flick turned scared green eyes on him. 'Thank God you were there. Thank you *so* much.'

Katie stood rooted to the spot above as Milo picked up a hank of shiny brown hair and moved it reverently off his shoulder. Katie's ever-suspicious mind raced. Had Flick known all along Milo would be there to break her fall? Had she timed the whole thing to make herself the centre of a drama?

'What's happened?' called Jack, racing onto the scene with Tess and Simon. 'Milo, you've dropped the beer, you clumsy ape.'

'He was busy catching me when I fell,' Flick called up in a tremulous, reedy voice, unlike her normal semi-coo. 'If he hadn't been coming up behind me . . . '

'You fell?' queried Simon.

Flick said nothing. She raised her head and allowed her gaze to drift and settle, like a fine green veil, on Katie. Everyone followed her gaze. Katie stared back at her sister, a sick feeling clawing at her stomach.

Milo escorted Flick up the stairs. 'Easy does it,' he murmured as she tested her ankle for support. 'Think your other half's been watching *Whatever Happened To Baby Jane*,' he muttered in an attempted aside to Jack. But being Milo, it came out in a semi-baritone and at last galvanised Katie into action.

'I didn't push her!' she yelled defensively, even then dimly aware that protesting too much would count against her. 'Silly cow fell arse over tit in her stupid, death-trap shoes!'

'That is *enough*, Katie,' ordered Tess, her robust figure going rigid with disapproval. 'Flick's had a nasty fall. She could've been seriously hurt. Can't you think of her for once?'

But Katie was sure that Flick, without saying a word, had planted a collective thought among those present, perhaps even Jack. That Katie Gibson had deliberately and cold-bloodedly shoved her kid sister down a flight of stairs.

Rage pushed discretion aside. She turned to Flick as she limped by with Milo. 'I didn't fucking push you, you pathological liar. But I wish I had.'

'Katie, give it a rest,' begged Simon, with a younger brother's sigh of forbearance. 'Haven't you done enough for one day?'

Jack looked at Katie's white face. 'Can everyone please calm down? And kindly remember, Katie's had a shock, too.'

Katie gripped the stair railing, trying to steady her breathing. She must remember, she had an ally in Jack. He didn't judge her by her fixed place in family folklore.

Milo scurried back down the stairs to retrieve Flick's diamanté handbag, her tiny gold lighter, and one broken-heeled shoe. To Katie, the petite elegance of Flick's possessions underlined the same qualities in the woman herself. And her helplessness at the hands of her big, butch, murderous sister.

'I'm OK, it's OK.' Flick began limping towards the flat. 'Lucky I learnt to roll in gymnastics at school.'

'Very fucking lucky!' yelled Katie, unable to bear the act any longer. 'You know I didn't push you. How can you tell such a lie and live with yourself?'

'But, Katie.' Flick looked moist-eyed and puzzled. 'I never said that. I wasn't going to, you know, go into details, in front of people.' She darted a coy look at Milo.

'What pigging details?' hollered Katie.

'Well, you have got a bit of a temper,' sighed Flick. 'And we all know it can get the better of you. Maybe I even have to take a bit of the blame for that big-nose comment. When that red mist descends—'

'It's descending now, you bitch!' screeched Katie. 'Have you seriously got the brass neck to stand there and say I shoved you. Have you?' Bellowing like a bull, Katie was dimly aware of a fine spray of saliva shooting from her jaws and landing on Milo.

'Steady on, old thing,' he murmured, looking at Jack.

Katie looked at Jack, too. And was appalled to see disgust on his face – for her, not Flick.

She tried to calm down. Jack had never seen her go off the deep end before. When she lost her temper, she wasn't one for firing off Dorothy Parkeresque shafts of wit while looking cold and imperious. She was the type who stamped and yelled and got a sweaty, screwed-up face from the effort. She was giving a very bad impression of herself, scarlet and bawling like a fish-wife. In front of Jack's work colleague, too. Oh dearie dearie me, how would he live this one down in the executive washroom? Chastened by her irrational hatred of everyone on the scene (all judging her, the bastards!), she willed her outburst to recede into cold, sullen fury. 'You've made everyone think I shoved you,' she said shakily to Flick.

Flick shut her eyes and leant on Milo's shoulder. He led her gallantly away from her madwoman sister towards the flat.

'For God's sake, can it, Katie,' begged Simon. 'No one's accused you of anything. You're getting all hysterical and in need of a rabies jab.'

'Thank you, Simon,' said Jack, with an edge to his voice. 'Let's go back to the flat and have brandies all round. The main thing is, no harm done. Come on, K.'

'No bloody way!' Katie charged past them and down the stairs, nearly coming a cropper herself on the spilt beer and shards of brown glass. She turned halfway down, looking up at the weary, strained faces of Jack, Simon and her mother. Tears thickened her voice. 'She's made you all think I might have done it. That just by being so mad and hysterical, while she's all calm and collected, I could have been mad enough a few minutes ago to try and break her neck. But there's only one lying, deceiving tramp in this family. And it's not me!'

And off she went into the night for a half walk, half run, sobs juddering inside her.

She heard Jack in pursuit. Diving into the street, she ducked behind the nearest railings and crouched behind a row of wheelie bins.

Once she'd heard him give up and retreat, she gave full flow to her tears, watched dispassionately by a black-and-white cat which had finished its inspection of the bins. She welcomed its non-intrusive company. 'It's not just now that's upset me,' she sniffed, wiping her eyes on her sleeve. 'It all goes back to Steve. Even though I should be over him – am over him – since Jack came along.'

The cat licked a paw.

'She's a bit like you,' said Katie. 'Retractable claws, good at schmoozing to get her own way. All the feline graces. I'm more like a dog. I never see the kick coming.'

She reached out a hand towards the black-and-white fur. The cat began to purr as she stroked its head with a shaking hand. The rhythm of its purr soothed her. Its eyes were huge and green, empty as a shark's. And then, to justify her assessment of its self-serving fickleness, it lashed out half-heartedly with extended claws, scaring her off. She withdrew her hand and watched it slope away.

By the time she returned home, shivering with the

cold and cramped in every muscle, the flat-warmers had left. The glass and beer had been cleaned off the stairs, although the smell would linger for days to come.

Jack was clearing up in the flat. As she came in, he looked up, sat down on the new sofa, and beckoned her over. Her self-respect gone by then, she threw herself on his shoulder and cried some more. His arms crept carefully round her.

'That bitch really has it coming to her,' she sniffed. 'I *didn't* push her. I'm not evil or sneaky like that. But everyone will think I was waiting for my chance to pay her back over Steve.'

'Why would they think that? Steve was ages ago and you didn't scratch her eyes out at the time.'

'I could've been stewing,' she trumpeted into a hanky. 'Plotting my dastardly revenge, seizing the first chance I got.' She looked up at him. His jumper was smeary with her tears. 'You don't think I pushed her, do you?'

''Course not, sweetheart. She was teetering near the stairs in those shoes. It's easy to see how it happened. Come on, now.' Tenderly, he wiped her face with a clean hanky. 'A stiff drink and an early night. No harm was done, except possibly to Milo's wallet. He had to buy that beer.' He looked thoughtful. 'I'd better offer to go halves. Don't suppose Flick will cough up.'

Katie sighed, relieved to have his backing, but also aware that 'no harm done' remained the final, dismissive judgment of all who'd witnessed the incident. To anyone but her, it was a storm in a teacup, those handbags at ten paces she'd tried to avoid for the sake of her dignity. No one else would analyse it deeply enough to conclude that Flick had achieved her objective: making mud stick. It seemed clear that Flick had slipped – no one nosedived deliberately down a flight of stairs to show someone else in a bad light – but by God, she'd exploited the little drama for all it was worth.

In the months that followed, Katie had asked herself why everyone (meaning her family) was so ready to believe the worst of her, and yet they (meaning, she supposed, Tess) had never taken Flick to task for her behaviour with Steve.

Not that the Stairs Incident was alluded to, ten months down the line. Tess was used to the role of silent observer in her daughters' lives. Simon treated the hostility between his sisters as a big joke. He'd once suggested they settle their differences with a wrestling match in jelly, and he'd sell tickets to it.

Apart from Jack, only Nikki offered unswerving loyalty to Katie. In fact, Nikki, being female, went one better than Jack and got suitably outraged, offering to go halves on hiring a hitman to take out Flick.

But to Katie's way of thinking, all those present – and certainly Milo, an outsider – must have harboured at least a grain of doubt. Did she or didn't she shove her little sister? Was she capable of it?

It was yet another reason to fear and loathe the power of Flick. She could bend the minds of others with one tragic roll of those green eyes. She was worse than vindictive. She was dangerous.

On Sunday, when Jack's car turned into Alderney Road for their lunchtime visit to Tess, Katie's stomach gave an all-too-familiar lurch. Flick's red mountain bike stood against the hedge. Katie had heard she'd taken to travelling further afield on two wheels. Not that she'd be asking her sister why. She'd leave the small talk to Jack and the dinner-table repartee to Simon. Thank God Si was going to be there, a natural talker cheerfully insensitive to the nuances of veiled barbs and strained atmospheres.

As they got out of the car, Tess appeared from the side of the house, carrying a potted geranium. She was wearing an apron over her purple two-piece. 'Jack, how relaxed you look after your holiday, despite the luggage episode. Come in.'

Tess led them into the house. Jack handed over a bottle of Greek wine and answered dutiful questions about the holiday. Katie handed over the lace hankies and followed nervously, wary of Flick – not to mention Don Gibson and the strangers comprising his new family – lurking behind doorways or under big cushions.

To Katie, 23 Alderney Road was just a house, not her family home. It would never be a repository of childhood nostalgia, of tennis racquets thrown in the hallstand on summer evenings. She was glad. Ultimately, she'd have less to mourn.

Into the dining-room, and still no sign of *her*.

Tess poured sherry. Backfiring out front announced the arrival of Simon in his banger, a recent graduation present from Tess. Insofar as she allowed sentiment to get the better of her, Tess's only son was her clear favourite.

He strode in with an armful of Sunday papers, all boyish grin and sticking-up hair. 'Afternoon, campers.'

'How's life in the Trotskyist paradise of Lambeth social services?' teased Jack.

Simon had gone to university in his early twenties after bumming round Europe on a motorbike, fruit-picking and working in bars. Since his graduation, he was back living at home and training to be a social worker.

'Not an ice-pick in sight so far,' he grinned. 'These going spare?' He grabbed a sausage roll off the plate carried into the room by Tess.

'Mum,' complained Katie, 'I'm a vegetarian.'

'They're Linda McCartney's,' defended Tess.

'Even the gristle tastes authentic,' endorsed Simon with his mouth full.

Katie sat down. She was past reminding her mother that she hated the taste of meat, not just the unethical fact of its production.

She watched her mother bustle in and out with plates, knowing better than to offer help. Now sixty-one, Tess Gibson, née Houlihan, hadn't looked for help since the day she kicked her errant husband into touch and raised his three children alone. Don had paid maintenance, of course, until Simon's gradu-ation. Tess had never gone out to work. Her home was her fortress; her refusal to go to pieces was her life's work. Katie admired her mother, but was slightly in awe of her survival skills. She was pretty sure she'd go to pieces and end up in the nearest funny farm if Jack, in years to come, took up with a Tanya-alike. But Tess and Don had managed a civilised, almost antiseptic break-up. If there had been flaming rows and a Don entreaty for one last chance, the Gibson children hadn't heard any of it.

Tess didn't replace him. No 'uncles' came and went on overnight stays. She never bad-mouthed her ex – she never referred to him at all. It was doubtful they'd spoken since the day he shipped out, his golf bag clanking against his knees, his children hanging silently over the banisters to record the solemnity and scary implications of the occasion.

Tess and Don had treated them beforehand to some half-baked Disneyesque speech about Mummy and Daddy not wanting to live together any more, but still loving them all very, very much. Which struck a hollow note when Don went to America and seemed to forget he had children in London.

Katie hadn't been left scarred for life and she doubted if Simon had, either. He'd been only two at the time. As for Flick, who could say? Flick was like Tess, an iceberg whose visible one-third bobbed above the surface, either hoping you wouldn't probe for the two-thirds beneath, or wouldn't realise that what you saw was the sum total. Either way, Flick and Tess were master illusionists.

Now Tess peered past Katie, through the french windows and into the back garden. 'Where have they got to?'

'They?' It had to be Don and co. Flick must be out there, too, laying claim to being number-one daughter, taking them for a pre-dinner turn in the garden.

Katie's heart began a muffled thud. She was still brimful of her engagement news, but she didn't share Jack's keenness to hog the limelight in such a suddenly extended family.

'Here they are,' sang Tess.

The french windows creaked open. Katie felt a draught on the back of her neck and turned slowly. Her smile was clamped in position, her hand primed to shoot out and greet Legs Up To Her Armpits Tanya and two transatlantic step-sisters.

Flick stepped daintily through the open window. Followed less daintily by a tall, stooping, shaggy carthorse of a man.

'Everyone,' said Flick, 'I'd like you to meet my fiancé, Dan Avebury.'

Chapter Four

Loitering in the garden with Flick, Dan Avebury had geared himself up to make a relaxed, cool entrance. Not that he wanted to make an entrance at all. He'd have been happier sunk in the depths of an unobtrusive armchair indoors, watching Flick's family arrive one by one. But he knew Flick did want to make an entrance. She had a theatrical flair for seizing the moment.

That was why she'd dragged him round her mother's garden, and then to the tiny greenhouse, pretending Mrs Gibson was interested in growing a fig tree. 'Alma or Osborne's Prolific?' he'd asked. 'They're best under glass. Brown Turkey and Black Ischia are better outdoors. Now if she had a conservatory, she could grow the mistletoe fig, *ficus deltoidea*.'

At which point, he'd forced himself to shut up. He always droned on like a fool, way past his listener's attention span. That was what came of trying to be helpful. There was a fine line between enthusiasm and harassment, and he only knew he'd crossed it at the garden centre when punters started falling over shrubs in their haste to get away.

As they stepped through the open french windows, he reached clumsily for Flick's hand. But she was one step ahead of him. 'Everyone, I'd like you to meet my fiancé, Dan Avebury.'

He nearly fell flat on his burning face. 'Hello,' he mumbled.

There was a short silence. 'And on that bombshell!' squawked Flick's brother in an excellent Alan Partridge impression.

'Simon,' warned Mrs Gibson. Dan had met her earlier. She came forward and introduced the rest of the family formally. Simon was lanky and gave him a matey wink. Katie, the megabitch of popular legend, looked harmless, if a little stunned. She was very pretty in a wholesome way, with streaked hair and a tan. Last was Katie's boyfriend, a self-assured-looking bloke called Jack. He had a dry handshake and a tight, judgmental smile. Reserving judgment on Simon and Katie, Dan decided Jack wasn't his type. He was too terrified of Mrs Gibson to form a definite opinion on her. He was just relieved when Flick linked her arm through his and resumed control of the situation. 'Lovely spread, Mum. Hope you weren't starting without us.'

'As the orgy said to the bishop,' chortled Simon. 'What's this ruddy wedding business? Bloody hell, as the man of the house, where's my shotgun?'

'Like I'd tell *you*,' pouted Flick playfully.

Jack cleared his throat. 'Actually,' he began, 'the funny thing is, when Katie and I were on ho—'

'Look, there's a – a hedgehog in the garden!'

shrieked Katie and made a desperate lunge at Jack, shoving him towards the french windows. 'At least I thought it was a hedgehog. Maybe it was a pile of leaves.'

Jack looked startled. Not half as startled as Dan felt. Maybe the megabitch was also a loon.

Everyone jumped again as a cork popped nearby. 'We haven't said congrats yet,' declared Mrs Gibson, holding a frothing bottle aloft. 'I kept this for the first of my children to make me a mother-in-law. Let's have a toast. To Pippa and Daniel!'

'Dan will be fine,' said Dan shyly. He stood there, feeling a total berk, as Flick's family raised their glasses. Katie drained hers in one go.

'And by the way, Si,' said Flick, tossing her hair. 'This isn't a shotgun job.'

'You mean I can't even horsewhip him?' Simon asked sadly. He turned to Dan. 'I hope you've been careful of my sister's honour. More careful than she's been, anyway.'

'Simon, you've started early, even for you,' complained Tess. 'Let's all sit down.'

For some reason, in trying to look at no one in particular, Dan met Katie's eye. He sat down, blushing, and knocked his cutlery off the table.

'Heard you lost your luggage, Jack,' said Flick. 'Put in a claim yet?'

Jack gave her such a dazzling smile, Dan wouldn't have been at all surprised if he practised it in front of a mirror. Smug git, he decided.

'No one gives a toss about my luggage. We want to hear about you and Dan the man here.'

'Too right,' nodded Simon.

'Dan's a garden designer,' revealed Mrs Gibson. 'Isn't that right, Dan?'

'Er, yes,' he agreed, 'by training. At the moment, I work in a garden centre. Doing, you know, more everyday stuff.'

'He knows everything there is to know,' put in Flick. 'What's that rose, Dan? The one that's useless in a bed, but great up against a wall?'

'Can't remember,' panicked Dan, glancing in terror at Mrs Gibson.

She patted his arm. 'Flick thinks I'll keel over and die on the spot at the mention of anything rude. She seems to forget how she got here.'

Dan could have died on the spot. Flick had never mentioned that her mother, despite being a Catholic and having a Queen-addressing-the-Commonwealth hairdo, was quite . . . liberal.

'How did you two meet?' asked Jack, passing Dan the buttered rolls.

Dan took one clumsily and got butter on his trailing cuff. 'Erm, well, you know . . .'

'We've met on and off at the garden centre for the last couple of years,' replied Flick smoothly. 'Every time Stempson's do a fashion shoot for the store catalogue, I have to pop down there and pick out background foliage. Dan's always been a great help.' She smiled at him. 'It's only recently we stepped up a gear.'

A short silence descended, during which Dan squirmed. He scraped the butter off his cuff with a serviette. He knew what they were thinking, the stuck-up bastards. What did a beautiful, sophisticated woman with a great job see in a hulking great navvy like him? He threw his head up defiantly, only to meet Katie's eye again. But she didn't look stuck-up at all. Her gaze rested softly on him. He smiled gratefully.

'So this is a whirlwind romance,' persisted Simon. 'But you knew about their engagement before today, didn't you, Ma?'

'A little birdy might've told me,' conceded Mrs Gibson.

'I told her last week,' said Flick. 'Because I got this fantastic idea, which Mum agrees with. Dan and I are going to get married as soon as poss, and move into Cloverley.'

Katie gasped.

'Blimey,' said Simon. 'I didn't know it was still standing.'

Dan decided to make his pitch for why he and Flick should take over Cloverley House, Mrs Gibson's childhood home. It was a rambling wreck of a farmhouse near a village called Marsham in Kent. The house was still owned by Mrs Gibson and stood (just about) on a scrubby acre of land. The surrounding land – Cloverley's only valuable asset – had long since been sold off.

'Me and Flick have been to look at it,' explained Dan. 'And it seems to us, if someone, could, you know, make a go of it . . . it could . . .' He trailed off, alarmed by the sound of his own voice in the attentive room.

'Look,' interposed Flick patiently, pointedly excluding Katie as she turned to Simon and Jack. 'Cloverley has a big old garden and Dan's a garden designer. He's the perfect person to restore it. And I'll do up the house, restore it to its former glory.'

Simon snorted. 'Former glory? It's a heap of stones. You'd need a fortune to do it up. Anyway, it's cursed. There be ghosties in tham thar hills, ooer, missus!' He hopped off his chair and pulled his jumper over his head to make an impromptu Dracula cape. Then he loomed over Katie, 'oohing' inside the cowl of his jumper until she lost patience, muttered, 'Get off, you berk,' and shoved him away.

'But seriously,' frowned Jack, 'you two really think you can restore Cloverley? I've never seen the place, admittedly . . .' He shrugged eloquently.

Dan felt goaded enough to respond tartly, 'Well, we've given it a thorough once-over.' He faltered under Jack's challenging gaze. 'It's got loads of potential. Soil's a bit chalky in Kent, of course.'

'Bit far for commuting,' muttered Katie, her first direct comment.

'I'll give up the garden centre job,' said Dan.

'And I'll commute to Stempson's for a while, see what happens,' flicked Flick. 'I might even go free-lance. Any more questions? Only Dan and I would like to pause for eating.'

'Just the one,' piped up Simon. 'You said as soon as possible for the wedding. When did you have in mind?'

Flick counted off her manicured fingers. 'Five Saturdays from now, in Hampstead register office. Not a big do. *Close* family and friends only.' Dan might've imagined it, but her green eyes rested briefly on Katie.

Simon's eyebrows lifted. 'Thought you'd object to the lack of a proper church do, Mum.'

'Don't stir it,' pouted Flick. 'Dan and I have

sounded Mum out. If she'd been cool on the registry office idea, we'd have reconsidered.'

'I've had time to think, over the years,' said Tess, smiling at Dan. 'It's not the setting that counts, is it? It's how sincere the two people are, and I've been to some beautiful civil ceremonies in my time.'

Simon winked at Jack. 'So now you know. You and Katie can really push the boat out. How about a bungee-jumping ceremony for you two?'

Katie stood up and announced she was off to the loo. Flick smiled. As Katie's flit had delayed the start of lunch still further, she pushed back her own chair and shimmied into the garden for a cigarette.

In their absence, conversation drifted back to Cloverley House. Simon seemed hell-bent on dissuading anyone from having anything to do with it while Jack, who'd admitted never seeing the place, nodded sagely at every offputting remark.

Dan was forced to revisit a history he already knew. How Mrs Gibson's Irish father, a farmer from the ould sod, had been defeated by Cloverley's running damp and grudging crop yields. 'In Ireland, he only had the Black and Tans to deal with,' Simon pointed out. 'Over here, that house defeated him, swallowing every penny he made, for roof repairs, damp coursing – Mum was lucky not to get rickets and worse, growing up there.'

'It's a money-pit,' nodded the smug Jack.

Dan opened his mouth. He could've knocked them off their self-righteous perches with a few choice words. But no, he'd promised Flick. Their future plans were *their* secret.

'No offence, mate, but I give you six months in that

place before you chuck in the towel,' finished Simon.

'Tops,' added Jack.

'You don't know what you're talking about,' said Dan bluntly.

Jack and Simon drew back, frowning.

'What Dan means,' said Mrs Gibson, touching his arm, 'is that you have to take the root-and-branch approach. My father, God rest him, could only afford a bit of patching here and there as he went along. He'd no sooner fixed a few roof-slates than the rain would be dripping into buckets again.' She gazed nostalgically into the middle distance. 'This is Cloverley's last chance before it falls into rack and ruin. If Daniel and Flick want to take on such a big project, good luck to them.'

'But Grandad knew what he was doing,' snorted Simon. 'At least he was born rural. Which only goes to show.' He adopted another foolishly menacing voice. 'It was that house, I tell you. There be malice bred in its very stones.'

'Give it a rest, Si,' ordered Flick, returning from her cigarette break. 'If only someone *had* fallen to a mysterious death from an attic window, we could rope in passing coach tours and charge them for tea and a tour.'

'Surely a podding serving-wench was turned into the snow one Christmas Eve and cursed Cloverley House and all its descendants with her dying breath?' said Simon, looking disappointed. 'Maybe I'll pop down to Marsham and see what I can dig up in the village library.'

'Be *our* guest,' said Flick, her little finger creeping onto Dan's wrist. 'You can even come and stay with us. After the wedding, Dan and I are moving into a cottage in Marsham while the builders do up Cloverley.'

'I hear Marsham has changed,' said Katie in a high, breathless voice, gliding back to the table. 'Gone all heritage-mad. There are signs everywhere saying "here stood ye oldy parish pump".' She blushed. 'That true, Dan?'

'It's got all that,' said Flick dismissively. 'But it's still a rat-run for tankers on their way to the motorway. We might even join the Marsham bypass campaign.'

'That would be very political for you,' said Jack mildly.

Flick blew him a kiss. Dan tensed as Jack fielded the kiss and blew it back as a soft raspberry. Not yet attuned to Gibson family dynamics, Dan was unhappy at any signs of intimacy between the best-looking couple at the table. He glanced at Katie to see if she was put out, but she was busy topping up her wine-glass.

'I do not believe it,' raged Katie in Victor Meldrew mode on the way home. 'Upstaged yet again. That bloody cow!'

Jack slumped grimly over the steering-wheel. 'And he was a wanker.'

'I mean,' Katie raged on, 'how would Mum like it if we gave her a few weeks' notice of our wedding? Which we can't do now. It'll have to be a wedding the total opposite of Flick's or everyone will say I jumped on her bandwagon. Grrr!'

'And I didn't like the way he was looking at you,' grunted Jack.

'Was he looking at me?' she asked, glad it was too

dark in the car to reveal her blushes. 'Can't say I noticed.'

'He had difficulty finishing his sentences. Did you notice? Not that he had anything worth saying. What does Flick see in him?'

'Sex?' suggested Katie. Intrigued though she was by Flick's unlikely fiancé, she had more grumbles to get out of her system. 'And now, of course, we can't even announce we're getting married until the dust has settled after Flick's. God, if only I'd told Mum when I phoned her the other day. Now everyone will think I'm rushing to the altar because Flick set the trend.'

'I don't see why we should wait,' said Jack irritably. 'We could sneak off to Las Vegas or do it on a Caribbean beach, then come home and tell everyone. That's different enough from Flick's.'

For the rest of the drive home, they gave this idea half-hearted consideration. Katie pointed out that they were skint after Rhodes, that Tess and Freddy might be offended by an offstage wedding, and that if you got married on the sly you did yourself out of wedding presents.

Jack found a cogent response only to the last obstacle. 'We come back and throw a big party. We lay on the booze and grub, and the guests bring presents.'

'It's a bit mercenary,' said Katie sadly. Weddings had suddenly lost their appeal.

Dan accompanied Flick back to Hampstead, loading her bike on to the tube. He didn't like her cycling in traffic. He was peeved that she'd cycled to Balham at all, when she normally restricted her journeys to short, local trips.

It also meant he hadn't been able to meet Flick en route to her mother's, and get her to calm his nerves. Instead, he'd caught the train from Richmond, near his bedsit, then waited for her outside Balham tube station.

Now he wanted to know what she thought of his performance at lunch. Had he passed muster with her mother? He guessed that Mrs Gibson was used to finding thrusting executive types on her daughter's arm.

He gripped Flick's bicycle as the tube swayed and lurched. The carriage was nearly empty. After a bit, when she still hadn't said anything, he risked, 'Your mum probably expected a thrusting executive type.'

Flick gave a little sigh and flicked her hair playfully into his face. 'Mum's prepared for anything. She's very open-minded.'

'Thanks,' he said, crushed.

'Oh, Dan.' She snuggled against him, making him feel wonderfully mellow and all-powerful at the same time. 'You big old softy. How could she not like you?'

'I've got dirt under my fingernails,' he reminded her. 'I'm one step up from a jobbing labourer.'

She stood on tiptoe to kiss his neck, which went blotchy with excitement. 'Stay at my place tonight, Dan.'

Dan looked down at his large, ungainly feet. His dad said he walked as if he was getting used to snow-shoes. 'You sure?' he asked.

She didn't make a habit out of asking him to stay overnight. He reckoned she was right to be disciplined about it. They both had a lot to sort out before the wedding. They needed their space (strictly speaking,

Dan didn't need his mouldy bedsit space, but he appreciated why Flick needed hers). Anyway, they'd be together soon enough, living in Marsham while they rebuilt Cloverley.

'Sure I'm sure, you big hairy dope,' said Flick.

He loved being lovingly insulted. He felt a rush of happiness. Unbelievably, he had Flick. Now he couldn't wait to get his hands on Cloverley, on that garden lying sunk under brambles and neglect.

'Dan?' laughed Flick. 'You're always looking at your feet. Look up, not down, my dad used to say.'

He blushed. 'When I was a kid and Dad started one of his rants, I used to look down at my feet in case eye contact made him worse. They say you should look away from an angry dog because it sees eye contact as a challenge. And if you smile, all it sees is your teeth.'

'Leave your dad to me,' said Flick. 'And give us a kiss.'

He wheeled her bike when they got off the tube. As they walked to her flat, he thought about telling her that he owed his interest in gardening to his father. When he was ten, Phil Avebury had locked him out of the house for a whole chilly Saturday, to teach him respect for his elders and to make his bed when he was told to. In an attempt to distract himself from the cold, Dan had allowed himself to be fascinated by the life at his feet – beetles and earthworms and roots – jostling for space in the darkness between green blades.

But it was a bit self-indulgent to go on about himself, he realised. Especially when Flick's family were more intriguing.

'Katie looked harmless,' he said, once they were in Flick's elegant flat.

'Looks can be deceiving with that one.'

He followed her into the kitchen. 'Are you going to invite your dad?'

Flick pulled the ice tray out of the fridge, popped out a cube and rolled it across her temples. 'Nope.'

Dan looked at her adoringly. 'Headache? Want a massage?'

'Just a bit tired. And you needn't worry I'm pining for Dad to give me away. We were never close. He never remembered birthdays after he left. Sometimes, he'd get wind of a big event, like my eighteenth, and send a fistful of dollars in a card. Doubt he'd come if I asked him.'

'As long as you're not just being brave,' said Dan, all concern.

Flick slammed the fridge door. 'For Chrissake, Dan! He's a louse.'

He stepped back as if he'd been shot. Or stupid enough to make eye contact with his father.

'I'm sorry,' she sighed, and her eyes went all big.

She held out her thin arms and Dan stepped into them, giving her a self-conscious bear-hug. His heart ached for her. He'd forgotten what an ordeal lunch had been for her, too, all those questions being fired at once. 'Sorry to go on,' he said. 'I just can't imagine what sort of bloke walks out on his family without a backward glance.'

'What's so hot about an ever-present father? Look at Phil.'

'See what you mean,' he said cautiously. Not for the first time, he resolved to stay out of the whole fathers minefield. It wasn't as if any good could come from comparing notes. Don Gibson: cheating bastard. Phil

Avebury: bastard. The pair of them were best left in the back of the memory drawer. Though that was easier said than done, when Phil was still around. He'd been the first to hear about their wedding plans. They'd called round the day before with their big news.

Phil had asked two key questions: 'When?' and 'Who's paying?'

Once they revealed their plans for a registry office ceremony and the lowest of low-key receptions, he'd become quite affable, going so far as to offer Dan the cost of new shoes for the big day. New shoes!

If it hadn't been so insulting, Dan would've laughed his socks – and shoes – off.

'You're all right, Dad,' he'd responded with the words he knew Phil wanted to hear. 'I've got the whole thing sorted. You just turn up. Treat *yourself* to new shoes,' he'd added mischievously, emboldened by Flick at his side.

'I'm going for a bath,' she announced now, padding past him out of the kitchen. 'Be an angel and make us a few crustless sarnies.'

'We could share a bath,' he offered daringly.

'We could, sweetheart, if there was anywhere to dangle your legs. I think we'll have a sunken, circular bath at Cloverley,' she added. 'And a Jacuzzi. And a big claw-foot bath where you can slough off your artisan dirt when you come in from the garden.'

'Um, OK,' he agreed in all seriousness, though a profusion of baths suggested separate bathing would be the order of the day at Cloverley, too. 'Sarnies coming up.'

After her bath, she joined him on the sofa, wrapped

in a flowery kimono and smelling of bath salts. She sat down next to him, ignoring the tea he'd brewed to complement the sandwiches. Her face was pensive and her eyes huge. 'I've been thinking while I marinated in the bath, Dan. I want to tell you about me and Katie. I want you to know the whole story.'

'Flick, I know that—'

'Listen first. You're an only child, like Jack. You're bemused by the scab-picking brothers and sisters go in for. Katie and I never got on, which isn't unusual. But now she hates me, all because of that Steve bloke I told you about.' She paused, studying her pearl-pink nails.

'I know,' remarked Dan, feeling comment was expected.

'You reckon?' she said glumly.

'Yeah I do. You told me. He was going out with Katie, then he met you, and kaboom. I know it must have pissed off Katie big-time – but these things happen. She's well over it now. She's got Jack.' Relieved for his sake that Steve Wotsit was no longer the love of Flick's life, he stroked her knee through flowered silk. 'How could I blame you?'

'Everyone else does. In my family, I mean. And good ole Katie will have given chapter and verse to anyone she's ever met. My sister, the superbitch man-stealer.'

'Because you, er, didn't resist the attraction?' hazarded Dan, feeling like a man asked to walk barefoot across hot coals.

She nodded and sighed, flicking hair off her shoulder. 'You see, he told me he and Katie were on the verge of splitting up anyway. That it wouldn't come as a shock to her if he went off with another woman.'

Dan held his tongue, on the tip of which teetered an observation that the identity of the other woman had probably been the prime cause of shock.

'Like a fool, I let myself be reeled in,' said Flick bitterly. 'I can't honestly say it was more than lust at first sight. I went against my better judgment, but that's what happens when you believe a bloke's weasel words.'

Dan nodded sagely. He painted a quick thumbnail sketch in his head of Steve Wotsit, debauched seducer of innocent young women.

'I mean, it was never going to last,' she went on, clutching the flowered lapels of her gown round her shoulders. 'I always knew that. We had nothing in common. He'd been doing a PhD for about a hundred years, living off his auntie and pissing his student loan away down the pub. I bet he still hasn't finished his thesis.' She looked down at her nails. 'Katie would've bought into all that penniless student crap. She'd never have twigged him for the lowlife sponger he was. She's too naive, which is good news for insecure men, like dear old Jack.'

Dan swooped on this digression for some light relief. 'What do you mean? What's insecure about Jack?'

'Everything,' retorted Flick. 'He can fool everyone but himself with that Mr Cool act. Jack's ashamed of his background and lives in terror of his public-school chums digging it up. Katie's meat and drink to a bloke like that because she goes in for all that soothing the ruffled brow nonsense. In exchange, Jack extends her the courtesy of allowing her to be his girlfriend.'

Dan balked at the sneer in Flick's tone. He hadn't heard it there before.

'But sod them.' She looked up at Dan with a fluttery-eyed gaze. 'I'm ashamed of taking up with Steve. The worst of it is, I'm ashamed for my own self-respect, not because it might have hurt Katie.'

'No "might have" about it,' said Dan, with uncharacteristic sharpness. 'It must have knocked the poor woman for six. They'd been going out for what – over a year? And you swiped him from under her nose, then threw him over after a two-week fling. Like you said, though, it was only a bit of lust.' He was losing his train of thought and righteous indignation under Flick's steady gaze. 'I suppose Katie reckons you could have walked away from the situation. If he was gonna leave her anyway, it didn't have to be for you.'

Her eyes glittered. 'Right Mr Moral Majority, aren't you? I'm not proud of going off with Steve, but at least I outed him in his true colours before she went off and married him or something. *And* I'm the one who persuaded him to tell Katie about us. I didn't want to go sneaking around behind her back.'

Dan, surprised at the force of his indignation on Katie's behalf, struggled to cope with the twists and turns in Flick's revelations. Her confession was couched in strangely defiant humility – and now it turned out she'd been doing a public service.

She took a deep breath. 'I'm telling you this to let you know my standing in other people's eyes. I have no illusions, Dan, and I don't want you to have any, either.' Her brio evaporated and, to Dan's horror, her eyes filled with tears. 'I wish the past could be wiped out and that I was a better person. Someone worthy of you.'

He pulled her towards him, galvanised by tenderness. 'Flick, sweetheart, so you made a mistake. Nobody died. You can't go on torturing yourself. I didn't get the impression at lunch today that anyone hates your guts. Not even Katie. I was expecting her to be Lucrezia Borgia, but she seemed like, you know, she had a side you could appeal to.' A Shakespearian quote bubbled up from his subconscious. 'Her quality of mercy wasn't strained. Know what I mean?'

Flick cuddled up against him. 'To coin my own phrase, I was young and I needed the adulation. I was flattered that Katie's boyfriend preferred me. Don't you think – I know everyone else does – that she's prettier than me?'

'You serious?' Dan was beginning to enjoy himself. She'd never clung to him like this before, making him feel so necessary to her happiness. 'You and Katie have different kinds of beauty. I know which I prefer.' He kissed the top of her head loyally.

'And you don't hate me over the Steve thing?' she asked in a small voice.

'I *love* you, Flick.' He crushed her to his ribs.

'Because I'm not little miss perfect and I can't live with that image if we're going to be married.'

'Don't want you to be perfect. God knows I'm not.'

'And while brutal honesty is no defence or excuse, I just had to remind you that everyone has the odd skeleton in their cupboard.' She brushed her button nose against his. 'Do you forgive me?'

'You know I do. I'm not Katie, caught in the thick

of it, so I can see it from your point of view. I know there are always two sides.'

'Give us a kiss,' murmured Flick. Afterwards, she rested her chin on his shoulder and stared into space. A satisfied little smile played on her feline face.

'Come in, the pair of you,' a tremulous Freddy greeted Jack and Katie in Hendon. 'Tea's nearly mashed. Pull up a pew and tell the old man about your holiday.'

He led the way into the living-room. Through the open kitchen door, Katie glimpsed three of everything laid out on the worktop – powder-blue cups, saucers, teaspoons, and even three biscuits, huddling together for company on a willow-pattern plate. Suzette's handiwork, she guessed, prepared before she left.

Katie dropped into an armchair. It was chintzed right down to the valance. Feeling something crackle, she slid her hand down the side and drew out a copy of the *Racing Post*. Freddy, on his way to the kitchen, paused to look guilty.

'Dad,' complained Jack, swiping the newspaper. 'You haven't!'

'Just the odd flutter, son.' He looked stubborn. 'You need some comforts in life.'

'You're not gambling with your pension?' asked Jack.

Freddy's liver-spotted fingers clutched his baggy oatmeal cardigan. He wore it, rain or shine, like a hairshirt. Katie felt sorry for him, and annoyed by Jack's sharp tone.

Freddy was a small, stooping man with watery blue eyes. Scraps of white hair clung to a balding scalp, making him look older than sixty-three. It was possible, now and then, to see echoes of the handsome man who had once inhabited this wreck.

'Leave him alone, Jack,' begged Katie. 'So what if he enjoys the odd flutter? It's up to you what you do with your pension, isn't it, Freddy?'

Freddy almost straightened inside the cardigan. 'It is just the odd time, son, when there's a big race on. I don't bother otherwise.' He shuffled off.

Jack chewed his bottom lip moodily. 'Listen, K, just remember one thing about Dad and Suzette. She does all his meals and laundry, and doesn't take a penny for bills. Her old man left her provided for and, I'll say one thing, she's not grasping.'

'Is this Suzette's late husband?' Katie picked up a photo on the polished sideboard. A thin-lipped man with military bearing held in his stiff embrace an untidy-haired woman with a gap in her front teeth.

Jack peered over her shoulder. 'Suzette and Brian on their wedding day. He worked on the railways with Dad.'

'He looks like a wife-beater.'

'Listen, don't rock the boat for Dad, K. Where else would he find a billet as cushy as this?'

'Can't you be a bit nicer to him, though? I mean, he's right. What's the point of being alive if every pleasure's cramped out of existence by you, Suzette and the must-have-a-purpose-in-life brigade? He's worked hard all his life, surely he can do what he likes now, even if it means doing nothing, or stuff you don't approve of? He's too old to go playing squash, in case you hadn't noticed.'

She hadn't meant to sound so sharp. Jack's mouth downturned sulkily.

She replaced the photo and moved restlessly to the piano. It was just for show, the closed lid covered in a strip of fringed lace weighted down with more photos. 'Did Brian play?' she asked, depressing a foot-pedal. It rose back slowly, spongy from lack of use.

'Family heirloom of Suzette's,' he muttered. 'She sees it more as a dust-trap.'

Katie waded through the photos until she found the one she was looking for, hovering out of sight in a small, oval frame. It was a photo of Jack's parents on their wedding day, Freddy's sole attempt to stamp a shared presence on the room.

In this grainy photo, Freddy looked heartbreakingly handsome, his hair as darkly blond as Jack's, if not as thick. Already, at twenty-eight, he had a slight slope to his shoulders, as if stooping to receive burdens yet to come.

Jack's mother, Janet, had been another sturdy, mousey addition to the yeoman stock, adulterating the Gold genes still further. Thank goodness, thought Katie with a surge of possessive pride, her Jack was a throwback to the first, attractive Gold, the one who'd ditched 'stein' but kept and passed on his looks.

'Tea's up,' announced Freddy, puffing through the doorway with a laden tray.

Jack sprang up. 'Let me, Dad. I should've offered in the first place.'

They met in the middle of the room, bumping into each other. There was a brief tug-of-war over the tray, the crockery rattling in protest, until Jack gave up and went back to his chair, bumping into a pouffe on the way.

Katie felt for them both. She knew Jack wouldn't be

happy about her witnessing that little scene. In the moments since their arrival, Jack's confidence had begun to evaporate. He was embarrassed by his father.

If that had been the whole story, Katie might have disliked Jack. But it was more complex than that. Jack was a driven man, impatient of self-inflicted failure, which, unfortunately, his father epitomised. So a son's love battled with exasperation and even resentment. Freddy did nothing to help himself, since he was clearly afraid of Suzette, a woman who rationed the number of biscuits he could offer to guests. No wonder Jack had poured himself into a different mould. Becoming the opposite of Freddy, socially and politically, must have seemed like the best way of avoiding being a chip off the old block.

'Look,' mumbled Jack. 'Sorry to go off on one about the gee-gees, Pops.'

'Found a soft spot for the working man?' joked Freddy, winking at Katie.

She smiled back, happy that Jack was making an effort. 'How's your sciatica?' she asked.

'So-so, now the weather's looking up. The circulation in my foot's not the best, but no point pestering the quack. He won't refer you to a hospital unless you've bits falling off. You pay into the system all your life, and when you need it, his lot have closed every hospital in sight.' Pointing a mock-accusatory finger at Jack, he broke into a hacking cough.

'Be fair, Pops,' said Jack mildly. 'Your lot are in power now.'

'Don't get me started on Blair,' wheezed Freddy. This was as animated as he got and it played havoc with his chest.

'OK, we'll look at our holiday snaps instead,' soothed Jack, reaching into his jacket pocket. 'You should come with us one year. What do you think, Katie?'

''Course,' nodded Katie, driven to martyr-like munificence by the thought of liberating Freddy from Suzette for a week. 'Suzette could do her own thing for a week, maybe go off with her friends.'

Freddy took a sip of tea. He wrinkled his lips over his small, pointy teeth. 'She don't mince words, your girl, Jack. She only wants my company if I'm not part of a certain couple.' Katie blushed furiously, but Freddy said thickly, 'Thanks for thinking of me, love. We all need a break from the other half now and then.'

Katie perched on Freddy's arm-rest to talk him through the photos. Already, she could barely remember the days they recalled, of hot beach, white stone walls and herself a blaze of primary colours against the Lindos acropolis.

'Look at that sunshine,' sighed Freddy. 'Looks lovely, right enough. No pictures of the pair of you together?'

'Oh, we don't bother,' said Katie. She wasn't going to drop Jack in it by telling Freddy that he didn't trust passing plebs with his state-of-the-art camera.

'We decided to get engaged while we were away,' said Jack, taking Katie's breath away with the casualness of his announcement. 'Only, it's not official. Katie's sister got in her own announcement the other day, so we're keeping shtum until her wedding's over.'

'That's great news, son! Good lad, good girl.' Freddy's eyes moistened.

Katie touched his arm shyly. 'You're the only

person we've told so far. So if you wouldn't mind keeping it to yourself . . . '

'Won't even tell Suzette,' he said loyally, though Katie guessed that keeping secrets from Suzette was second nature. She wondered how long the *Racing Post* had been down the side of the chair.

'Getting married,' he said in wonder. 'Well, I won't say "about time", but it is.' He wiped his eyes quickly on the corner of his cardigan. 'Anyone need a bit of fresh air? I've got those hydrangeas up and running.'

'I'll wash up,' offered Katie. 'I'll handle the cups like fine china,' she assured him ironically, and began gathering up the remnants of the tea party. She felt she should give father and son some time alone.

From the kitchen window, she enjoyed a clear view of them standing under a pergola at the bottom of the neat little garden. Jack's tall frame was lowered towards his father's stooping one, as Freddy gestured, talked and rearranged his cardigan. For the first time, she noticed a parental tenderness in Jack's stance; that reversal of roles as parents slipped into second childhood. Now Jack was the father-figure, appearing to listen intently to the babble of a less focused mind, while part of him was probably disengaged and thinking – worrying – about Freddy's future.

Except, thought Katie with a little chill, Freddy didn't have the unformed, hopeful future of a child.

Sighing, she swirled bubbles over Suzette's powder-blue crockery. Close kinship was scary in its power to enslave, to demand rather than inspire commitment. Maybe she was better off not knowing Tess too well. And being reassured by the solid self-sufficiency that characterised what she did know of her mother.

Chapter Five

It was happy hour in the cocktail bar, and Katie had never seen Nikki happier. She was halfway through her third Hairy Nipple – presumably a post-feminist complement to the Hairy Navel – with the fruits of a day's clothes-shopping clustered in bags around her feet. They had come 'up west' for the day on the tube, reliving their teenage Saturdays.

The day out was Doug's idea. He'd offered to babysit for a whole Saturday and send Nikki off to recapture her lost youth and sparkle.

On previous occasions, Katie and Nikki had tried the girly day out with Sarah in a sling or push-chair, sometimes Max trotting alongside, but it wasn't the same. Instead of purely selfish indulgence, the day revolved around keeping the children happy, or at least sated with food, drink and sensory experiences.

Nikki was grateful for Doug's offer to babysit, but suspicious of his motives. 'After this, will he expect me to stay indoors for the next ten years?' she asked Katie. They'd visited old stomping grounds in Oxford

Street, trying on skimpy clothes and tutting aloud at the prices. It was allowed at their age. They'd even tried on clothes in a communal changing room, which Katie would never have braved on her own, all too aware of her orange-peel thighs. Nikki displayed her cellulite with pride. 'Gives these teenagers some idea what's coming to them,' she declared.

After this public service, they'd slipped into £500 ballgowns in Liberty's, pretending to the po-faced assistants they were serious about buying them.

Katie eventually began to enjoy herself. She rarely ventured into central London any more, preferring to potter tamely around Crystal Palace. Nikki, resplendent in green mohair jumper and canary-yellow capri pants, was the perfect companion to take up west on a Saturday. Her bulk and vividness acted as a buffer between Katie and the swirling street masses. Nikki even talked her into buying a pair of useless, desirable pink jelly shoes.

She'd told Nikki about Flick's upstaging wedding announcement, but until flopping into the cocktail bar there'd been no time for analysis.

As soon as they sat down, Nikki slapped her forehead. 'We should have gone shopping for your wedding outfit.'

'Not sure if I'm buying or recycling,' Katie had admitted.

Now Nikki, slurping the dregs of her Hairy Nipple through a twisted straw, was ready for more lowdown on Flick's wedding. 'So what's he like,' she demanded, 'the man who's captured the frozen organ that passes for your sister's heart?'

'His name's Dan. Late twenties, like Flick, shaggy

hair, prematurely grey in places. He's a garden designer, currently lugging bags of peat moss about in a garden centre. He's really sweet, but very much the honest artisan. Hardly Flick's ideal husband. God knows what her Hampstead circle will think. I can't believe she's compromised her image and written off her market value by settling for Dan. She *claims* she's not pregnant.'

Nikki looked thoughtful. 'Flick either goes for a high-powered mirror image of herself, or, if she doesn't fancy the competition and beating off other frozen-hearted hussies with a stick, chooses a low-powered lapdog. Like this Dan.'

Katie considered. 'But he didn't seem a helpless ball of Plasticine in her evil hands.'

'*And* she's got her mitts on the ancestral home,' said Nikki.

'Oh, she's welcome to that. We spent summer holidays there when Grandad was still alive. I loved seeing Grandad and for once I had my own room, but I never got a wink of sleep in it. Soot fell down the chimney most nights, thumping like something coming to get me. Gives me the goolies just thinking about the place.'

Nikki, however, was more interested in Flick's lovelife. 'I think I've got it sussed. Flick's after a lapdog, deffo. One who'll turn a blindly adoring eye when she sneaks off to bonk her preferred type, a stiff called Jeremy or Rupert who works in PR. Hubby will put up with anything to keep her. And the trade-off is, he gets to live in the haunted house. Isn't that place a dream come true for a garden designer who's been short of gardens to design? He's marrying your sister for her top-soil.'

'But despite Flick's guff about doing it up, they'd need megabucks to make Cloverley habitable.'

'Precisely. He'll be so busy mending and patching, he won't have the time or energy to keep tabs on Lady Muck's exploits on the side. She won't be there, anyway. She'll be in bed somewhere nice and warm with Rupert or Jeremy.'

'But why bother getting married at all? Or why not find a rich lapdog?'

Nikki shook her head. 'She's got a third string to her bow I haven't worked out yet.'

'Poor Dan,' said Katie after a pause. 'Maybe someone should warn him.'

'As long as it's not you,' snorted Nikki. 'More drinks all round. Waiter!'

She dithered over the menu. 'Haven't you got a Painted Lady?' she asked, eyeing the waiter's tight trousers.

'That's a butterfly,' he said in a bored tone. 'I think you mean a Pink Lady.'

'That's it.' Nikki shut the menu. 'Pink and ladylike, just like me.'

The waiter looked at Katie.

'Coffee, please,' she requested humbly, feeling she owed him a display of demure sobriety by way of compensation. Anyway, she'd had enough of sickly cocktails. She wasn't a woman who could hold her drink. Neither was Nikki, but Nikki was naturally loud in voice and appearance. It wasn't easy to spot when she was skew-wiff; her colourful plumage was her camouflage.

'Where were we?' said Nikki. 'Oh yes, keep your hot little mitts off Dan.'

'As if!' protested Katie angrily.

'You've got that look on your face. The Stephen Sheridan look, and later, the Jack Gold look. Jesus! *You don't fancy Dan?*'

'Shush, no. Don't be stupid.'

'You can't crap in your own sandbox, Katie, however much you want to get even over Stephen. I mean, look at me. I find Jack fanciable. Strictly as poster fodder. He's not my type, if you see what I mean, but I can see what other women get their knicks in a twist about, and I wouldn't mind a piece of the action if it was going. Just a quick snog on a pile of coats at a party, you understand. Then I'd want to rush back to the kitchen and make sure Doug was still holding my drink. Now that, you see, is fancying with inbuilt security measures.'

'I don't see how,' said Katie grumpily. 'You still want to snog my fiancé.'

'Oh, purlease, you're missing the point. You wouldn't be fancying Dan 'cos he's gorgeous. You'd be convincing yourself you fancy him, so you can use him, take what's not yours.'

'I'd never do that!'

'And who could blame you? But as' – hic! – '*individuals*, we have to liberate ourselves from the tyranny of family and its past injustices. From all those family anecdotes and in-jokes that define who we are, even to ourselves.'

'Liberate. Right. Thank you, Che,' muttered Katie, wishing now that she had ordered another cocktail. It was the hypocrisy she objected to. Nikki's parents had retired to Cornwall years earlier. Her sister lived in Spain. Her dealings with *tyrannus familias* were limited to bearable-in-small-doses fleeting visits.

'Jack is more important to you than family could ever be,' continued Nikki, on a roll. 'He got to know you in the context of desirable woman, not loopy sister or difficult daughter. Now, setting your cap at Dan would be a backward step – saying that all the anger and hurt Flick caused you is still eating you up inside. That you've let her win.'

Katie was desperate to change the subject. As their drinks arrived, she judged the time was right to turn the spotlight on Nikki. She fished in her shoulder-bag and drew out a folded square of paper. 'I saw this in Mum's local paper, Nik. I think it could be what you're looking for.'

Nikki unfolded the paper and peered at the job ad, seeking a deputy manager/ess for a health-food shop. Then she peered across at Katie. 'Isn't this where you used to work?'

'Yes. It says "CVs to Frank Melvin". Frank's the owner, my ex-boss. I could put in a good word for you, and it's part-time, so you could sort something out with Doug or a childminder. Not that I want to pressurise you. If you hate the idea, just say so.'

Nikki's dark eyes brewed tears. 'I don't know. I've lost my confidence, Katie. I've become a useless, domesticated lump. I can't even do mental arithmetic when I'm handed change in a shop.'

'Now don't exaggerate, Nik.'

'You think I'm exaggerating?' Nikki flung back her head and gave Katie the full diva look. 'You've got *no* idea, with your cosy Dinky life, taking your employ-ability for granted. Maybe you secretly think a mother's place *is* in the home, picking rusks out of the carpet, though you'd never dream of giving up your freedom to restock the species.'

Katie rolled her eyes. Nikki was being daft. But her tearful eyes and heaving bosom suggested that Nikki was also aware of this fact. She wanted to escape the Gordian knot of her unreasonableness, but couldn't see how. Katie would have to extricate her. She seized her best friend's wrist. 'Listen, fat-arse. You're bright, funny, hardworking and capable. Your brain hasn't turned to mush, Doug's nuts about you, and you've got two gorgeous kids. Your arse is not fat but, in fact, nicely covered. In a minute, I'm going to tell you to count your blessings.'

Nikki squirmed theatrically. 'Please, not that.'

'Then give up the dying swan routine. And take the ad home, sleep on it.'

'OK, I will,' sighed Nikki with a watery smile. 'Thanks.'

'Don't mention it.'

The May evenings were getting longer, but it was still dark when they rolled off the tube at Balham, and found Jack waiting for them. 'Had a good day?' he asked, casting a nervous look at Nikki.

She flopped against him, decorating him with bags. 'I assume you're giving me a lift to Streatham, Jack? Oh my God, you're sexy.'

'Er, so are you,' replied Jack with stuffed-shirt politeness, and looked put out when both Nikki and Katie shrieked with laughter.

'Time to change shift at Fort Bissett,' sighed Nikki, as the car pulled up at her house. 'Thanks for a lovely day out, Katie. I'll think about that job, let you know if I apply so you can alert that Frank bloke. I dunno, though. Do you think I'm up to it?'

'You could run a major industry with one hand tied behind your back,' promised Katie, suppressing a disloyal yawn. Nikki's pleas for reassurance were a symptom of domestic incarceration. She tended to brood rather than act, often wandering over the well-picked bones of meagre anecdotes or incidents. Going out to buy a pint of milk often became an epic travelogue, lacking only the dog-sleds and the need to drink her own pee.

'She's drunk,' complained Jack as they drove away.

'She's a bit merry. Big difference. And who'd begrudge her?'

'You're a saint, listening to all that self-pitying claptrap.'

'Oh, Jack, it's not like that at all. She bolsters me when I'm down. We prop each other up, provide succour and support.'

He looked a little sulky. 'I thought that was my job.'

Back home, the living-room was a tip. Jack had unloaded the washing machine and covered every available surface with damp sheets. The washing was usually Katie's domain. She flopped against a sheet straddling the sofa and kicked off her shoes.

Jack stood casually by the mantelpiece, one arm draped across it, gesturing meaningfully towards the gilt-edged envelope propped against the clock. He was excited about the invitation. He was impressed, too, and couldn't wait to tell Milo. He wasn't sure Katie would share his excitement, though. He would never want her to be like Flick, but he secretly wished she had just a little of her sister's sophistication. Nikki wasn't exactly a byword for sophistication either, although Jack liked her upfrontness. And that Doug was a good bloke. Jack wouldn't have minded getting to know him better.

He stroked the edge of the card as Katie said unexpectedly, 'Jewellery shops are open on Sundays, aren't they? I thought we'd go shopping for an engagement ring tomorrow. What do you think?'

'I think only places like Argos and Woolie's are open. Unless you want a ring from either of them?'

'Oh.' Disappointment twisted sharply inside her. He was right, but that didn't stop the first fluttering of panic. Deep down, she was beginning to wonder if his proposal *had* come back to haunt him in the cold light of day. By sabotaging his attempt to make the announcement at Tess's, she might have given him time to think twice.

'This came today, late post,' he said with apparent nonchalance, picking up the stiff square of card.

'A wedding invite?' asked Katie. 'Mum said Flick wasn't bothering. It's word of mouth only.'

'It's an invite to dinner,' said Jack and paused. 'At L'Etoile, on Thursday night.'

Katie looked blank.

Jack sighed. 'One of the poshest restaurants in London.'

'Who's invited us there?'

'Mr P Avebury, father of the groom. He's hosting an intimate do in honour of his son's nuptials.'

'Oh, God. Well, it won't be so bad with Mum and Si there. And close friends of the happy couple, I presume.'

'Actually, your mum phoned today, a bit put out. Seems we're the only two invited.'

'Oh *God*,' repeated Katie with more urgency. 'Flick's doing this to spite me. She knows I don't know my finger-bowl from my foie gras. She wants to show me up in front of a lot of snobs.'

Jack began to laugh, which made her fume more. 'Come off it, K. Flick can't make every move in life after calculating its embarrassing effect on you. I rang her after your mum's call and turns out it's all Dan's idea. His dad asked him to nominate a couple of guests and he chose us.'

'But why? Hasn't he got any friends of his own? He's going to need them, married to Lady Macbeth.'

'Poor old Shaggy,' snorted Jack.

'Why do you call him that?'

'It's Simon's idea. We both reckon Dan looks like Shaggy out of *Scooby Doo*. Did you notice the size of his feet?'

'You know what they say about men with big feet,' sniffed Katie.

'Big feet, big shoes,' replied Jack coolly. He smiled. 'L'Etoile! Personally, I can't wait. Can I go ahead and RSVP Shaggy's dad? Come on, it should be a laugh. The grub's free and the starving millions won't take it personally if you stuff your face with overpriced haute cuisine for one night.'

'I suppose,' she conceded, seduced as ever by Jack's effortless manipulation of her. Topped off with the Killer Smile.

Katie was on the phone to Nikki. They were discussing clothes. Katie was regretting not buying a posh frock on her Saturday up west.

'What about the green thing you wore to Sarah's

110

christening?' asked Nikki.

'Sweat patches under the arms that never came out.'

'The blue, beaded mini-dress?'

'When I sit down, it makes my knees look fat.'

'But your knees will be under the table.'

'We can't assume anything. Complacency is the enemy.'

'All right, that red, vampy number.'

'Wearing it to the wedding, de-vampified with a jacket.'

Nikki sighed down the phone. 'This isn't easy. I can't even see the damn clothes.' A thin wail pierced the background behind her. She turned away to yell, 'Doug, don't forget her ears. We're out of cotton buds, so use the corner of the towel.' She turned back to the phone. 'You could borrow something off me.'

'Er . . .'

'Sorry. Momentarily forgot I'm mistaken for the Hindenberg by low-flying aircraft.'

'My hips are bigger than yours,' Katie rushed in, fence-mending. 'I'll have to buy something new. Sod, I've only got three days.'

'Any chance of me being invited to the wedding?' asked Nikki wistfully. 'Just once I'd like someone to say, "you *shall* go to the ball, Cinders".'

'You're well out of it. The reception's at Mum's, a buffet for twenty-five, as requested by Flick. It's got all the makings of a royal street party; brown tea and sandwiches with flags in. When Jack and I get married, it'll be a proper sit-down do with compulsory flying-saucer hats, and you'll be the first name on the guest-list.'

'When's that likely to be?' muttered Nikki.

'Look, we can go up west any time. If Doug can't or won't babysit, Jack will.' Worried by the recklessness of this offer, she said, 'I still don't get Flick's wedding. do you? I thought she'd want the works. A big summer wedding, so next year at the earliest. Flashbulbs popping, colour-coordinated going-away outfits and a hundred white doves released on cue.'

'I had most of that,' groaned Nikki. 'Excluding the last three things you mentioned. Anyway, point is, my dad flogged a kidney to pay for my wedding and look what it led to. Broken dreams and broken sleep.'

'Oh sod off, Nik, and apply for that job. It's tailormade for you.'

Having dispatched her friend with equal measures of encouragement and briskness, Katie had a final rummage in the wardrobe. Nope, nothing. She'd exhausted her limited options. *Unless . . .*

It was a long shot. She might have chucked it out in a fit of pique disguised as spring cleaning. But if she remembered rightly, she'd balked at cutting off her nose to spite her face, reluctant to chuck a posh frock on the scrapheap or even let it go to Oxfam.

Taking advantage of Jack's absence, she climbed on to a chair and scrabbled about in the top shelf of the wardrobe. Belts and scarves rained down on her head, along with odd shoes and stuffed toys.

Then her hand grasped it before she saw it. Gauzy material, as fine and silvery as a fisherman's net spread out to dry in the sun. With a little whoop of excitement, she drew the dress towards her and stared at it in silence.

Steve had bought it for her as a twenty-sixth birthday present. The only gift of taste and value he'd ever got her. He'd rolled up at the flat on the eve of her birthday, a flat, fawn-coloured box clamped to the armpit of his Goth jacket. She'd recognised the designer name scrolled in fine gold letters across the lid. He'd been very pleased with himself, winking and grinning as she prepared to raise the lid. 'What is it?' she'd asked unnecessarily.

'Well it's hardly a flat-pack elephant! Come on, bach, put me out of me misery. Tell me if I chose right.'

Suddenly excited, she'd dived through layers of protective tissue paper and lifted out a dress.

'You're a 10 on a good day, aren't you?' Stephen had asked eagerly in his Welsh burr, too keyed-up to wait for her own spontaneous reaction. 'I'll slit my wrists if it's the wrong size. And it's classy, right? That's what the woman in the shop said. Goes with any colouring, and I thought, with your brownish skin . . .'

What she'd thought, first, foremost and ungratefully, was that Flick would have looked great in it. With spooky prescience, her boyfriend had picked the sort of floaty yet minimalist, tasteful yet look-at-me cocktail dress favoured by Flick. The size 10 thing was also worrying. True, she could squeeze into a ten on a good day, as Steve had tactfully put it, but she didn't really want to. Not when size 12 was a perfectly acceptable size to be (she'd finally come to realise).

But still, it was a beautiful dress and it did ooze class. 'It's lovely,' she'd cried, a bit theatrically (he hadn't noticed). 'It must've cost a bomb. I'll only wear it on a special occasion. Like my birthday.' This had been a heavy hint (which he hadn't taken) that she'd like to go out for a posh meal on her birthday.

Not that she'd really minded when he didn't take the hint. He'd spent loads on the dress and it was churlish to look for Dream Topping with your Angel Delight, especially when you were used to Instant Whip.

She also knew, however, that she'd never wear the dress in front of Flick at a family function. She'd have stood silently accused of copying the maestro.

So the dress, reverenced and coveted at first, then rejected as indelibly linked to its purchaser, had been consigned to a hanger at the back of a wardrobe, making its way, by dint of a few years and a couple of moving upheavals, to the back of the wardrobe's top shelf, rubbing shoulder-straps with leg-warmers, striped dungarees and cork-heeled espadrilles.

It never made its debut appearance. A few weeks short of Katie's twenty-seventh birthday, Steve left her for Flick.

But none of that mattered now. She was a different, confident, secretly engaged woman, who had the collar-bones to wear this dress and appreciate it. And she could still, on a good day, carry off a size 10. She stood in front of the bedroom's full-length mirror and held the dress against her, convincing herself of these facts. It was a layered shift dress in three overlapping panels of charcoal grey, shot through with silver thread and beads. The spaghetti straps *were* a bit dodgy with her meaty shoulders, but perfect for showing off her tan.

And what the hell, no one had seen her in it. Whereas Jack and Flick had seen everything else in her evening-wear collection. She sniffed the dress for must or damp and hung it on the back of the wardrobe door to air.

*

'What do you think?' Flick did a twirl for Dan. 'Too over the top?'

'No. It's fine.' Dan cringed at his choice of words. Fine? She was sex on legs! She was wearing a thing called a bustiere, in ice-blue (apparently) satin, over skintight black satin trousers and square-toed embroidered shoes. Her hair was piled up in a loose, shining coil, threaded with tiny, ice-blue stars.

He huffed and puffed inside his only suit and ran his finger around the inside of his shirt collar. He looked at his finger, expecting to see a residue of grime. They hadn't even left for the restaurant and he was sweating like a pig.

'Dan,' said Flick, slipping into a teeny black jacket. 'Are you sure you're OK with the Steve Sheridan thing? Maybe I was mad to tell you.'

He bounded over and folded her carefully into his arms. 'Look, Katie's got Jack now, hasn't she? So it all worked out in the end. It's all water under the bridge, end of story.'

Her frosted pink lips pursed anxiously. 'Sure?'

'Never been surer of owt.' He adopted a gruff Yorkshire accent.

'Good,' she smiled up at him. 'Could you stand a little well-meant advice? Relax, sweetheart. It's just dinner. Phil's not planning to eat you.'

'Not without giving me a roasting first,' acknowledged Dan with one of his rare flashes of gloomy wit. 'You've only met him once, but you already know how to handle him. All my life I've been bumbling over the invisible trip-wire that sets him off.'

'He has a go at you because you let him,' said Flick with devastating confidence. 'And by the way, don't let slip in front of Katie we told him about the engagement before we told Mum. She's already pissed off at not being invited tonight.'

Dan looked edgy. 'You know what a tight-wad Dad is. He stipulated two guests only, and I thought we owed it to Katie to make an effort. You know, wave a big olive branch about. My dream is to get you two acting like sisters.'

Flick laughed flutily. 'We *are* acting like sisters.'

Dan gave up and took himself into the bathroom for a final squirt of antiperspirant and talc down his boxers.

But when he emerged, Flick wrinkled her button nose and crushed his remaining confidence by observing, 'Sweetheart, you can't go out smelling like an accident at a perfume counter.' After she'd stopped laughing (in a tinkly, benevolent sort of way), she made him take off his shirt. He used his half-naked state as a pretext to get playful (anything, frankly, to delay the night ahead), but she pushed him away gently and told him to check out the spare room wardrobe.

Reluctantly, he padded into the spare room. And found three immaculate men's shirts in ivory cotton, swinging in the near-empty wardrobe. He was taken aback, but too nervous to consider asking Flick where they'd come from. He slipped one on grudgingly. It fitted him well and felt good, he had to admit. Normally, he grabbed a polyester/cotton three-pack off a shelf in Bhs.

'Just the ticket,' purred Flick when she saw him. 'Just as well I always over-shop. I couldn't resist buying three at once.'

'Oh. I thought they were left here by someone,' blurted Dan, and kicked himself.

Flick brushed threads off his jacket. 'Men's shirts make perfect night-shirts. Don't worry, I'll be going for a more trad look on honeymoon.'

Dan willed himself to relax. Once he got this evening out of the way, the only hurdle would be the wedding day itself.

Katie arrived at the restaurant feeling guilty as well as awestruck. She'd told Jack she'd bought the silver-grey dress on her day out with Nikki. That she'd been saving it for the wedding, but then realised it was inappropriately evening-dressy, and decided to wear it to L'Etoile instead.

Jack looked wonderful. Usually smartly dressed on the right side of raging vanity, he *had* splashed out on new threads; an Armani suit, no less. He'd bought it in his lunch-hour at a place recommended by Milo. Katie hadn't asked the price. It wasn't her money, and she knew she'd echo the figure in a horrified, censorious voice. Besides, he never interrogated her that way.

He was a bit shame-faced about the suit, though. He'd made her swear never to reveal this act of decadence to Freddy.

Now Katie had never felt prouder, as Jack escorted her across thick carpet to their table. She swung her beaded Lulu Guinness bag from her hand, basking in the admiring looks cast Jack's way. The reflected glory was all hers to enjoy for a few precious seconds – until she saw Flick.

Her sister was hard to miss. Her piled-up hair

glittered icily with tiny blue stars. She was leaning forward, her pushed-up boobs almost falling out of a bustiere, talking earnestly to a squat toad of a man sitting on her left.

Katie was so captivated by this tableau, she almost forgot to look for Dan. Who, in any event, was doing his best to look inconspicuous, a gambit that failed when one of his cufflinks fell off and bounced across the table.

Retrieving it, he rose to make formal introductions. 'Er, Dad, this is J-Jack. He's with Katie, who is – this is her – Flick's sister.'

Dan sat down abruptly. Katie followed suit, not waiting for Jack to pull out her chair for her. She didn't like the way Flick was staring at her. Or, more accurately, her dress. Dammit, she shouldn't have worn it! Now she'd have to brace herself for the inevitable snide remark, along the lines of 'suits you surprisingly well, that dress, considering it was designed for a much smaller woman'. *Like me, you fat cow.*

Dan's dad sat back and lit a fat cigar. 'Phil Avebury,' he growled. 'Father of the groom, for my sins.'

He was, thought Katie, a dead ringer for Jabba the Hut in a suit. Yellowy, lizard-like eyes flicked back and forth between her and Jack. Assessing, prying for armour-chinks. Katie was repulsed. She expected him to unfurl a long, darting tongue and snaffle a passing fly. Touching the rows of heavy silver cutlery in front of her, she glanced surreptitiously at Dan to check he bore no resemblance to toad-features. To her relief, she was met by the comforting sight of his shaggy hair and homely face. He wasn't weatherbeaten, though. More like washed smooth by the elements, his unlined skin pink and white. Why hadn't she noticed that before?

His warm grey eyes found and reassured her. She smiled. Out of the corner of her eye, she saw a beringed hand wriggle possessively on to Dan's sleeve. Flick was sporting a whopper diamond solitaire.

'Nice ring,' said Jack.

'My late wife's,' grunted Phil Avebury. 'Before that it belonged to my mother. When the wife died, couldn't get it off her, even with butter. Right bloody hoo-ha. In the end, had to chop it off. What? What?' He looked from one aghast face to another. 'Not as if she could feel anything. Christ Jesus almighty!' Suddenly, he let out a bellow of laughter that shivered all the crystal on the table. 'Bloody fell for it, didn't you? Hah! Didn't need to chop off her finger. She never wore the bloody ring towards the end. Had it nice and snug in the vault, waiting for young Philippa to come along.'

Flick swatted his arm. 'You're an old monster, Phil.'

'It's the way you tell 'em, Dad,' said Dan with a spurt of sarcastic vigour.

'Christ almighty.' Phil Avebury's reptilian eyes swivelled towards his son. 'Milk teeth instead of fangs. What this fine specimen of a woman sees in you is anyone's guess.'

Dan blushed scarlet. 'Mine too,' he admitted. He seemed to crumple from within.

Katie, silently rooting for him, had hoped for a sturdier comeback.

'You promised to behave, Phil,' Flick chided him, half nanny and half coquette.

'Can't help it if flower-boy's the bloody daughter I never had.'

He dug a fresh cigar out of his breast pocket and patted it again for his lighter. But Jack got there first. He'd spotted the gold lighter on the table, nestling under a damask napkin, and swooped it under the brown torpedo. 'I see by your tie-pin you're a Chelsea fan, sir.'

Phil grimaced round his lit cigar. 'Board member as well. Do you think there are too many bloody foreigners in the team?' He settled his malevolent gaze on Jack.

'I think it's the right blend. Italian artistry, Gallic guile and English grit. Of course, Zola was an inspired buy.' Jack leant back in his chair and steepled his fingers. 'The team dynamo, as it were.'

Katie stared at him. What did Jack know about team dynamos? He hated football. And how could he suck up to this horrible old git? Unless Phil was doing a star turn as a horrible human being, he *was* a horrible human being. No wonder Dan was so shy. It was amazing he'd turned out normal, let alone nice. And now he was going to saddle himself with Phil's female alter ego.

Phil pointed his cigar at Jack. 'Makes a change, talking to a man who knows his game, not a man who deadheads begonias for a living. Where are the bloody waiters?'

One glided up to the table.

'Right,' said Phil. 'I take it we're all ready to order? What's the dish of the day, sonny jim?'

The waiter's face tightened. 'The chef's specialité du jour is mussels in a garlic and wine sauce. Sir.'

'Mussels! Christ Jesus, washed up on the beach with the raw sewage. I'll have steak *au poivre* with new potatoes. And an ashtray.'

'Yes, sir.'

Thanks to a combination of cigar smoke and the raw sewage remark, Katie found her appetite ebbing away. Still, she had to make the effort, for Jack's sake. She didn't want him thinking she'd erred on the side of minimalism to take a stand against the epicurean indulgence of her fellow-diners. She dithered, blushed, and eventually ordered a black-bean salad with monkfish.

Phil's unwelcome gaze came to rest on her. 'Can't believe you two are sisters. Not a bit alike. One dark and thin as a pin, the other fair and built for comfort, not speed. What's the milkman look like down your mum's way?'

'Give it a rest!' hissed Dan, as Katie cringed and Jack came close to frowning in displeasure.

Phil's little yellow eyes gleamed mischief. 'Now what've I said? I can't stop speaking as I find, just because the rest of the world's got its corset laced too tightly.'

Dan suddenly thumped the table hard enough to make the cutlery skitter. 'For one evening in your life, give everyone a break. This is supposed to be a dinner for me and Flick, so just lay off insulting and – and insinuating! And you're not supposed to be smoking this end of the restaurant. And Flick's given up fags 'cos I think it's a filthy habit.'

Katie gazed admiringly at Dan. But Jack shifted uncomfortably, Flick frowned slightly, and Avebury ground out his cigar, chuckling, 'Touché, flower-boy, touché. No offence, Kitty, Katie, whatever your charming name is. I'm a bloody monster, as Philippa's already told me once tonight. 'Course you two girls look alike. Two stunners. Two peas in a very lucky pod.'

'Excuse me.' Katie rose tremulously. 'Just off to powder my nose.'

Her flight was delayed as she untangled her Lulu Guinness bag from her chair-leg. Then she almost ran for the loo. *Built for comfort, not speed.* How could Jack sit there and let her be talked about that way?

She heard pursuing footsteps and dived behind a pillar. Only then did she turn. To her surprise, her follower was Jack. For some reason, she'd expected (and half-hoped) it would be Dan.

'Katie, don't let him get to you.'

'For God's sake, Jack, why are you all over him like Swarfega? The way he talks to Dan and rubbishes other people. He's horrible.'

'Yeah, but he's *the* Phil Avebury. Katie, he's worth a fortune! One of the country's richest self-made men.'

She stared at him, light dawning. 'You admire him, even though he's a horrible old reprobate who just insulted your fiancée.'

'Oh come off it, that's neither here nor there. You can't take people like him personally. He's a wind-up merchant. I guarantee you he's worked twenty-four-hour days since he was a tea-boy somewhere. Dan's the one born with a silver spoon in his mouth, the real parasite. One day, he'll inherit wealth he did nothing to create.'

'How can you make that comparison? While old Phil's probably cooking the books and fiddling the taxman, Dan's working creatively with his hands. He's putting loads back into society compared to Phil.'

Jack folded his arms. He looked truculent. 'He can afford to dabble, with Daddy's millions sitting in the bank. Doesn't matter how he passes the time while he waits to inherit. Fair play to Flick. Avebury's a widower and Dan's the only child.'

'Doesn't Daddy have her sussed as a gold-digger?' asked Katie.

'Probably pleased as punch she's a career woman with a healthy income.'

'Did you recognise him as soon as you saw him?'

'No. It didn't click until I felt the weight of his lighter. Solid gold, to match the Rolex on his wrist. That's when the name rang a bell.'

'And that's when you started pretending to like football.'

'Come off it, K.' He pushed a wayward shoulder-strap on her dress back into place. She shuddered pleasurably. 'I have to suck up to clients all the time,' he explained. 'I can't afford to wonder whether they're kind to furry animals.'

Suspicion welled up in Katie. 'It'd be a huge feather in your cap at work if you got Phil as a client.'

'Obviously, he's spoken for. He's not exactly the sentimental type, but he might put business my way if I was family.'

'But you're not.'

'Will be when we get married.' He kissed her nose. 'His daughter-in-law's brother-in-law. Close enough.' He looked down at her serious expression. 'I'm joking.'

Katie fiddled with her bag. Jack was so handsome and she was so easy to manipulate. 'Come on,' she sighed. 'We've been away too long, they'll know we've been talking about them.'

'OK. But just ignore Phil. He's from the same mould as Flick. One of life's takers, and blow who gets trampled in the process.'

When they returned to their seats, they found that Phil, puffing his latest cigar, had moved on to baiting the happy couple. 'As you're not up the duff, Philippa, what's the bloody rush to get spliced? Apart from the fact flower-boy here has a stonking great trust fund he can dip into any time.'

'Dad!'

'Well, you have!' Phil turned to Flick. 'I suppose you already know he got the key to his trust fund when he hit twenty-five this year? I'm sure a girl like you did her research.'

'Dan has mentioned it, but it's very ungallant of you to,' replied Flick smoothly. 'I'm a success in my own right. I'm sure you've done your own research to verify that.'

Phil chuckled approvingly.

Flick's eyes sparkled. She was enjoying sparring with Phil, Katie realised.

'You shoved Dan out of the nest at sixteen, told him to find his own way without handouts from you,' Flick went on. 'And he did. He's a brilliant garden designer.' She clutched the sleeve of a very embarrassed-looking Dan. 'His job's a vocation and vocations are notoriously badly paid.'

'So why,' challenged Phil, 'doesn't he set up his own business and get on with it? What's he waiting for since he came into the trust fund? Why does he work in a bloody garden centre?'

Dan opened his mouth.

'He was thinking of doing just that when I met him,' said Flick.

Dan shut his mouth.

'So now we're going the whole hog in one go. We're getting wed and doing up Cloverley, but we're not into excess for its own sake. Neither of us is interested in a society wedding, shoving smoked salmon and Bollinger down the necks of freeloaders. It's the same with Cloverley. We want to do it up as an investment, as well as a family home.'

'Well', grunted Phil, 'that makes sense. Having dosh doesn't mean you need to spread it on thick to impress nosebaggers. I must have done something right.'

Fascinating as this was, Katie found it surreal that Dan just sat there, allowing himself to be discussed in the third person. However, Phil and Flick hadn't finished locking horns. 'Just be thankful, Phil, you old monster, that he's marrying someone who can take care of herself,' said Flick, tossing back tendrils of chestnut hair. 'And your son, if need be.'

'No need to go for the bloody Oscar, Philippa. Like I said, I don't know what you see in him, trust fund or not.'

'I love him,' said Flick quietly. Katie watched Dan's features melt, and felt very afraid for him.

Phil laughed, a touch nastily. He could see straight through Flick's bravura performance, and Jack was looking at her with sardonic admiration. But poor old Dan was destined to fall for it, hook, line and sinker. Katie felt sick. She decided to give the chocolate tartuffe a miss.

Only Phil had dessert. Then he insisted on coffees and brandies all round. 'Got to push the boat out. This is my contribution to the wedding. When are the hen and stag nights?'

'We're not bothering with that out-of-the-ark stuff,' replied Flick. 'This is our first and last blow-out before the big day.'

Phil lit his fifth pungent cigar. Full of good food and wine, he struck Katie as slightly mellower. He caught her eye. 'You two jumping the broom any time soon?'

'Not thought about it,' she answered quickly, in case Jack chose that moment to make his pitch for family membership.

Phil laughed. 'If I'd remarried and had a few more brats, flower-boy might be sharing the spoils with them after I snuff it. Never had much use for the old s-e-x. Lot of bloody fuss about nothing. All I need now is Dorrie. She comes in and does for me twice a week.'

'Dad's sister,' explained Dan to Jack and Katie. 'Since Uncle Sid died, she does the housekeeping and cooking for Dad.' He added pointedly, 'She's a nice woman.'

'Cut from the same "meek shall inherit the earth" cloth as his mother,' growled Phil. He flung down his stained napkin like a gauntlet and reached into his jacket for what proved to be a mobile phone. 'What's Vic's bloody number, flower-boy? Hang on – got it. Now. Jack, Kitty, back to my place with these two for a nightcap, is it?'

Katie shuddered, reaching for her bag as she waited for Jack to politely decline.

'That would be very kind of you, Sir,' said Jack.

Chapter Six

Phil Avebury's chauffeur-driven Daimler waited for electronically controlled gates to swing open. Katie gripped Jack's hand. Her annoyance had worn off and excitement set in at the prospect of seeing where Dan had grown up.

She tried to absorb every detail, from the plush white leather of the Daimler seats to the brass pineapples topping the gateposts. Nikki would want to know everything.

Phil sat in the back of the car with the rest of them, his stumpy legs just skimming the floor, unhappy about being driven. 'Only use the bugger now and then, when I've been out on the town,' he growled, nodding up front towards the deferential chauffeur, Vic. 'Rest of the time, he does the garden.'

Dan tensed at the word 'garden'. He'd been tense throughout the journey, his big, square-fingered hands dangling between his knees. All he needed, thought Katie, was a hat to spin in his hands, like Joe Gargery tongue-tied in the presence of a gentlemanly Pip.

As soon as they drove through the gates, she thought she knew why Dan had tensed. Wood View House, in leafy Surrey, was a good mile away from the nearest mansion, so she'd expected to see lawns, trees, flowers, a profusion of spring greenery. Instead, a wilderness of crazy-paving zig-zagged up to the oak door of a redbrick mansion.

It was a terrible sight, the slabs of paving relieved only by a silent stone fountain in the centre. This rose in three tiers, topped by a little stone dolphin, its jaws agape in petrified suspense to gush forth water. Phil's mansion looked out on a prospect of dead, unyielding stone, yet his son was a garden designer. It had to be spiteful revenge on 'flower-boy's' chosen career.

Even Jack and Flick were subdued as the gates clanged shut and the car halted on an apron of gravel. Katie couldn't take her eyes off the flags of virgin stone, unmarked by weed or footprint.

Inside the house, Vic dismissed to garage the car, Phil gave them a grand tour, clearly proud of the gold taps, deep carpets and hand-blocked wallpaper. It was all tasteful, Katie conceded privately, in a decorating-by-numbers way. It was bought-in good taste. The sort she'd have to resort to if she won the lottery.

They reassembled in the main lounge, where Phil splashed Scotch into glasses. Jack looked at his watch. 'I'll call a taxi to take you home when you're ready,' said Phil. 'Probably two taxis, as you're going in different directions. Unless you're staying the night?' He darted his question at Dan, who looked to Flick for his signal before replying, 'Going back to Hampstead with Flick.'

Phil beckoned Jack to the window. The others followed out of curiosity.

'Get a bloody load of this,' said Phil and pressed a switch on a small black box he held. The curtains swished open. Another switch illuminated the stone fountain in a shower of harsh light. The dolphin had never looked sadder, more exposed. 'Is the fountain on in the daytime?' asked Katie hopefully.

'No, it isn't,' replied Phil shortly, turning to Jack. 'Into wine at all, Jack?'

'I know my Chablis from my Chardonnay,' replied Jack, unfazed.

'Thought you might. Ever seen a decent wine cellar?'

'Never had the chance to.'

'Well, this is your lucky night.' Phil rubbed his hands. 'I don't give guided tours as a rule, but anyone who's bloody coming, fall into line. I know you'd rather drink that gnat's piss you call real ale, flowerboy. You up for a cellar tour, Philippa? Kitty?'

Katie sat down abruptly on a squishy sofa and fell into its depths. 'No, thank you,' she squeaked, having meant to sound haughty and dismissive.

'Right then. Anyone who's coming, look lively.' Phil surged out of the room, followed eagerly by Flick, with Jack bringing up the rear. He gave Katie an apologetic half-shrug. She ignored him. She hadn't liked the Jack she'd seen tonight, fawning over Phil, ready to sell his soul for a tainted shilling.

She became aware it was just her and Dan in the room.

Dan blinked at her from under his shaggy fringe. 'Jack should be honoured. Like Dad said, he doesn't show off his plonk collection to just anybody. They'll be gone ages. What's the difference between a wine buff and a wine bore?'

'Dunno.'

'Me neither. Once Dad gets going, Jack and Flick will be knocking back the booze to stay awake. I like your dress.'

'Er, thanks.'

A few more seconds ticked by. Dan sprang to his feet. 'We don't have to sit here. I'll show you my sort of secret den.'

Katie rose cautiously. Replete with food and brandy, she'd been nicely positioned to snatch forty winks until the wanderers returned.

He led her down the hallway, along a passageway and down a flight of stairs. It got cooler as they descended, the wallpaper giving way to bare stone walls and the faint smell of old cooking. At the foot of the stairs, he pushed open a heavy door that squealed its protest. 'Come on,' he exhorted, glancing over his shoulder.

She followed him into a pitch-black room. 'Hang on.' She heard him stumbling about, and suddenly the room was lit by the soft glow of an oil-lamp, Dan's endearingly shaggy hair haloed above it. 'Sorry it's so cold. There's an old range that usually gets going if kicked in the right place.'

He disappeared into the shadows, leaving Katie to sink down on a wooden settle. It was a kitchen in a time-warp, complete with butler sink, a scarred table of dark oak and a matching dresser, empty of crockery, carved with wooden curlicues. The light flickered over heavy curtains patterned with huge sunflowers. Further along the settle, she found big, old, patterned cushions, smelling of mildew. 'We saw your dad's kitchen already,' she said into the gloom.

'Hang on.' Dan's muffled voice was cut off by a tortured gurgling. 'I think I've got it going. There's still some wood inside, but it won't last long.'

He padded over and joined her on the settle. His features seemed larger and softer in the soft light. He smiled at her, calm and poised. Normally, in Flick's company, he seemed suspended between excitement and dread, as if life with her sister was one long adrenaline rush and you couldn't have one without the other. Here, in his natural habitat, he was no longer a bumbling assemblage of arms, legs and oversized feet.

He kicked off his shoes and spread his toes towards the warmth curling out of the shadows. 'This was Mum's kitchen,' he explained, slipping a cushion behind her. 'Dad was too mean to put in mod cons. He only built a poncy kitchen upstairs when Aunt Dorrie took over and couldn't be doing with all the hard labour.'

'Wouldn't your mum have liked a modern kitchen?'

Dan pushed his hair out of his eyes. 'I'm not sure. She died when I was five.'

'I'm sorry.' She was, too. If anyone had needed a sympathetic parent to cancel out Phil, it was sensitive Dan.

He took a deep breath. 'Mum was Dad's house-keeper before they married. She was from the Ukraine and never learnt much English. They weren't equal partners in the marriage. He wanted a kid – a son, I suppose – but he was too busy to go and look for a brood mare and he's got a thing about women being on the make. So Mum was the practical answer. She already worked here, and she was honest and trustworthy. She carried on being his housekeeper after they married.'

Katie was stunned. 'You mean she provided a son and heir, but carried on being a servant?'

'Well, yeah. But that's what she expected of marriage. She didn't have any family to fall back on and she'd had a hard time of it 'til she fetched up here. I remember sitting here drinking my orange juice, and she'd be down on her hands and knees, scrubbing the floor. When Aunt Dorrie came to visit and offered to help with some horrible job, like cleaning the range, Mum would have none of it. I reckon she didn't trust another woman to clean into the corners.' He waved a hand around the kitchen. 'There's this, a pantry and a back bedroom where Mum went back to living after she had me. I stay in it now when I come over. It's all that's left of the original house. As Dad got better off, he built on top of it. Hey, would you like a drink?'

He swivelled round suddenly and nearly collided with Katie. In the cosy warmth, she'd unconsciously edged towards him. Now she slid back along the settle, embarrassed.

'A cup of tea would be nice.'

'Sorry, there's no leccy. This old bit has separate wiring from the rest of the house. Expect to turn up any day now and find it all bricked up. That's why I keep the lamp here.' He dived off the settle and began rummaging under the sink. 'Mum used to keep a little something here, for medicinal nips, she said. Why should the wine buffs have all the fun?'

Katie heard him clattering aside what sounded like

a mop and bucket. At last he emerged, frowsy with cobwebs, clutching a square-necked bottle of violet glass. He pulled out the stopper and sniffed, recoiling briefly. 'I think it's Ukrainian moonshine. Mum used to swear by it. Probably relieves the pain of housemaid's knee.'

He took a swig, blanched, and passed the bottle to Katie. When she sniffed it, the spikily aggressive aroma brought tears to her eyes. She could only describe it as the smell of Dettol crossed with cherry brandy. After a moment's hesitation, she decided to be brave, and took a sip.

The liquid exploded in her mouth, hot as acid, barbed with nameless flavour. Tears streamed from her eyes. She flopped back woozily, hardly aware of Dan slipping another cushion behind her. 'Phew! What was your mother's name?'

'Irina.'

'Why did she die?'

'Cancer, I think. It was never discussed. I remember her making jam tarts for my fifth birthday. She had to sit down to roll the pastry and her breathing was funny. I was licking the jam spoon, splodging it everywhere, but she didn't seem to notice.' His voice thickening at the end, he cleared his throat.

Katie rubbed his back and passed him the bottle. 'I'm sorry, Dan. Jack lost his mother to cancer when he was sixteen. He doesn't talk about her much. It's still raw to him.'

'Yeah, well, wasn't like Mum used to sing me to sleep with lullabies. She had a short fuse. Actually, a few years back, Aunt Dorrie said she reckoned Mum might have felt ill for a couple of years without doing anything about it. That would explain a lot. She never slowed down on the work front and she was always cross and out of breath.'

'Did Aunt Dorrie look after you when your mum died?'

'I think she and Uncle Sid were up for it, with Dad away on business so much. But all three of them had a big row after the cremation. I was up in my room, so didn't get details. I think they offered to move in here, and Dad told them where to get off. Of course, he'd have suspected their motives. Dad thinks everyone else is like him, taking the quickest route to the fastest buck.'

'But your aunt looks after *him* now,' pointed out Katie.

'Uncle Sid stormed off after the row, dragging Dorrie with him. She came back on the QT to visit me at weekends. I don't think Uncle Sid would have approved. She and Dad patched things up properly after Sid died.'

'Poor you.'

'It wasn't so bad. Dad got hired help in, a big woman with chin hairs who walked and talked like a bloke. She hit like a bloke, too.'

'Oh Dan, that's horrible.' Upset, Katie took another swig of booze. Her tender heart bled for the unloved Dan Avebury. No wonder he couldn't tell real love from fawning avarice.

'Honestly, it was OK,' insisted Dan. 'I was lucky. A lot of kids in that boat get shunted off to boarding-school. I ran wild here, except for the odd time Dad decided to check up on me. Then he'd end up having a go.'

They shared more sips. Katie was getting used to the drink's bitter taste – though she was vaguely aware she'd lost the use of her legs.

'What's with the crazy paving?' she asked, her voice echoing loudly inside her head.

'Just Dad's idea of a low-maintenance outdoors. He gets chronic hay fever. Funny, you asking him about the fountain. It *used* to flow all day. Mum made a special point of asking for it. The fountain's the only thing left from the original garden.'

'He must still have tender feelings for your mum, then.'

'Now there's a thought.' Dan shuddered theatrically. 'I think I prefer him in evil-capitalist mode. Dad wouldn't know how to have a tender feeling. He'd turn it into something else, like indigestion.'

Katie sniggered. Dan looked at her in amusement. 'You will come and visit us in Cloverley, won't you? With Jack,' he added as an afterthought.

'Cloverley!' spluttered Katie. 'Nothing there a trust fund can't put right. How much loot have you got? Sorry,' she winced as he sucked in his breath. 'Very vulgar of me. Take no notice. But tell me, did your handy little windfall coincide with my sister's sudden interest in you?'

'Shut up,' he said gruffly.

'Well, come off it.' Katie could feel the metaphorical gloves sliding off. 'Even you must have your suspicions. Was your dad featured in the paper as Businessman of the Year just before she came on to you? Or did someone at the garden centre drop a word in her shell-like that Dan, Dan, the compost man was an eccentric millionaire, a prince in pauper's mien?'

'Put a sock in it,' he muttered. 'I've never tried to hide who I am from anyone.'

'Bet you never played it up, either. Did people at work know your relationship to Phil?'

'No,' he replied after a short pause. 'Drop it.'

'I can't. I share your dad's bewilderment. Why haven't you used your dosh to set up in garden design before now?'

'Because . . .' He leant forward earnestly. 'I wanted to prove I could do it by the long road, not the short-cut. I thought, if I worked hard enough and did a good job, I'd get on.' He shrugged. 'I was coming round to seeing there's nothing wrong with getting a head start, and then Flick came along and made Cloverley an option. I'm gonna do the place up, then get commissions on the strength of it.'

'Right. Well, good luck.' She tipped up the bottle and sucked down the last drop of addictive nitric acid.

'You don't sound as if you mean that,' said Dan.

'For Chrissake, you know what I think of Flick. She's Cruella de Ville with knobs on. What more is there to say?'

'Say nothing then,' he snapped, and Katie bit her trembling lip. She felt she was going to burst into tears at the drop of a hat. She felt weird. So he'd be bonkers to marry Flick – in her opinion. But some people found happiness in a bonkers lifestyle. Look at Irina, scrubbing floors while wearing a diamond the size of a roc's egg.

'I'm sorry,' she told Dan. 'It's just I can't see you living happily ever after. I especially can't see Flick as lady of the manor.'

'She's not inviting your dad to the wedding,'

muttered Dan in a pointed change of subject. 'Or even telling him she's getting married.' He put the empty bottle on the floor.

'Big deal,' snorted Katie, and mucus shot out of her nose. In the darkness, she bent hurriedly to extract a clean tissue from her bag. The sudden movement hit her a hammer-blow of dizziness. 'Christ, my head,' she groaned. 'What were we on about? Dastardly Don. Oh yeah, he used to send money in cards now and then. Funny, he hardly features in family photos back when he *was* part of the family. It's like he was always standing off to one side.'

'Flick told me about going off with Stephen Wotsit,' muttered Dan, exploding a bigger bombshell.

She dabbed furiously at her eyes. 'My mascara must be black ink by now,' she said through gritted teeth.

'She admitted she was in the wrong, Katie. She could have lied or kept quiet.'

'Let's give her a fucking sainthood, why don't we?'

'Katie, I—'

'Look, get this into your head, will you?' Katie clutched her own aching head. 'She's after your money!' She clutched his knee. 'You're a lovely bloke but she doesn't give a toss about that. You're all her Christmases come at once. Excuse me.' She burped indelicately into her hanky. She was saying things she'd regret. If he repeated this lot back to Flick, it could start World War Three.

'I love her,' said Dan in a slurred voice. 'I don't care why she chose me, I'm just glad she did. I'm not such a great catch in ways that matter. Dad knows that. Let's face it, he'd probably have disinherited me by now if it wasn't bad for his share price.'

Katie said nothing. She'd said too much already.

'All right, Flick and me are different,' admitted Dan. 'Doesn't mean we're wrong for each other. Look at us, you and me. We're alike in loads of ways, but doesn't mean we're right for each other. Does it?'

Katie tried to sit up straight. He had a point there. They *were* alike, each the sidekick of a more glamorous, go-getting other half.

That was how it worked. Jack and Flick needed her and Dan for more than ego-boosting comparison – in Flick's case, maybe for more than money. They needed someone who wasn't in direct competition with them and, in Jack's case, a partner who'd save them from all-out vanity and arrogance by shoving nicer qualities in their line of vision – humility, kindness, patience, all-round good-eggness. While this should have disturbed her, she acknowledged the trade-off. She and Dan gained advantages, too. They could each depend on a confident partner to protect and defend their interests.

But most shattering of all, if Jack and Flick were alike in some ways, that meant Flick *wasn't all bad*. Jesus, could she cope with that concept? Why was she having deep thoughts at all? It wasn't fair. Why couldn't an excess of alcohol leave her in a mental haze to match her uncoordinated limbs? 'Dan,' she said groggily, realising she had to share her insights. 'Me and you, alike. Not alike, them and us. It's all clear now.'

'Good.'

'No, listen. You and I would drive each other mad. See, we're too nice. The world doesn't need any more niceness. It's nice people who dither about and do sod all, 'cos we're afraid to get our hands dirty making difficult decisions. So we let the hard bastards run the world – people like Flick, and even Jack. And then we say, God, they're not very nice, are they? Which is precisely the point. They don't care if they're hated as long as they're wielding power and getting things done.'

'Nice guys finish second, you mean?' said Dan, distilling her amazing insight into a cliché.

'Whatever. Point is, you are right for Flick. Maybe. And I'm definitely right for Jack. God, that makes me so happy.'

'Good,' he said again. This time, he sounded wistful. 'I wish the nice people could sometimes give each other a try, though.'

She was silent for a minute. 'How do you mean?'

'If all the nicies paired off, they might achieve things and take decisions as double-acts.'

'No. See, we act as a brake on the nasties. Stop them running amok and remind them they should have morals.'

'Sod morals,' grunted Dan. 'Can I kiss you?'

'No.'

'Go on.'

'Get stuffed. I mean that nicely.'

He went for it anyway. It was her fault, she realised afterwards. All that stuff about real men going for it. She'd provoked him into proving he was more than a moral sounding-board for Flick. She also knew it was her fault because she'd enjoyed it. Eventually.

She could still have fought him off after the first kiss. He was every bit as drunk as her and couldn't have found his way out of a paper bag without an A to Z, much less grappled with the intricacies of her bra-straps, if it hadn't been for fifth-columnist help from her scheming libido.

It had waited a long time for anything illicit to come its way. Katie had kept it on a short leash all these years, under strict orders from her brain that she was a one-man woman. She knew her libido secretly saw her as a one-man-at-a-time woman. At least, it did tonight.

Her shoes dropped to the floor. The straps of her dress fell away with the same effortlessness and she felt herself floating away in an out-of-body experience.

Then lassitude gave way to something else. Lust. Pure and simple. She liked kissing Dan. It was different, daring, big, bold and exciting. The forbidden fruit tasted exotic and she wanted to tuck in with gusto.

And somewhere, at the back of her deliciously addled mind, she wanted to pay back Flick. Just talking about Steve had raked over the old, painful feelings.

This was candy-sweet revenge, snogging the face off a bloke she might have fancied anyway, had they both been free agents.

But now the pleasure had a wicked edge. She didn't know herself. Her instinct was showing her the way and, for once in her life, she let instinct be her guide and elbow aside reason, conscientious objection, moral anguish – all those plodding, boring bits that were so Katie-like and had no place here in the soft light with Dan.

Not that she was waiting for violins to strike up or fireworks to explode. This was an interval of lust with a payback punch. And by God, she was up for it.

Dan definitely was. He was kissing her shoulder now, her neck, invading her mouth again . . . She kissed back greedily, surrendering to her sensations. She guided his hands down the sides of her clinging dress, smoothing her own across and under his shirt.

The lamp flickered on the empty bottle rolling at their feet, and finally guttered out.

Cuddling her limp form in the taxi home, Jack was stricken with guilt. 'I'm sorry,' he said yet again, kissing the top of her tousled head. She had played a blinder all night. For starters, she'd splashed out on a beautiful new dress rather than risk letting him down. He hadn't liked to say so at the time, but none of her pre-existing gladrags had been up to L'Etoile standard. Then she'd endured being called Kitty all night by Phil in what appeared to be a calculated snub. Phil was too sharp to forget a name so easily.

And finally, he'd left her for well over an hour in the less than scintillating company of old Shaggy, while he and Flick swirled mellow old ports round their palates and vied with each other to flatter Phil.

The upshot was that he'd discovered her crashed out on the squishy sofa, practically comatose with exhaustion, Dan slumbering on a nearby armchair.

Poor Katie. She wasn't one for late nights and competitive socialising. Jack felt ashamed for neglecting her, while his disinterested, ambitious side reflected on a successful night out.

'Where are we?' Katie asked, finally lifting her head off his shoulder.

'Nearly home,' Jack assured her tenderly.

Katie fought a rising tide of nausea. The motion of the car . . .

'Sorry for leaving you on your tod like that,' said Jack humbly. 'Was Shaggy blindingly dull? I admit, old Phil must be a nightmare of a father. I suppose if your dad's a self-made zillionaire, you have to put up with a certain am—'

'I'm going to barf,' Katie announced.

'Brandy never agrees with you,' he couldn't help reminding her, as he tapped the taxi-driver's shoulder. 'I blame myself. I should've monitored how much you were drinking at dinner. Normally, you're so good at self-regulation, K.'

She tottered out of the car and retched not once, but twice. She was aware of Jack standing perilously, heroically close in his Armani suit. He twisted her hair out of harm's way and held it back. Blast him, she thought vaguely. Why did he have to show his caring side now, after being a right-wing brown-noser all night?

'I'm sorry,' repeated Dan in a low voice, as Flick silently handed him a cup of black coffee. Back at her flat, they'd just had their first row. Dan had stomped drunkenly indoors, tried to tear off his clothes with some difficulty (watched dispassionately by Flick), then lost his temper and demanded to know *the real reason* she kept men's shirts in her spare room.

'I have three lovers,' she'd coolly replied. 'Each of them likes to keep a spare shirt here, so they can go straight to work in the morning after a night's unbridled shagging.'

It was the 'shagging' that did it. He'd collapsed,

deflated, on her velvet chaise-longue. 'Sorry. I dunno. Oh God, I'm sorry.' And then he'd burst into tears. Childish, boo-hoo tears of incoherent regret and self-pity. The tears of a drunk.

Flick stood watching him for a bit, then padded away, returning with the cup of coffee.

'I'm sorry,' he repeated.

'For sounding off at Phil a couple of times over dinner? He had it coming. I just never noticed how much Dutch courage you were soaking up before-hand.'

'No,' said Dan slowly, gripping the coffee. 'Not for that.'

'For what, then?' She stood over him, hands planted on black satin hips. She was all angles and sharpness to match the impatience in her tone.

He realised he couldn't tell her. Consoling himself that her sharpness denoted a strength of character he lacked, he mumbled, 'Just for being a pillock half the night in front of Dad. For being me, I suppose.'

'Oh Dan.' This was the pathetic last line of defence she clearly expected of him. 'It went really well. I know Jack and Katie found out about the money, but that doesn't matter.' She turned away, briskly unpinning her hair. 'Did you see Jack in action? My God, he was so transparent. Phil knew what he was up to. It was like watching a cat toy with a half-dead mouse.'

'Jack a half-dead mouse?'

Flick grinned at him over one bare shoulder. 'Point is, you could put a tin can on top of a dunghill and Jack would go scrambling up to check if it was made of gold. I think Katie was embarrassed. *I* would have been. Jack wasn't exactly subtle.'

Dan half listened, the rest of him replaying his conversation with Katie. How much of a dunghill-scrambler was Flick?

Before he'd met Katie, Ulterior Motives had never crossed his love-filled mind, but perhaps they should have done. His self-assessment to Katie had been an honest one. He wasn't a great catch, aside from the money.

Flick began to peel off her clothes, tossing them carelessly into corners. Usually, Dan found her striptease erotic, the more so because she carried it out with an air of distraction, as if he wasn't there. Tonight, though, he just felt worried sick.

He drained the coffee, put down the cup, and picked up one of her shoes. 'Do you really love me, Flick?' he asked quietly.

She whirled round, her small white body naked and her green eyes compelling. 'Why don't you come to bed and I'll show you?' She padded over to him and hauled him to his feet.

He stood reluctantly. 'I can't,' he said.

Her eyes narrowed. 'Brewer's droop?'

No, he felt like saying. I can't get it up because I've only recently had sex with your sister. Probably. Maybe. If only he could remember!

'I'm tired,' he mumbled.

'No problem. Let me do all the work.' She ground her naked hip-bone against his fully clothed one.

'I need a quick wash,' he realised in panic, pulling away. He needed to check for incriminating evidence in his boxers.

'What for? I like dirty sex.' Again she was too quick for him, and her hand vanished down the front of his trousers. Her exploratory fingers were chilly and should have chased away his erection, but the bloody thing responded with a life of its own. Oh God, if she went on feeling down there, she'd find out if—

'Come on, Dan. Let's go to bed.'

There was no arguing with that tone. He'd made his bed, now he'd have to lie in it and come up with the goods. He followed Flick into the bedroom, where she bounced matter-of-factly but expectantly into bed. He undressed hurriedly in the dark, kicked his clothes into a corner, and jumped in after her.

'Your chest is wet,' said Flick, sliding her hands across it.

'Manly sweat?' he suggested. Sweaty nerves, more like.

It was OK while they were doing it. He was good at not thinking of anything in particular, apart from how beautiful and satiny Flick felt. He'd never understood blokes who needed to delay gratification by dwelling on images of hoovering the car.

But afterwards, Flick, unusually for her, wanted to cuddle. As she snuggled against him, he felt a wave of self-loathing. Oh God, he had jeopardised everything by giving Katie massive leverage against a hated sister: 'I slept with your fiancé at your own pre-wedding dinner. That's for Steve Wotsit, you bitch.'

His best hope lay in the instinctive niceness of Katie's character. Would she tell Flick and cut off her nose to spite her face? It depended on how much she wanted to keep smug old Jack. He wished he knew her better. As opposed to intimately.

'I think I've got alcohol poisoning,' muttered Katie,

pulling her ancient black beret further over her face. 'Whatever it is, it's worse than a hangover.'

'Is that why you're done up like Truman Capote?' demanded Nikki from the water's edge. She was hanging on for grim life to Sarah as her small, chubby hands lobbed bread inexpertly at the ducks.

After ringing in sick at work, Katie had phoned Nikki and asked to pop round. Unfortunately, Nikki had arranged to meet her in the park and 'make the most of this lovely day'. Katie didn't give a stuff for the loveliness of the day. She resented the lack of cloud cover. The sunshine hurt her eyes and a nice downpour would at least have matched her mood.

So far, she had given Nikki chapter and verse on the dinner at L'Etoile, from the Steve Sheridan dress to the discovery of Dan's true identity as modest millionaire, and, finally, a highly edited account of the visit to Maison Phil.

'Pass me the bag of brown bread,' ordered Nikki. 'I've got an interview at the health-food shop next week.'

'Brill, Nik. I'll get in touch with Frank and sing your praises.'

'You mean, you haven't already? I assumed I'd got this far because of rampant nepotism.'

'I sort of got distracted with the dinner. Which is great. You're there on merit.'

'Oh fuck,' panicked Nikki. 'That means the standard of applicant was really crap. So it's a crap job nobody wants.'

'No it isn't.' Katie put a hand to her throbbing forehead and let her troubled gaze roam over the duck-pond. So far, she and Nikki had shared every meaningful secret that had affected their lives. But sleeping with Dan had put her beyond the pale.

If she *had* slept with him. She couldn't remember that bit. Which only made it more sordid. What she *did* recall clearly was an overwhelming urge, stoked by Ukrainian rocket fuel, to settle her old score with Flick. She reckoned that made her capable of anything.

No, she couldn't tell Nikki. She couldn't even tell her best friend about her late-night bathroom search for a damp patch on her inner thigh. Unable to verify anything, she'd settled for flapping at both thighs with a wet sponge, nearly falling into the bath and cracking her head. Very funny – unless it was happening to you.

All her adult life, Katie had taken her own integrity for granted. So had Steve Sheridan and now, Jack. She had let herself down, forgotten temporarily who she was . . .

A deflating beach ball bounced painfully off her nose. 'Max, look where you're chucking it, you careless little sod,' shouted Nikki.

'Sorry, Auntie Katie.'

'No harm done, Max.' No harm done, least said soonest mended, it takes two to tango . . . Supposing Dan decided to confess all to Flick? Start the marriage with a clean slate? Oh God, that would be typical of him.

Nikki flopped onto the seat beside her. 'Waste of time being jealous.'

'I'm not.'

'How much is he worth?'

'Well, Jack reckons he must have a tidy ten mill in

his trust fund. A trust fund seems to be a personal pot of gold with a few strings attached. The trustees have to ratify withdrawals or something. But I don't think it's a problem for Dan to get his hands on dosh since he came of age. Presumably he'll also inherit the company and the ancestral home one day.'

'It's a fucking lie that money can't buy happiness. I know what I'd do with a cartload of dosh. I'd go travelling for a year and leave Doug at home with a choice of comfort-women or geishas or whatever you call them. Then, when I got back, he'd be too shagged out to want sex ever again. And I'd get a proper job just as the money ran out.'

A fat tear slid down Katie's sunglasses and dripped onto her sleeve.

'Oh fuck,' said Nikki. 'I know what you mean. Life's a crock of shit. Max, pull that duck's backside again and I'll leather yours.'

Max came over, half dragging, half carrying his baby sister. Straddling Nikki's lap, he grabbed her sulky mouth and yanked it up at the corners. 'I know a joke,' he said.

'Let's hear it,' said Katie.

'Keep it clean, son,' added Nikki.

Max curled his fist into a make-believe microphone. 'Police are 'vestigating a man found dead in an ice-cream van. He was covered in raspberry sauce and Flakes. Police say he may have topped himself.'

Katie burst out laughing. Nikki exploded at the same moment. They sat on the bench, cackling, dangerously close to real tears.

Max beamed proudly.

*

It was two weeks and counting to the wedding. Tess was holding an evening counsel of war at 23 Alderney Road. Jack had arrived with Katie, then drifted into the lounge to watch a penalty shootout with Simon, who was supposed to be in charge of 'freshening the pot'. Which left Katie alone with her mother.

'I thought Flick and Dan would be here,' she said accusingly.

'They've hired a U-haul and gone down to Marsham with their things,' replied Tess. 'They finally got the keys to the cottage. It would be nice if the boys could drag themselves away from the telly, but there you are.'

Tess flapped pages covered with her large scrawl. 'I'm putting you in charge of the bar, over there by the sideboard. Could you buy the booze, plastic cups, and look into hiring proper champagne flutes, twenty-five of them, for the toa–' She looked up from her jotter. 'Don't you want to write this down?'

'I'll remember. Booze, cups, champagne.'

'And champagne *flutes*. Are you all right?'

'Yeah, why wouldn't I be?'

Tess flapped her pages briskly. 'You seem a bit curly round the edges. Not my Katie at all.'

Katie squirmed. There must have been times in the past when her mother had laid claim to maternal instinct and ownership, but not for years and years.

She was spared any further need to dissemble when the door edged open and Jack came in with a laden tray, rattling teacups. 'I knew you'd be parched.'

Tess moved paperwork off the coffee table to make space for the tea. 'Does Freddy have any strong food preferences, Jack?'

Jack looked startled. 'He's not expecting an invite, Mrs G.'

'Well, if you're as good as family, so is he. Flick has included him and Suzette on the guest-list.'

Jack's expression grew guarded. 'Suzette won't come.'

'So what about Freddy?' Tess licked a pencil-stub and poised it over her jotter. Jack looked to Katie for guidance. Feeling spectacularly unworthy of taking the moral high ground to plead Freddy's case as a guest, she looked away.

'He won't know anyone,' said Jack lamely.

'He knows me,' snorted Tess. 'He can get to know the others. I'll take him under my wing. Does he have false teeth? I have trouble with grape pips under my plate and I'm iffy with sweetcorn.'

'He's got teeth,' said Jack, embarrassed.

Katie accepted her cup of tea, avoiding Jack's eye as he smiled entreatingly at her. He was still making it up to her for behaving like Gordon Gekko on speed (his words) at L'Etoile, and later at Phil's.

Alerted by the sound of pouring tea, bat-eared Simon loped into the room. 'Nice one, Jack. Any digestives going? Mum, you're not doing those bacon and prune monstrosities, I hope.'

Tess studied her jotter. 'I did have devils on horseback as a starter.'

'Let them eat Pringles,' pleaded Simon and threw himself into an armchair, nearly slopping his tea.

'Now I think of it, we'd better have thirty champagne flutes,' decided Tess. 'In case of breakages. OK, Katie?'

'But Mum, for heaven's sake, Flick works for a

department store,' objected Katie. 'Can't she just borrow what she needs from the homeware section?'

'She's bogged down already, wouldn't you say?'

Katie gritted her teeth. 'What's the split between beer, wine and spirits?'

Tess tore a page off the pad. 'I've written it all down. Beers, wines, mixers, fruit juices.'

'What's Shaggy's dad like?' Simon asked, and Tess sniffed. She still hadn't recovered from the slight of her exclusion from dinner at L'Etoile.

'He's a fat toad who smokes cigars,' said Katie. She looked at Jack, who was sipping tea with a philosophical air. It wasn't their job to reveal Dan's promising financial situation. Tess was already offended, and was bound to be more so when she learnt that Phil could have paid for a highly catered wedding ten times over. Let Flick be the bearer of hurtful news – eventually.

Tess looked around the room, frowning. 'I'd forgotten about smoking guests. If I left the french windows ajar, they could step outside.'

Katie imagined Phil's cigars littering the patio, and the grass beyond, like fat worms. 'You could just ban them, like an airline. Better fit a smoke alarm in the downstairs loo.'

'We'll see,' said Tess, knowing she'd cope with all eventualities. 'Most guests are friends of Flick who've been here at least once before. Dan's side seems a bit lightweight.'

That figured, thought Katie sourly. A few half-decent friends would have set Dan right on Flick. He was the juiciest fly ever to wander into her web.

'Buy the booze at Tesco's, Katie,' said Tess. 'I'll give

you my club card. Keep it under two hundred pounds and I'll write you a cheque.'

'No need for that, Mrs G,' said Jack. 'It'll be our wedding present to Flick and Dan.'

'Well, that's nice of you,' said Tess, looking at Katie for confirmation.

Katie struggled upright in her armchair. 'Our present. Right. No sweat.'

'My mate Larry can get some knock-off spirits,' offered Simon. 'And what about your mate, Jack – Milo? Doesn't he do booze runs to the Continent?'

'We don't want knocked-off anything,' declared Tess, licking her pencil-stub. 'We'll store the drink in the garage, assuming there's room next to Flick's boxes.'

Katie felt grudging interest. 'Isn't she moving all her stuff to Marsham?'

'She's got a lot of it,' replied Tess. 'And the cottage is fully furnished. Oh, and while I think of it, Katie, don't forget the olives, cocktail cherries and swizzle sticks.'

It had gone ten before they escaped. 'You don't mind, do you?' Jack asked on the drive home. 'Maybe it's more than we wanted to spend, but buying the drink is less hassle than trawling round Debenham's looking for antique cake forks.'

'Has she got a wedding list at Debenham's?'

'Where have you been? She hasn't even got a wedding list at Stempson's. It's all part of her masterplan to show Phil she's not a gold-digger. She'll just buy everything she wants after the wedding.'

'It seems clear Phil thinks the sun, moon and stars shine out of her colonically irrigated bottom.'

She felt him peering at her. 'You OK?' he asked. 'You look peaky. Time of the month?'

'What else could it be?' she asked sarcastically. 'If a woman's pissed off, it's only because she's hormonally unstable.'

'Are you? Pissed off, I mean.'

'I'm not anything.' She blinked back tears. The guilt was like a boulder crushing her, even though the details of her night with Dan had faded away with her hangover. But that didn't help. Her imagination supplemented her memory banks with wild-woman behaviour. Perhaps she'd egged Dan on, suggesting things she fought shy of when sober. The only thing she could remember clearly was coming to on the wooden settle, with her dress half on. But at least on. As was her underwear. She'd kind of blacked out during the heavy-petting stage. As for Dan, she found him slumped across her lap, face flushed and lips endearingly apart, like Sarah taking a nap.

She'd struggled to the sink, turned a tap and stuck her face under the bracingly cold trickle. Cupping water in her palm, she'd dashed it over Dan's face, making him open a bleary eye. 'Wha . . . ? Not getting up yet. Too tired.'

She'd needed him awake to interrogate him about what had (or hadn't) happened. To get their stories straight.

Hauling him upright, the first thing she'd seen were his trousers in tell-tale disarray. Battling her shock, she'd settled for more cold-water treatment. This time, she'd filled the empty booze bottle and doused it liberally around Dan's face and neck, slopping most of it down the front of his shirt.

It had done the trick, sort of. He'd come to, sat up, straightened his clothing and then stared groggily at her, awaiting further instructions.

So she'd prodded him up the stairs and into the living-room, shoving him into an armchair while she collapsed on the squishy sofa.

A few seconds later, he started snoring.

Next thing she knew, Jack was gently shaking *her* awake. Soon after that, the taxis arrived. She'd had no chance for a quick tête-à-tête with Dan, an 'Oh my God, what have we done? We must take this secret to our graves' conversation, so she could have checked they were on the same wavelength.

Now, in the dark of the car, she curled her fists until the nails dug into her palms. If Dan's guilt was anything like hers, he was bound to make a clean breast of it. Which meant Flick wouldn't waste time making sure Jack knew. He'd probably get the gist of it when Flick called round to gouge her eyes out.

Oh God, she'd have to tell him. And not just to head Flick off at the pass. She couldn't keep Jack in the dark. She loved him. She vaguely recalled a gobbledygook conversation with Dan in which she'd pointed out her essential compatibility with Jack, and his with Flick. She'd meant every word of it. The bizarre thing was, that had been the catalyst for her and Dan to test the nature of their incompatibility. They were a pair of tarts, end of story. Well, almost end of story. Drunk tarts weren't as bad as the other sort – were they?

But back to loving Jack, something she badly needed to prove, to herself and to him. Honesty and taking responsibility for mistakes mattered to him. If she confessed all, now, before her guilt became a festering stump of a third limb she dragged everywhere, there was a slim, outside chance he'd respect her openness and courage.

Clutching at this chance, she turned to him, banishing the alternative scenario from her mind. 'Jack,' she croaked. 'I have been feeling off-key recently. It is because of our night out. It's not what you think. It's—'

'I don't want you and your mum thinking I'm ashamed of Freddy,' he blurted out in the same instance. 'I know it looked like I wasn't mad keen on him coming to the wedding. It's just I know what he does and doesn't like. A formal do with a bunch of strangers is his idea of hell.'

'If he doesn't want to come, I'll square it with Mum. Jack, look, I have to t—'

'Bloody hell!' Jack hit the brakes and her seatbelt snapped taut against her shoulder. Dazed and shocked, she took a few seconds to realise they'd had a near miss. She peered through the windscreen as Jack leapt out of the car. They were almost home. She recognised the stunted trees of Garden Close.

Jack had gone to check on the old dear who'd stepped out in front of them. A hunched figure in a mac, clutching a suitcase tied with string, white hair tossed on a pink scalp like sea-spray against coral. But as Jack took a mackintoshed elbow and guided the old dear to the pavement, Katie did a double-take. She'd know that hunched stance anywhere. It was Freddy.

Chapter Seven

'I've made him comfy,' said Katie. 'We can kip either ends of the sofa. Sorry, but Freddy obviously has to have the bed.'

'No need to apologise when it's my father who's dropped us in it.'

They peered through the crack of the bedroom door. Katie was touched by the sight of Freddy's white head lying so trustingly on their pillow, in their flat. His eyes were shut.

Jack pulled the door closed. 'I'll talk him into going back to Suzette's first thing in the morning. That's if she'll have him.'

'But Jack, he wouldn't be here, all his worldly goods tied up with string, if he hadn't come to the end of his tether.'

'His tether's very flexible when it suits him,' muttered Jack, toe-poking the battered suitcase. 'Must have had a row and done a runner. I'll get it out of him in the morning.'

Keeping her counsel, Katie headed for the airing-

156

cupboard to find blankets for the sofa. Although she'd never met the scary Suzette, she felt she knew her well enough by reputation. She couldn't imagine Freddy besting her in a heated argument or storming into the night to teach her a lesson. No, it looked for all the world as if Suzette had shown *him* the door. Perhaps Jack didn't want to consider that possibility.

So far, Freddy had given little away. His flight from Hendon had taken its toll. While Jack stood glowering and biting the side of his thumb, Katie had coaxed Freddy into opening his suitcase to extract nightwear and essential toiletries.

She returned from the airing-cupboard to find Jack staring at the phone. 'We'll have to ring her and let her know he's here.'

'I suppose.' They were both in uncharted water. What were the rules of engagement when your sixty-three-year-old father ran away from home? Did he count as a missing person? Or was Suzette the last person he'd want notified of his whereabouts? A logical thought struck her. 'Jack, Suzette would have rung here by now if she was looking for him. It's the first place she'd try.'

'You're right. So it's the worst-case scenario. She's chucked him out.'

Katie looked at him with tenderness, sullied by her omnipresent guilt. She saw Jack, yet again, as the broodingly concerned parent of a disappointing child.

But for her own sake, she was temporarily grateful to Freddy. He was a crisis demanding action, a distraction from her guilt, and a third person in the flat, making confessional privacy impossible. She had a stay of execution from losing Jack.

'What will I do with him? Long-term, I mean.'

Katie plumped a cushion. 'You're not on your own with this.'

He looked at her with such pathetic gratitude that she wished the ground would open up and swallow her. He hadn't a clue that her magnanimity was borne of sheer relief. When he picked up her hand and silently squeezed it, she thought, yet again, 'This is the moment to come clean. Throw myself on the mercy of Jack's court, his Solomonite sense of fair play—'

'I'm not going back,' announced Freddy from the bedroom doorway.

They spun round to face him.

'I'll be out of your hair soon as I'm able,' he mumbled. 'Salvation Army hostel will do me.' He broke into his trademark hacking cough.

'Don't be daft,' muttered Jack. 'Daft and dramatic. Salvation Army indeed. As if I can't look after my own.'

'I won't be a burden, son.'

'Bit late for that.'

'Would you like a glass of hot milk?' Katie asked Freddy hurriedly, throwing a warning look at Jack. Freddy didn't have a highly developed sense of irony. He'd take Jack at his sardonic word.

Freddy shuffled his feet. 'Thanks, but better not. I'd only be using your toilet at all hours.'

'No flushing after eleven-thirty,' muttered Jack. 'By order of the residents' association.'

Freddy looked alarmed, then bewildered.

Jack sighed. 'I was joking, Pops.'

'Still, I'll try not to go. You hear all sorts through the walls in these flats.' He hesitated, as if awaiting permission to fall out. Then, quickly, he padded back into the bedroom and shut the door.

'Honestly, Jack, he'll lie awake half the night now with a throbbing bladder, afraid the neighbours might hear him peeing.'

'That's his lookout.' Ruffling his springy hair, Jack raised tired blue eyes to her. 'OK, I'll admit it, I'm not handling this well. I'm a lousy son. I'll take him out in the morning to that greasy spoon near the station. He'll love it. A couple of slices of fried bread and he should open up.' He squared his shoulders. 'Then we'll work something out.'

Katie could see him willing his confidence to return. Was that how he operated at work? Take the knocks, absorb them and bounce back with a strategy before anyone scented weakness? Poor Jack. She reckoned Milo and co were probably like animals in the wild, liable to turn on a wounded pack member and finish him off so he didn't slow them down. She was glad she didn't have a high-pressure job. On the other hand, Jack now had his agenda for the morrow. Deal with Freddy; solve the Freddy problem.

She wished her own problems could be timetabled so efficiently. But still, she continued to feel sorry for Jack, locked into his little certainties about how to deal with things and people, then ticking them off in boxes as dealt with. She had a suspicion that Freddy, like her gnawing guilt, wasn't about to go quietly.

In Dan's dream, Flick was standing on the far side of a green lawn, wearing a floaty, ankle-length green dress, her fragile arms held out to him. He wasn't close enough to see her face, but he could feel her green eyes reeling him in. He knew she was looking at him with longing and love.

Trouble was, to get to her he had to walk around his father, who was sitting at a table heaped in gutted birds, waving a dead pigeon on the end of a giant toasting fork. 'Try some of this red meat, flower-boy!' shouted Phil. 'Make a man of you yet. Aw, what's the matter, sonny jim? Afraid to get too close? Afraid to get spliced to Cruella de Ville with knobs on over there in case she always holds the whip hand?'

Dan tried to ignore him and keep his gaze fixed on Flick. Seeing his predicament, she'd begun to float towards him on invisible castors.

'Why not listen to your father for maybe the once?' asked a voice at the other end of the table, and Dan turned to see his mother. Her large pale face was smooth, moon-like and unsexed beneath the blue headscarf she always donned for cleaning. She'd made a fastidious workspace for herself amid the dead, blood-leaking birds, and was polishing a candlestick in the shape of a dolphin. 'Maybe he is right about people, your mad father,' she went on. 'Maybe you need to put your foot down with people from the word go. Like he did with me.'

'Mum,' croaked Dan. 'Don't take his side.'

But Irina went on polishing and wouldn't look up. So he turned to the approaching Flick. Her arms were still extended, her smile soft. But when he looked into her eyes, they were as hard as green marbles.

'Why?' he cried. 'Why did you have to tell me the nitty-gritty about going off with that Steve bloke? It got me thinking you might not be the person I took you for. So I went and got drunk and listened to Katie doing you down, and ended up doing stuff with her.'

'Dan,' she said, with a sly smile. 'You know why I told you about Steve.'

'No I don't.' He looked stubbornly at his feet. At all the life slithering about in the grass. It seemed furtive rather than purposeful all of a sudden.

Her arms slid round his neck. He was afraid to look up and be turned to stone by her Medusa stare. But when he did, he met the soft, blue-grey eyes of Katie.

'She told you because she could,' murmured Katie. 'She warned you what she's really like once she knew she had you. She gave you a chance to back out, knowing you were already hooked. Makes her look like she has a conscience. Clever, but that's my kid sis for you.'

As Katie's arms tightened round his neck, he tried to back away. The arms became a stranglehold. Katie's face dissolved, becoming a hard, green-eyed mask topped by a hairdo of waving snakes, an emerald eye glittering from each of their foreheads. 'Get off!' he yelled.

He woke up suddenly and gasped, disoriented, trying to remember where he was. Gradually, his heart-rate slowed. The shadows of the Hampstead flat re-massed into familiar shapes. He turned on his pillow, and started. Flick's eyes were wide open and staring at him, like a dead person's.

She touched his trembling chest through his T-shirt. 'Couldn't sleep either? Must be pre-wedding nerves. I just want the whole thing over and done with.'

Dan stared at the ceiling. 'Sure you won't die of boredom and isolation out in the sticks?'

'It's in my blood. All my ancestors were close to the

land.' She raised herself on one elbow so that her hair poured over his chin. 'Stempson's will keep the door open for a bit. I'm not shutting the gate totally on my old life.'

'Mmm.'

'What's the matter, Dan? Recently, I mean?'

'Look – can I just ask – erm – I can't stop thinking about you and Steve Wotsit,' he blurted. 'Katie's Steve,' he added, for good measure.

Flick stared down impassively at him. He felt at a disadvantage.

'Thinking what, exactly?' she asked, cool but playful. 'That I might go back for a rematch? I loathe the bloke. He was an aberration, a cheap shot at Katie. It's bad enough that she's punishing me for ever and a day. Am I to be punished by you for the rest of my life?' Her eyes glistened.

''Course not,' he said miserably. 'But if I had a similar skeleton in my cupboard, would you take the same view? That it was a moment of madness? One I shouldn't go on being punished for indefinitely?'

The suggestion of tears vanished from her eyes. 'Something you'd like to tell me, Dan?'

'No! Yes! No.' He broke into a sweat. 'It happened – a long time ago,' he mumbled, taking refuge in a story book beginning. 'I was drunk. I was out of my head, to be honest, and so was she.' Heat flooded his face. 'Wouldn't have happened otherwise. She's got too much taste.'

'Where are you going with this, Dan?' Flick sounded deceptively bored, but he knew she was waiting, like a scorpion under a rock, to deliver the telling sting.

He swallowed hard and made the mistake of looking into her eyes. They were as hard and green as he remembered from his dream. And how much greener would they get, fired by jealous rage, when – if – he told her the truth?

He was close to achieving something for the first time in his life. Marrying a woman his father approved of, a woman who knew all the stuff he didn't about getting on in the world. And not least, a woman he was crazy about, who was beautiful, sophisticated, witty, ballsy, and capable of great tenderness.

He took a deep breath. 'It was me and Maggie,' he mumbled.

Maggie was the manager of the garden centre.

'We had a – thing. A one-off legover situation. Before you and I got together, obviously. It's just . . . I had to tell you. She's a married woman, after all.'

'I see.' Flick stopped tormenting him with her all-seeing eyes and flopped back on her pillow. She giggled.

'Is it cause for amusement?' he asked, sounding mildly offended as a way of increasing his cover. He hated himself for this. Christ, how easy it was, once you started telling lies. Maggie was a down-to-earth, apple-cheeked woman in her mid-fifties who wore the same anorak, day in, day out.

'Well,' giggled Flick again. 'She's ancient and smells of manure, but I suppose some men go for that.'

'She's not that bad,' huffed Dan, irrationally defensive of a lover-who-never-was. 'She's got nice – teeth.'

'Oh, Dan.' Flick bounced away to her side of the bed. 'I think you were only doing a public service. Her husband ran off years ago, didn't he? As long as you haven't bedded Barbara.'

Barbara was Maggie's seventeen-year-old daughter.

'What do you take me for?' he asked indignantly (he was really getting the hang of it). 'I just wanted to tell you,' he added lamely, addressing her back.

It shrugged eloquently. 'That's all done and dusted, then. Past lovers ticked off and put into cold storage. Don't worry about it. G'night, Dan.'

'G'night, Flick.'

'Maggie!' she giggled, this time to herself and emitted a long, tolerant sigh into her pillow.

Dan kept a vigil for the next hour or so, denied sleep by a mixture of self-disgust and astonishment at his facile lies. He accepted now that he'd never be able to tell her about his lapse with Katie. She'd think it was his revenge for Steve Sheridan as much as Katie's.

And in a way, it had been.

He remembered the first time he'd seen Flick coming to talk to him at work, gliding across a seeded lawn, professional but waif-like in her two-piece suit. He'd glimpsed her from time to time since he'd worked at the centre and thought her the image of fragility and sweetness, perfection and loveliness.

Even though their meetings were occasional and strictly businesslike for nearly two years, and then on unequal terms, his faith in her perfection had never wavered. The professional distance between them only underlined her poise. Her reserve strengthened the case for underlying vulnerability. He had dreamt so long of good things.

Good things that had finally come his way this March, when Flick first took him to one side, and suggested they get together in a more informal capacity – perhaps over coffee – to discuss the floral backdrop for Stempson's next fashion show.

She was right about the ex-lovers ticked off and accounted for. Well, not in so many sordid words. They'd reached a coy compromise of agreeing that she'd notched up fewer than Madonna and he could account for a handful more than the Pope.

As Flick's breathing deepened beside him, he mopped up a brief rush of silent tears with the edge of the sheet. He rarely cried. Not even as a child. His father couldn't abide cry-baby males. He hadn't been allowed to his mother's cremation, so he didn't know if he'd have blubbed on that occasion. He reckoned he would have felt like blubbing, then seen his dad watching him and wet his pants instead. So really, his dad had spared him.

Jack decided to wait until Freddy had demolished a stack of fried bread and a mug of milky tea. The caff was heaving with builders, nurses who'd just come off the night shift and hungover men in suits. Jack was rattled by all this teeming life at the unearthly hour of eight-thirty. Freddy seemed to be revelling in it. His eyes were as wide as a child at a funfair's. Between the delights of his greasy fry-up and the profusion of people, he didn't seem to grasp that Jack had brought him here for a man-to-man talk.

'Dad,' he began heavily.

'Son,' retorted Freddy warily.

'What's going on with you and Suzette?'

'Nothing's gone on for a long time. You know that.'

Jack shifted awkwardly in his chair. 'I mean, why walk out now, unless you've had a falling out?'

'We haven't argued. You'd have to communicate first, to have a row.' Freddy dropped his third sugar cube in his tea, smiling proudly at his cryptic utterances.

Jack's irritation rose, grease settling like Scotch mist on his suit. He knew he'd arrive at work ponging like a workman's vest. 'It may interest you to know that I'm popping round to see Suzette after work to get her side of the story.'

'It doesn't much.' Freddy watched in apparent fascination as a child in a buggy threw his pacifier on the floor. His mother picked it up, wiped it and handed it back to him, only for the little boy to throw it down again, repeating the whole process. 'Would you look at that?' chuckled Freddy.

'Dad, this is serious,' said Jack.

'It's not, you know. Nothing's serious at my age.'

'What does that mean? You're not long for this world, I suppose.'

'I mean, I've made a right royal screw-up of things so far. How much worse can it get?'

Jack flushed angrily. 'It can get a lot worse for me.'

'How so, son?'

'Nothing. Doesn't matter.' Jack decided to stare around as well. He'd get nowhere as long as Freddy kept up this resigned and philosophical act. Which, to Jack's way of thinking, was just a cop-out. He looked at his father's hoary old head. At this moment he hated the bloke. But underneath the hate lay a jagged edge of guilt, and beneath that, the softer, blurred edges of regret, tenderness, even love . . .

'You mean,' said Freddy, 'I could make things worse for you by coming between you and Katie. I know that. She's a very patient girl, as it happens, and she'd give me a long bit of rope to swing on before she got tired of me. But I'm not completely daft, lad. I don't want to stay with you for ever. I just want to get out and about – stretch my wings.'

Jack stared at him. 'You weren't in Wormwood Scrubs. Unless . . .' He hesitated. 'Did Suzette ill-treat you?'

Freddy coughed. 'We ill-treated each other. Emotionally, like.'

'If you're going to go all agony aunt on me,' said Jack crossly, wondering why his father's flit had to coincide with this exasperating descent into Confucius-like utterances. Oh, to be at work with cut-and-dried men's men like Milo. Right on cue, his mobile phone rang. He answered it with relief.

'Problems,' he told Freddy happily, at the end of a rapid and coded conversation. 'I have to dash. Katie give you a key for the flat?'

'Yes, thanks. All right if I wander round for a bit before I go back?'

Jack smiled. 'You're not under curfew, Pops. Go out and stretch those wings. But don't take off,' he added, worrying he'd been too negative up to now. 'We'll talk some more tonight.'

'Look forward to it,' said Freddy gloomily.

Jack stood up, threw a tenner on the table, nodded curtly and shot off. Leaving Freddy free to order another round of fried bread.

On his way to the station, Jack's irritation gave way to weariness. He wasn't looking forward to visiting

Suzette. He didn't like her, although she was always charming to him. But she had never hid her contempt for Freddy, even in front of his own son. Now, though, she might have a handle on Freddy's current state of mind. Was this all about, God forbid, the onset of Alzheimer's? Or was his betting habit out of control again, after years of self-disciplined indulgence?

Freddy's presence would eventually take its toll on Jack's relationship with Katie. Look at the way they'd gently bickered over the old git when he lived at Suzette's. What would it be like when Freddy drove them mad in a small flat? Katie didn't know the half of it. She just saw Freddy as a sad, helpless old man. Which he was, when in need.

Jack passed a man begging outside the station and met his eye, thinking, I have no time for self-inflicted woes. Is it really beneath your dignity to flip burgers for a living? He was almost on the train when he thought of Katie's reaction to this every-man-for-himself philosophy. Sighing, he retraced his steps and slipped the man a two-pound coin. He was just glad Phil Avebury couldn't see him.

Tesco's on a Saturday morning was heaving. Katie steered a trolley around the booze section, 'helped' by Simon, whose assistance consisted of sudden darting forays down other aisles, returning with a copy of *Loaded*, several packets of silvermints, a jar of peanut butter and a bag of doughnuts.

'I'll pay you back at the checkout,' he promised, making sheep's eyes.

She sighed. He was in full 'love-me' mode. 'A few extras won't break the bank, Si.'

'How's Freddy? No sign of him moving on?'

'I'm not looking for a sign. He's only been with us five minutes and he's rattled enough after leaving Suzette.'

'So he's sticking to his story that she didn't chuck him out?'

'She didn't. Jack went round and checked it out. She came back from a friend's to find a goodbye note under the fruit-bowl. She was stunned, then angry. She doesn't want anything more to do with him. He had, as Jack put it, a cushy billet with her.'

'Yeah. Like a budgie in a cage has a cushy billet.'

Katie looked at him with respect. 'Exactly. Anyway, Freddy doesn't want to go back – assuming she'd have him back – and Jack and I are backing him all the way.'

'That sofa must be comfier than it looks.'

'Needs must,' said Katie stoutly. The sofa was a bed of nails, fittingly penitential for a scarlet woman. It was a shame that poor Jack was developing curvature of the spine as well, but at least conjugals were out of the question, solving her apprehension at having sex on a guilty conscience.

The laden trolley was proving difficult to push, so Simon took over. 'Thanks, Si, and thanks for volunteering to drive me here in the first place.'

She'd already done her grocery shopping. It was safely stored in Simon's car boot in the multi-storey.

'Can't have Jack giving up his Saturday-morning squash. Anyway, I wanted a word with you on your lonesome.'

Katie tensed. 'About what?'

'Promise me, Katie. No ruining this wedding to get

back at Flick over Steve. No sending Dan anonymous notes written with your left hand saying Flick was born Jeffrey and used to be a dog-handler with the Met. Promise.'

'Bloody hell! Did Mum put you up to this? What do you lot take me for?' A slow flush of anger crept up her neck. Did he but know it, she had the perfect ammunition to wreck Flick's wedding.

'No one put me up to it. I want to move out of Mum's and I want the wedding to go smoothly so she can have a nice memory to fall back on when I give her the bad tidings.'

'Talk about fancying yourself, Si. Mum's lived on her own a fair bit. She'll be able to cope when you do a flit.'

'That's just it.' He tugged at his explosive hair. 'It's where I'm flitting off to. Thought I'd try the States for a bit.'

Katie stopped in her tracks. 'America! You don't mean . . . Phoenix, Arizona, by any chance?'

'Might do.'

'You're off to stay with *him* and Legs Up To Her Armpits Tanya?'

His abashed look confirmed it. Katie was flabbergasted. 'I didn't even know you were in touch with him.'

'He initiated it, just in the last year at uni. He reads the English papers on the net and saw my name on the back pages, that time I rowed for the college and we beat Cambridge. He didn't even know I was at university – well, you know what he and Mum are like for keeping in touch.'

'They don't,' nodded Katie.

'It's not like Mum's ever passed on his Phoenix address and phone number to us,' said Simon. 'And I'd never have the nerve to ask her after all this time, though I doubt she'd turn a hair. You and Flick already have his contact details?' he asked curiously.

'Never had any interest in finding out,' said Katie. 'Can't vouch for Flick. I always imagined his address would be easy enough to come by if I needed it.'

'He started writing to me at uni,' continued Simon. 'Just "Simon Gibson, care of Nottingham University" at first. Can you believe it? Hadn't a clue who that first letter was from when it turned up in my pigeon-hole. He'd only featured in my life up to then as a sperm-donor.'

'Keep your voice down, Si.'

'He wrote along the lines of "You don't know me but I used to be your father", only with lots of Yank gush about reaching out and healing the wounds of the past. I think he's seen a shrink.'

'I don't want to imagine him shrunk.'

'Once I'd had a good chuckle, I got thinking. The randy old git is my *father*, after all. He's been inviting me over from the word go. I think he's suffering from only-son syndrome.' He tried to look apologetic, but only succeeded in looking relieved it was all out in the open. 'He's offered to fix me up with a job if I come out for a year and says I can live with him, Tanya and the girls initially. I may be a mercenary toe-rag but why shouldn't I get something out of it, if he's offering? I'm not cut out for this social work lark,' he added defensively. 'Battered this and battered that, as our late-lamented Saint Di put it. It's all getting me down. I'd rather shoulder my spotted hanky on a stick and go west to make my fortune.' He tried his matey smile on Katie, but she was frowning, still digesting his news.

'Well,' she said, as another trolley clanged into them; they were blocking an aisle. 'Have you told him about Flick's wedding?'

'No way. That's Flick's shout, and she seems hell-bent on keeping him in the dark. She *and* Mum would probably go ballistic if I went around dishing out info unilaterally. Anyway, if Dad got in touch with Mum over that, she'd find out I'd been supping with the devil behind her back. How do you think she'll take it?' he asked in all seriousness. 'And when should I tell her?'

Katie tried to marshal her thoughts. Her brother had been in treacherous contact with Don Gibson and Legs Up To Her Armpits Tanya for the past year. So what? It was his life. And in all fairness, he'd only been protecting their mother by keeping it under wraps.

She tried to feel hurt that Don was displaying a belated but nonetheless zealous interest in his only son, but frankly, she couldn't have cared less. 'Maybe wait until after the wedding to tell Mum, Si. As long as you're not flying off the day after?'

'Not till a few weeks after. I was going to suggest Freddy move in as a lodger, keep her company.'

'Nice thought but bad idea. Too much scope for clash of personalities and the fallout lingering over me and Jack. Freddy needs to be protected from strong women, by Act of Parliament if necessary.'

He nodded absently. 'Thanks, Katie. If everyone reacts as sanely as you, it'll make things a lot easier for me.'

'Hmm.' Katie felt older-sisterly towards him. He wanted everything to come easily to him. He expected laconic charm to smooth every path before him, and most of the time it did. Take the way he'd got round her. A second before his announcement, she'd wanted to brain him with tinned salmon for calling her a potential wedding saboteur.

Simon left her on the pavement of Garden Close with her grocery shopping. He was taking the booze straight back to Alderney Road. He hadn't offered to help her wrestle six full carrier bags up three flights of stairs. She'd forgotten to ask him, too busy mulling over his news.

Anyway, it wouldn't be the first time she'd lugged the shopping up, although Jack usually insisted it was his job. He wouldn't be back from squash yet, but Freddy was in. Maybe Freddy would like to feel useful by carrying up a bag or two.

Balancing this against the likelihood of him getting a stroke, Katie buzzed the intercom. No answer. She buzzed again. Finally, she dug her front-door key out of her handbag and struggled into the hallway, the key gripped between her teeth. She left two bags at the bottom of the stairwell and began to climb. Eventually, she got the other four up to the flat door.

As she let herself in, she smelt burning. Dropping her bags, she rushed into the kitchen. Nothing was actually on fire, but the air was dense with dispersing smoke. She saw the grill door on the oven ajar. Reaching inside with a tea-towelled hand, she found a smouldering, empty baking tray, and that led her to the swing-bin. She flipped up the lid and saw the charred husk of a garlic bread baguette. Beneath black crusts, herb-speckled butter oozed richly onto the bin-liner: Freddy's attempt at light lunch.

'I'm sorry, pet,' said a voice from the doorway. 'I brought these up.'

She turned to find Freddy on the kitchen threshold, carrying her two remaining grocery bags. 'I'm right sorry about the smoke, love. I put it under the grill and left it for half an hour, which I know is too long. I was watching the big race on telly, smelt the terrible smell and came running too late. I put the extractor fan on three, but it didn't help much. Sorry.' His shoulders almost slumped to the floor.

Irritation welled up in Katie. He'd deliberately compounded his guilt by including every detail that showed him up, like neglecting the frazzling bread while he watched a blinking nag race. It would also have helped if he'd read the very basic cooking instructions, which stipulated ten to twelve minutes in an oven, not under a grill.

But as she looked at him, she knew he expected the full weight of her opprobrium. He'd set himself up for it. He was engineering her to behave like Suzette. Well, she wouldn't. She had a pretty shrewd idea there was more to Freddy than an apologetic old buzzard who couldn't be left alone to change a lightbulb. He'd been fooling Jack and Suzette with that impression for years, but he wasn't fooling her.

'No harm done,' she said brightly. 'Reminds me, in fact. We must put a new battery in the smoke alarm. Fancy a cup of tea and a sarnie? I'm starving.'

He regarded her with wary hope. 'That'd be nice. I bought these.' He separated a scrawny-necked carrier bag from her bulging grocery ones. 'Just a few things to keep you and Portillo going. Wish I could pay me way more.'

'You're a guest, Freddy.' She took the proffered goodies, feeling like a cat-owner whose moggy has proudly thrown a decomposing sparrow at her feet. He'd bought a tin of condensed milk, a jar of fish paste, a jumbo box of matches and a packet of jam tarts in traffic-light colours. Anderson shelter provisions, thought Katie. How long since he'd been shopping in the real world?

She looked up to meet stubbornly hopeful blue eyes. 'It's ages since I had a jam tart,' she told him. 'Used to love them when I was a kid. Let's skip the sarnies and have a couple with tea. I won't tell Jack if you won't.'

Freddy shuffled further into the kitchen to have a stab at being helpful. She took two cups down from the cupboard. 'Be an angel and fill the kettle, Freddy. You know Jack and I back your decision to move out of Suzette's, don't you?'

'You might. Don't know about Portillo.'

'Oh, but he does.' Katie shut the cupboard door forcefully. 'It was always a dodgy situation. You had no formal tenancy agreement or anything. She could have chucked you out any time.'

'Don't know what tipped me over the edge,' he said, scratching his cheek. 'No, hang on, be honest for once in your life, Frederick Gold. There was something that got me thinking – you two getting married. Made me want to cut and run, but I'll be on my way soon as I can.'

'You're not a burden, Freddy.'

'Hear me out, love. After I burnt that garlic stuff, I ran again. Nowhere in particular this time, just down the road like a headless chicken. Didn't know what I'd say to you when I got back, so I stopped at a shop and bought a few fancy cakes and whatnot. Like an apple for the teacher.'

Katie's heart went out to him. He'd been a tiptoeing presence at Suzette's, afraid to so much as chip a cup. Now it was the same for him here. His son was a stranger to him in some ways, and maybe she'd been guilty of patronising him. 'Listen, Freddy, only one thing worries me about you staying here. Don't you miss Suzette's garden?'

'Probably more than it misses me. I was never much of a gardener, lovey. But it kept me out of mischief, especially on summer evenings with all the extra light. It was one of the few things I could do for Suzette, save her a few bob on getting someone in.'

Kate suppressed her own interpretation of these words; that Suzette had banished him to the garden for long hours. 'Maybe you could look at my straggly window-box,' she said. 'You still have greener fingers than me or Portillo.'

Freddy grinned. 'Know what, Katie? My boy could never do better than you.'

'Thank you, Freddy.' She hid the threat of tears by picking up the tray of tea and tarts and hurrying into the sitting-room.

She cleared a space on the coffee table, careful not to nudge Freddy's wedding photo. They sat in comfortable silence, sipping tea, until Freddy said, 'I want to tell you about myself. More than the lad knows, truth be told.'

'You don't owe me any soul-baring, Freddy.'

'I trust you. We're a bit alike, you and me.'

While she grappled with that bombshell, he continued sadly, 'Janet and I did our best by Jack. We kept up a united front, both of us going to his school nights and suchlike. He didn't know about my gambling till he was grown up. My *real* gambling, not the odd flutter I have now. I must have lost thousands in my heyday, if you can call it that.' He slurped tea, waiting for Katie's reaction.

'I didn't know,' she admitted. 'Jack's always so tightlipped about you.'

Freddy wheezed vigorously. 'And now you know why. He's ashamed of me.'

'That's not true.'

'The funny thing is, he still doesn't know the half of it.' He paused. 'I'm not telling you this next bit to show the wife in a bad light. Understand me?'

He looked so intense that Katie nodded.

'Back when Jack was a little 'un, I had a big win on the horses one day. A *big* win. When I rolled home that night, well-oiled, with the money burning a hole in my pocket, Janet called me every name there is. I can't tell you the feeling, pulling that wad from my pocket and showing off my winnings to shut her up. Might have been the biggest mistake I ever made.'

'Why?' asked Katie.

'I'll tell you. We were living in a poky flat, railway property. Jack, he'd have been eight or nine, slept in a bed I'd made out of an old trunk. So Janet grabs the money and says, "At last, you silly old fool, we can buy our own place!" And that's what we did. Went down to the estate agent feller, took a look at some nice new houses they were building in Whetstone and bought one, cash on the nail. A couple of grand a house cost back then, a nice house. There was a bit of money left, and Janet held onto it tight. She wasn't taking any chances with her and Jack's future.' He nodded approvingly at the memory of his wife's prudence. 'So there we were, set up in our des res, and we rubbed along half-happy for a few years. I still liked a flutter, but at least, from Janet's view, the house was bought and paid for.' His faded blue eyes grew wistful. 'This'll sound right mad. Twisted. But knowing there was less to risk, that I couldn't put us out on the street with one reckless throw of the rent money – well, took the edge off gambling for me. If that sounds mad, it's because gamblers are mad, selfish buggers. I just went in for the odd flutter after that.'

'Maybe you finally grew up,' pondered Katie, and blushed. 'I mean, maybe your windfall reminded you just in time what was important.'

Freddy smiled enigmatically. 'Nothing happened to rock the boat for a few years. Then I got this job offer in Australia. Did I ever tell you I had a hankering for Australia?'

Katie shook her head.

'More than a hankering really. A – what's the word? – yearning, I suppose. Mate of mine from school, Alfie Barker, had gone out there a few years before. He'd built up a nice little business, branches everywhere, and needed blokes he trusted to help him manage it all. He wrote me and offered the works. A house with two acres of garden, even a car! I suppose my hankering for wide-open spaces came from growing up in a sinkhole, ten to a lav. Maybe Alfie's, too. On school trips to Clacton or Southend, me and Alfie would look at the sea and imagine what lay on the other side. Not just France, but further-away places where pineapples didn't come in rings out of tins.' Smiling at his gauche childhood self, he gazed into space.

Eventually his gaze drifted back to Katie. 'Janet was having none of Australia. Said I could go on my own but I'd never see Jack again. You mustn't blame her,' he added hastily, as Katie stiffened. 'The only security she'd had was that house. She had local respect, too. She did the flowers in church and her boy was good at book-learning. But deep down, she was punishing me, and we both knew it. I'd given her too much grief down the years. She knew how badly I wanted Australia, so she was determined I wouldn't get it.'

Katie was captivated. So much drama and passion in a faded suburban marriage. All that double-crossing by a woman whose hands would have been busy shaping altar lilies into an Easter tableau. 'So you never went to Australia.'

'Stayed in Whetstone, working on the railways, last five years at Neasden Junction. Janet died when Jack was sixteen. She went quite sudden. Some people live years with cancer now, but Janet only lasted six months from the time she was diagnosed. She died at home.' He coughed.

'I'm sorry,' said Katie. 'Did you part . . . friends?' She blanched at the tweeness of her question, making them sound like occasional lovers who met under the clock at Charing Cross.

'It's illness that's the great leveller, not death,'

replied Freddy dully. 'When someone's that ill, everything that's gone before – good times and bad – count for naught.' He lapsed into silence, leaving Katie none the wiser. Perhaps Freddy was none the wiser himself.

After a bit, he picked up the thread of his story. 'After his A levels, Jack went off travelling for a year. I got restless on my own. When he came back, he got a job and moved into a flatshare. I said to him, "What do you think of me selling up and moving to Oz?" He thought I was bonkers. I said I'd split the money with him, but he got angry, didn't want to know. I stuck it out another while, but when Jack went off to college, I knew he'd need money for the next three years. He was too cute to get saddled with big debts, because he'd saved up a fair whack in his job. But I still had my excuse to sell the house. I did it – practically overnight. I meant to lodge half the money in Jack's account, to give him a head start after college. *Meant* to,' he repeated heavily. Then he seemed to falter, staring into his cooling tea.

'I think I can guess what's coming next,' said Katie gently. 'You gambled away the house money, didn't you?'

He nodded.

'But why?'

'The Aussies wouldn't let me in,' he replied bluntly. 'Even with my half for the house coming to a tidy sum, they must have seen me as a future burden on their health system. I dunno.'

'Couldn't Alfie have vouched for you?' asked Katie.

'I'd lost track of old Alfie by then. I wasn't planning to go over and work for my living, was I? Not at my age. There it was. No Janet to stop me going, but too late to get there. She must have been laughing her head off somewhere. I went a bit mad after that. In three weeks, I'd lost the lot, including Jack's half.'

'Three weeks!' echoed Katie with a small shriek. 'Why didn't you check out the emigration procedure before you sold the house?'

'You've no idea how a gambler's mind works, love. You always put the cart before the horse. It's expected.'

By whom? wondered a puzzled Katie. 'You should have gone over on a tourist visa first, to see if you even liked Australia.'

Freddy beamed affectionately at her. 'You're dead right there. That's what Jack said, only you put it nicer. He went mad when he found out I was homeless.'

Katie said nothing. Poor Jack. It must have been the understatement of the year when he revealed at their first meeting that he and his dad weren't bosom pals.

'I moved into a B and B. Clean, but a grim old place all the same. Jack fetched up to read the riot act. Partly to get him off my back, I took up Suzette's offer of lodging. Brian wasn't long dead and she wanted a bloke around the place.' He gazed in embarrassment at the tips of his threadbare slippers. 'We started an affair, I suppose you'd call it, just for a while. But I think she despised herself for being lonely enough to consider me that way. Then she despised me. Hard not to when I despise myself. This tea's gone cold.'

'I'll make you another.' The veil had been stripped away from the Gold family life and Katie was moved by what she'd heard. Freddy admitted his culpability. He hadn't emerged from the wreckage blaming other people or hating Janet.

Freddy trotted after her into the kitchen, nervous and subservient again in the wake of his confession. 'Like I said, Jack doesn't know the half of it, and I want to keep it that way. He knows I gambled away the house money, but not about Janet putting a stop to Australia. That's how it has to stay, as he was fond of his mother.'

'I understand, Freddy.' As she waited for the kettle to boil again, a disturbing thought struck her. 'Why did you say we're alike, Freddy?'

'Oh, you're not weak like me, lovey. If you were down to your last fiver, you wouldn't put it on a double-header at Newmarket and hope for the best. I mean we're both easy to rub along with on most scores. We take folk as we find them.'

'Right,' said Katie suspiciously.

'And here's another thing for your ears only, at least for the time being. I know Jack wouldn't approve. I've written to an old mate of mine—'

'Alfie Barker?' she hazarded, eager for a romantic ending.

'No, love. Bloke by the name of Sebastian Hatcher. We did National Service together. Peeled our own weight in spuds while a horrible sarge made us both cry for home. Posh bloke, but nice with it, always said he'd be off to Italy to open a restaurant as soon as he got out of our rain-filled foxhole, and he was. You could always trust old Seb to get off his backside and follow through.'

'Crikey. I suppose he married a local signorina and now he's a fat, contented grandpapa.'

'Not quite, love, not quite. He never married, and now he's retired from the restaurant, bought himself a little bar on some Greek island. Begins with an H.'

'Halkidiki?' suggested Katie.

'That's the bugger. Excuse my French. We kept in touch and he's been on at me to pay a long visit. So I've written to see if he'll have me. They say it's dirt cheap to live out there. If Seb can't find a use for me, someone will employ me as a hotel porter, cellarman or whatever.'

'Right,' said Katie doubtfully, glancing at Freddy's slight, life-battered frame. And as for that cough . . .

'But like I say, don't tell Jack. I'll tell him myself if and when Seb gives me the nod.'

'Mmm,' agreed Katie, distracted by pleasant thoughts of revolutionising Freddy's wardrobe, ceremonially burning the cardigan, sending him off to his successful friend with a bit of dignity and some new slippers.

'Have you never been abroad, Freddy?' she asked. 'Despite your wanderlust?'

'I've been to Calais and back, shopping at the hypermarket with Suzette. But that's not what you'd call abroad.'

'You'll love the Greek sunshine and way of life,' enthused Katie, already picturing him playing back-gammon in the shade of a spreading olive tree. There wouldn't be that many crates to hump about, surely, in a small taverna? She'd better hold her horses, though. Freddy was back to square one if Seb, like Alfie Barker, had vanished in the mists of time. 'You say you've written to Seb. So you've got his current address and everything?'

'I think so.' A shadow of doubt crossed Freddy's face. 'It's a couple of years since our last Christmas cards. But he'd have dropped me a line if he was moving on.'

'Can you phone him?'

Freddy looked stubborn. 'I've written now. Don't want to pester him to death by phoning as well. Anyway, how would I get hold of a Greek phone directory to find his number?' This seemed to settle the matter for Freddy, who'd clearly never heard of international directory enquiries.

'Go for it, if it's what you really want. But staying here won't put us out, and you'll always be welcomed back.'

'Thanks, love. I know you mean it. With a bit of luck, Seb will get back to me by the time your sister's weddings been and gone. *Then* I'll tell Jack what I'm up to. Do me a favour, lovey, and act as surprised as him.'

'Well . . . OK,' she agreed hesitantly, loath to keep a secret from Jack concerning his own father. 'Are you sure he wouldn't approve of your plan?'

'He'd see it as another of the old man's hare-brained schemes. I want it to be the ace up my sleeve. For that, the plan has to pan out.'

'OK, I'll keep shtum. I'm sure Seb will get back to you soon.' She smiled at him gently, her warmth tinged with sadness. First Simon was shipping out on the sly, now Freddy. But she couldn't help feeling that her brother's plans were likelier to come to fruition.

Chapter Eight

'T hat's some outfit, lovey,' said Freddy appreciatively as Katie, already sweating in unladylike fashion, rushed around the flat making last-minute adjustments to her toilette. It was nearly time to leave for the registry office for the wedding of Philippa Gibson and Daniel Avebury.

'You scrub up pretty nicely yourself, Freddy,' she called over her shoulder, vanishing into the bathroom. As soon as she'd shut the door, Freddy marched into the bedroom to collar Jack.

'Dad! Don't you ever knock?'

'When are you giving it to Katie?'

'In my own good time.'

'I thought we agreed, before we left for the wedding.'

'There's plenty of time. Well, there would be, if you'd let me get dressed.' Having edged his father back over the threshold, Jack swung the door firmly shut in his face. Then he sat down on the bed in his shirt and boxers, grinding his teeth. This was a new and unattractive habit of his, probably leading to a severe case of lockjaw.

OK, so the little presentation he planned for Katie was Freddy's idea, but Jack resented Freddy having the idea in the first place. It underlined how well he and Katie were getting on. He wouldn't go so far as to say they whispered in corners, but they'd definitely formed an alliance. It should have pleased him – it was better than hostility – but he felt excluded. Why did Katie have to be so tolerant? And Freddy so full of ingratiating ideas all of a sudden?

Jack swung open the wardrobe door with his foot. He felt put upon and misunderstood, all because Katie didn't know the half of it.

Katie shot out of the bathroom and found Freddy ready and waiting, sitting carefully upright on the sofa. She had sent his faded brown suit to the dry-cleaner's, then pressed it herself to be on the safe side. The yellow silk hanky peeking from the top pocket was Jack's idea. 'Why don't you read the paper while you're waiting?' she exhorted, rushing past him into the bedroom – Freddy's bedroom, as things stood – the only room with a full-length mirror. She wanted to check out her strappy red dress, de-vampified with a cream jacket.

Getting dressed at all had been a feat of ingenuity, given that she and Jack now lived out of large carrier bags next to the sofa. They dressed in a synchronised frenzy each morning before Freddy surfaced and emerged without warning from the bedroom. He wasn't good at discreet entrances.

'How's it going?' she asked Jack, spying him behind the wardrobe door with one leg in his trousers.

'Don't ask. I thought you were him. He's already caught me in my boxers once.'

'I want your opinion. Jacket on or off?' She peeled off her jacket, did a slow twirl and put it back on.

'What's the difference? Apart from that spot on your back.'

'What!' She pulled the jacket off again and ran to the mirror. She craned her neck over her shoulder until her eyes bulged. There it was, a huge spot on her back, just to the left of one strap. God! She writhed and twisted, clawing at her carbuncled ugliness.

Jack watched her tenderly. 'It's only a tiny spot. Look, I'll kiss it all better.' He grabbed her and planted a solemn kiss on her blemished shoulder-blade.

Katie squirmed away and looked at him resentfully. He'd swept his dark blond hair into lightly gelled peaks and waves. Resplendent in his Armani suit and primrose-yellow shirt, he was the vision of loveliness she'd aspired to be.

'Don't humour me,' she grumbled.

'I wasn't. Mmm, your shoulder tastes of marsh-mallows.' He waggled his eyebrows ridiculously. 'Fancy a quickie?'

Katie smiled at him in the mirror. This was the first banter they'd had in ages. 'It would have to be a supersonic quickie. And I—'

Freddy burst through the bedroom door. They froze in attitudes of guilt, Jack's hand entwined slackly in her shoulder-strap.

'Phone for you, lovey,' Freddy told her.

'Thanks for knocking,' growled Jack. 'Again.'

She hadn't heard the phone. She hoped it was

Nikki. As she scampered out of the room, father and son looked at each other.

'What?' challenged Freddy at last, as Jack went on staring at him balefully.

'Don't "what" me,' muttered Jack. Realising the conversation wasn't about to get off the blocks, he developed an overwhelming interest in his tie-knot, and turned away.

In the living-room, Katie snatched up the receiver. 'Hello.'

'Katie, it's me. Dan.'

The blood froze in her veins. She cast a furtive look around her, checking that Jack and Freddy were still safely in the bedroom.

'Can you talk, Katie? I know I took a risk ringing you, but I was going to tell Jack I had to ask you something practical. That wasn't Jack who answered, was it? I couldn't leave things like they were,' he rushed on, before she could answer. 'Flick's gone out to terrorise the florist, who never sent round her bouquet.'

'Look, Dan—'

'I wasn't planning on ringing. But then she went out 'cos the florist's only down the road, and I was pacing around, and thought I'd better call you to see what's what.'

'Dan, you've managed to leave me on tenterhooks this long about what happened. Now you ring me to discuss it on your wedding day, for heaven's sake!' She waited, heart pounding in her ears.

'Katie, I can't tell Flick, I just can't. I thought about it, sure. But it would tear up your family and I'd lose her and I couldn't bear that.'

A bubble of relief popped deep in Katie's subconscious.

'This is dead hard for me, but have you told Jack? Are you going to tell him? I'm begging you not to.'

'I haven't told him . . . yet.' She gripped the phone. 'Like you, I've too much to lose, but I don't know if I can live with such a big lie, long-term. When Jack and I marry, I can't take my vows on a guilty conscience.'

'Not like me.' His tone was bleak rather than accusing. 'I've been thinking it over and what, um, happened – it meant nothing. '

'It was less than nothing,' she agreed quickly. 'To be honest, I don't remember a thing about it.' She paused hopefully. 'Can we be certain anything *did* happen? Something – you know – more than a snog and a grope?' She cringed, hardly able to believe she was having this conversation with Flick's fiancé on his wedding day. She glanced over her shoulder again. The murmuring voices of father and son were still reassuringly distant.

'I know that's clutching at straws,' she hazarded, as silence pulsed down the line.

'No way,' declared Dan in a burst of eagerness. 'And even if we did go further, we weren't in our right minds. If murderers can get off on temporary insanity 'cos they took drugs before the deed, I don't see why we can't be – what do you call it?'

'Absolved?' suggested Katie.

'That's the word. It wasn't premeditated or anything. I love Flick and you love Jack.'

'Yes, yes,' she nodded vehemently. She needed Dan to state the facts baldly, not couch them in philosophical musings. And part of her rejoiced that she could count on his discretion, ensuring she had nothing to fear from Flick. 'I find you attractive, Dan,' she risked telling him. 'I did from the start, but now I know it's because I see echoes of myself in you. It wasn't a physical or chemical thing. It's a metaphysical thing.'

'God, don't blind me with science on my wedding day. Let's agree we don't fancy each other. Not that you aren't gorgeous and everyth—'

'It's OK, I know what you mean.'

'And you promise you won't tell Jack?'

'I don't know about that. But I can promise that whatever I do or don't tell him won't rebound on you.'

'How you can guarantee that?' he asked doubtfully. 'It's like ripples in a pond. The more people who know, the more people will get to know.'

'Honestly, this thing can be . . . contained.'

'Would Jack dump you if he knew?'

Her stomach muscles knotted. 'I don't know.'

'Let me take an educated guess. He's a proud bloke and he doesn't see me as his equal. He'd think you did it to get back at Flick over Steve.'

'Maybe,' she mumbled. 'I think you should go now. You've tortured me enough.'

'Not deliberately. But you're right, I'd better go.' She heard a rustling at his end. 'My speech is crap. I'm not good with words, as you'll have realised from this phone call. I was going to move you to promise you'd take our secret to the grave.'

'Put it out of your mind, Dan. You've got to enjoy the day.'

'I'll try.'

They hung up with everything out in the open and nothing resolved. Suddenly weak-kneed, Katie sank onto the sofa. *Absolution.* Dan had spoken of it as a way of rationalising their guilt, wiping the slate clean by simply deciding to. But to her, the word resonated with its Catholic connotations.

If she took her secret to the confessional, it would be aired, shared and its secrecy still assured, but what about the plea-bargaining element? The price of a salved soul might be more than a string of Hail Marys – that was too easy. It might depend on telling Jack, giving him the choice he had a right to expect.

She was still brooding when the Gold menfolk came looking for her.

'Was that Nikki?' asked Jack cheerfully.

'Er, yes.' The minute the lie popped off her tongue, she met Freddy's quizzical gaze and remembered he'd answered the phone. Perhaps Dan had even given his name. She blushed.

Freddy's gaze shifted back to Jack and he plucked his son's elbow. 'Don't forget now.'

'Yes, all right, Dad. If you'd give me half a chance.'

'I was only saying,' grunted Freddy.

Katie was used to their peevish double-act by now. Jack was as irritated as ever by his father and babyed him with exasperated tolerance. But Katie had detected a subtle shift in Freddy. Now that she was his ally (and he had Seb Hatcher up his sleeve as a potential rescuer), he'd become less stubbornly meek. His shoulders had straightened a little, day by day.

Jack's had begun to sag a little more each day. Katie was almost afraid that Freddy, quite without meaning to, was leeching the confidence out of his son, sucking with invisible vampire teeth. She looked from one to another, wondering what they had to tell her.

'I've got something for you, Katie. Well, it was Dad's idea.' Jack gazed down at her with the Killer Smile. 'It belonged to Mum, and Dad thought you should have it as an early wedding present. For *our* wedding, I mean.' He drew a balding velvet box out of his jacket pocket and handed it to her. 'It's a brooch,' he explained, before she'd even raised the lid. 'Dad's been meaning to hand it over since we told him our news.'

Katie picked the brooch off its velvet pad. 'It's beautiful,' she gasped, and it was: a sea turtle in a mother-of-pearl shell, two tiny emeralds for eyes.

'Belonged to the wife's mother,' explained Freddy. 'Only worth a few bob, but looks the part. Janet always meant it to go to her daughter.' He looked at Katie with rheumy eyes. 'You're as good as her daughter now and, one of these days, marrying Jack will make it official.'

There was a stubborn endorsement of her in his tone that made Katie look away. Freddy might suspect she was lying about the identity of her recent caller, but he was laying his cards of loyalty on the table. A loyalty unlooked for, but apparently the dividend of standing by him in hard times.

She pinned the brooch to her jacket. 'Thanks, both of you.' She kissed both men on the cheeks. When she reached up to Jack on tiptoe to brush his cheek with her lips, he held onto her. 'Now you'll have a better reason to keep your jacket on than hiding a tiny spot.'

A pang of guilt struck her with almost physical

force. What a selfish cow she'd been, using Freddy's presence to delay telling Jack her secret!

But each day that passed made confession more difficult.

As family and guests assembled in the anonymous chambers of the registry office, Katie bagged a seat between Jack and Simon, who was bound to provide irreverent commentary.

The bride had gone for a rustic look. White slippers, white, high-waisted smock and a circlet of orange blossom crowning her loose sheet of chestnut hair. Her bouquet was white forsythia. Even from Katie's restricted side view, she was a shimmering vision of virginal minimalism.

'Tess of the d'Urbervilles meets the pre-Raphs,' hissed Simon to Jack. 'Anything that peasanty-looking must've cost a bomb. Shaggy looks like an estate agent in a housing slump.'

Katie examined the back of Dan's head, carefully groomed for the occasion. His well-cut suit didn't sit on him quite right. He looked as uncomfortable as the day he'd first come stumbling through the french windows at 23 Alderney Road. She shut her eyes and attempted telepathy. It's not too late, Dan. Run from your wife!

A guffaw ruptured the whisperings and shufflings and she glimpsed Phil, squeezed into a blue silk waist-coat, deep in conversation with Hoorah Henrys she didn't recognise. Flick's exes, possibly, or her retinue of male admirers from Stempson's. They didn't look like Dan's side. In fact – she did a quick reccy round the room – all the guests looked handpicked by Flick.

When the ceremony began, Dan stumbled over the words, awed by their meaning. Flick said her vows in a silver-bell voice, clear and unhesitating. More proof, to Katie's cynical way of thinking, that this marriage was a means to an end for her sister.

They were pronounced husband and wife.

Dan, moist-eyed, stooped clumsily to kiss his bride, knocking the orange blossom awry.

Katie sneaked a look at her mother, but Tess was not even close to mother-of-the-bride tears. She merely smiled with distant serenity, as if sensing Katie's curiosity. Seconds later, they were all spilling out into coolish May sunshine for the photos. There was no official photographer. The happy couple hovered on the registry office steps, Flick growing impatient for guests to take their snaps. 'Hurry up, Si,' she ordered her brother, the official chronicler for the Gibson albums, confetti from the previous wedding eddying round her white slippers.

Simon leapt around doing a David Bailey impression. 'Dan, look up. Flick, flash us a bit of leg with the old garter! Lovely-jubbly. Right, time for the family snapshot. Bride's first, I think. Oops, that means me. Jack!' he bellowed. 'Come and do the honours.'

Dan's family snapshot was a sad little tableau of himself, Flick and Phil Avebury. Katie wondered where Aunt Dorrie had got to. Had she even been invited? As she looked around for Jack, a cloud of evil-smelling smoke drifted over her. She turned to meet the reptilian gaze of Phil.

'Well, young Kitty, what do you make of proceedings so far? I reckon he should've worn the dress.

If I know Philippa, she's more used to wearing the trousers.'

'Excuse me.' Stiff-backed, Katie walked off. Out of the corner of her eye, she saw Phil waylay Tess, and hoped her mother would give him short shrift.

She found Jack in cahoots with Simon, as she'd expected. They were well on the way to becoming conspirators for the day, detached from the bridal brouhaha.

'Where's Freddy?'

'Don't worry, I haven't abandoned him, he's gone to the gents,' replied Jack. 'Are you coming with me or joining your mum in Phil's motor? He's giving her a lift.'

'Going with you, of course.'

'Nice one,' muttered Simon. 'With Mum off the scene, I can cram another of Flick's friends into my jalopy. Seen Trish, the one with the legs?'

'Too right I have,' chuckled Jack. 'With legs that long, she'll have to hang them out of your car window.'

'Or wrap them round me for safe keeping.' Smirking crudely, but still impish, Simon sped off, confident of compensating for his crap car with his personality.

Katie hooked her arm through Jack's. 'That went well,' she said cautiously.

'Taking notes for our own big day?' he teased.

She smiled. 'Call me bitchy, but I don't feel I've much to live up to.'

'I'd never call you bitchy where Flick's concerned. Just honestly judgmental. I'm happy to run the bar at the reception, you know. Let you mingle.'

'Er, you're all right.' She was looking forward to

playing barperson. It meant she wouldn't have to mingle with the Hoorah Henrys. 'I've been appointed by Mum, so can't be had up for dereliction of duty. Besides,' she added craftily, 'this will give you another chance to cosy up to Phil, if that's what you want. And there's Freddy to look after,' she finished, playing her trump card.

Shoe-horned into the narrow Balham house, twenty-five guests took on the proportions of fifty. Tess had locked away breakables and emptied the dresser of crockery, supplementing the furniture with garden and folding chairs from the garage. The table, laden with a buffet spread, stood against the french windows, which Tess had decided to keep shut.

The buffet queue shuffled forward, everyone admiring but resisting the crowning glory at the far end of the table. Instead of a wedding cake, Flick had commissioned a patisserie to make something called croque-en-bouche, a pyramid of cream-filled choux puffs, smothered in caramel icing and clouded in a golden web of spun sugar.

Katie wasn't keen. It looked like a leaning tower of cake from Miss Havisham's wedding banquet, the web a calling-card of busy spiders from the palace of King Midas. Still, it *was* very Flick, different and over-the-top. It even acted as a metaphor for Flick; it looked fragile but was probably impregnable, it lured with sweetness but repelled if you got too close.

Katie heaped her plate with a baked spud and a mixed salad, before scuttling off to the bar – an old sewing table covered in a paper tablecloth stamped with horseshoes. Bottles of champagne for the toasts were stacked underneath, ready to be opened by some obliging man (she had Jack and Simon on standby). She was soon busy. Jack rotated between her and Freddy, checking each was OK, breaking away now and then to pursue Phil.

Katie's static but prime position gave her a good view. She saw Simon chatting up Trish, and Phil stomping crossly towards the back door to join his fellow-smokers in the garden.

And she saw Flick and Dan. They never came near the bar. Flick alternated between sips of wine and swigs of Ballygowan from a full tumbler on the dresser, while Dan lapped his glass of wine like a nervous cat, eyes never leaving his new wife.

His face had a high, hectic colour. More than once, he ran a finger round the inside of his shirt collar. Flustered by constant offers of congratulations, he had difficulty balancing his wine glass and buffet plate while shaking hands.

Katie felt for him, but maybe he *could* be happy. Maybe love would find a way, if you believed sappy popcorn philosophy.

She wished she could get drunk to make the day go faster, but serving drinks slaked her own thirst for alcohol. As the room grew hotter, she drank water until her stomach felt bloated.

With the speeches about to start, Jack offered her a folding chair he'd swiped. 'Some woman went off half an hour ago to powder her chins and hasn't returned. I've been trying to cadge you a chair all afternoon. You should have had one from the off.'

'I don't mind standing. It's been fun here at the eye of the storm.'

He followed her gaze to a corner of the room, where Simon was gesticulating and Trish shrieking with laughter. 'Think your bro's well in there. Go on, my son.'

'How have you been getting on with Phil?'

'Hard to say. One minute he's asking me about work, the next he's telling me Tess is a fine figure of a woman for her age. I think he's harmless when pissed, so your mum should be able to handle him.'

Katie had stopped listening. She had spotted disturbing developments at the buffet table. It was Freddy. He was trawling through the remains of the food, wrapping portable items in bits of serviette, then pocketing them. A couple of samosas, a baked potato, split but unbuttered – oh God, now other people had begun to notice and titter. Did Freddy think he was invisible?

'Um, your drink need topping up, Jack?'

'Think I'll leave it till the toasts. Hope Simon keeps it clean as best man. You'd th–'

'Good bloody God,' guffawed a horribly familiar voice and the room turned as one to trace the source of Phil's astonishment. As Jack looked round, Katie cursed Phil from the bottom of her soul.

Phil pointed his wine glass at the hapless Freddy. 'Gather ye nuts while you may? Is that it, pal?'

Freddy blinked down at a mini pork pie hammocked on a serviette, halfway towards his trouser pocket. His jacket pockets were already full, pastry striations indenting the brown linen. He looked helplessly at Katie.

'Don't they feed you where you come from, you poor bloody blighter?' pressed Phil, as others turned tactfully away. 'Come on now, own up, who's been keeping their nearest and dearest on starvation rations? Or maybe the missus has got you on a bloody diet.' Phil patted his own ample stomach. 'Can't think why. Not a bloody pick on you.'

'That's Freddy,' piped up Flick's evil, silvery voice. 'Jack's father. He lives with Jack and Katie.'

'*Jack's* father?' Phil laughed with incredulity. 'No offence, mate, but you're not what I expected for Jack's old man. Is that the downstairs bog free at last? Gangway!'

As Freddy ploughed through the guests, cupping his crotch, Katie glanced at Jack. His face had a pinched, white look. Steady on, she urged him silently. It's no big deal. Don't let Phil make it one.

But, of course, she knew Jack would be taking this humiliation deadly seriously. Using her child–parent analogy, Freddy was like a no-hoper at a party full of competitively gifted children, fated to embarrass where others shone.

Tess came bustling to the rescue, champagne flutes on a tray. 'Right, we're almost ready to cut the cake thingummyjig. Freddy, you carry on there, I hate to see food going to waste. I wish a few more would follow your example, since Simon and I will never get through the leftovers.'

Katie silently applauded her mother's attempt at damage limitation. Freddy, in the process of unloading his food stash, shuffled nervously towards Jack. He got as far as touching Jack's sleeve, but Jack shook him off and strode away to claim a folding chair next to Simon. Katie met Freddy's gaze and threw her eyes skywards in a gesture of support. She strove womanfully to hide her own annoyance with him.

Dan made a hesitant, bumbling speech, short on content but burgeoning with unspoken feeling. 'Anyway, I'd just like to say, there's only ever been Flick – Pippa,' he wound up. 'And only ever will be,' he mumbled, gaze fiercely diverted from Katie. He plonked down on his chair, scarlet-faced, as Simon rose to play the part of best man.

Ever the showman, Simon played to the gallery with standard wedding-night jokes. Then he turned to the business of reading cards and telegrams. Katie's ears pricked up. She'd forgotten about absent well-wishers. Everyone, she noticed, was listening keenly, anticipating a missive from Don Gibson.

There was none. Hardly surprising, reflected Katie. Both Tess and Flick had clearly neglected to pass on the happy news. Keeping Don in the dark was a small but constant revenge for his lack of interest over the years.

Simon trawled through cards from half-forgotten relatives in Ireland and a warm salute from Aunt Dorrie, still not mobile after a cataract operation. He picked up the final card, winking at Trish before he read out: 'Flick and Dan, warmest wishes on your wedding day. From an old flame who still burns bright but knows when the better man has won. All my love, Stephen S.' Glancing quickly at Katie, he dropped the card and grabbed his glass of champagne. 'So now, I'd ask you all to raise your glasses . . . '

Katie had gone rigid in her seat. The last toast raised, she slipped off her chair amid the hubbub, and dived out of the back door. She headed for the dark, damp embrace of the garage, with its mildewing packing-crates and sad old rocking-horse. She wanted to be alone. She didn't even want Jack. Anyway, they'd probably have a supplementary row about Freddy, and she didn't want to think about Freddy.

She wanted to think about herself. And wallow in self-pity.

The day Steve came into the health-food shop, she'd been ready for a distraction. Steve was certainly that, a bloke Nikki would have described as too good-looking to be allowed out on his own.

He seemed refreshingly unaware of this fact. When he shuffled into the queue at the till and beamed at her, there wasn't a hint of self-aware come-hitherness in his magnetic blue eyes.

She was serving a harassed mother with a sobbing little boy entwined around her legs, being as gentle and patient as possible because the mother looked embarrassed and the child desolate.

Suddenly, a Welsh voice piped up, 'Wanna see me take my glass eye out?'

The little boy stopped crying abruptly. His mother and Katie looked up in alarmed fascination.

The good-looking man approached the counter. He now had the rapt attention of all three of them as he leant across the counter and curled his fist over his eye, miming a dexterous unscrewing movement. Next thing Katie knew, a round glass orb bounced onto the counter. She screamed at the same time as the mother and her delighted little boy, before all three realised it was just a marble shot through with a shard of blue.

Catching her breath, Katie had smiled at the man.

She always warmed to a man who took the trouble to divert unhappy children. Her grandad had been the same, hunting out treats or pointing out elephants and whales in cloud formations, to distract her from the sniffles after a row with Flick.

He'd bought a herbal spot cream, though his handsome face, with its quirky smile and dazzling eyes, was a spot-free zone.

'It's for my auntie,' he said in his sing-song accent, handing over the tube so she could scan the bar-code.

'Erm, this is for teenage acne,' Katie told him.

'Acne? No! I thought it was denture fixative, bach.'

He made 'denture fixative' sound like something lyrical by Dylan Thomas.

Katie had been mesmerised, a slave to her preconceptions about soulful Celts.

So when he put back the spot-cream, retrieved his marble and asked her if she was free for dinner that night, she said yes.

Over dinner, he told her right off that he was a penniless student who lived with his aunt. She hadn't minded. There was always a catch with a good-looking bloke. Too often, the catch was insurmountable; he was gay, bisexual, alcoholic, bisexual and alcoholic, terminally screwed-up by an ex and seeking revenge on all women, reused his tea-bags . . . So living with his aunt and 'not having a pot to piss in for the foreseeable future, bach' were minor-league drawbacks to Katie.

By their second date – at the cinema – she even plucked up the courage to ask him if buying the spot-cream had been a ruse to talk to her.

'Of course not,' he'd laughed in embarrassment,

leaving her with the happy impression that she'd rumbled him.

In his neediness, he'd been the opposite of Jack. Jack had a horror of appearing clingy, even when a display of sentimental attachment might be appropriate and reassuring. Like the time he insisted on going alone to the dentist for root canal treatment, shrugging off her concern as unnecessary smother-love, even though they both knew he was terrified.

On the plus side, Jack had never needed rescuing from rainy doorsteps or propping up with the loan of never-returned tenners.

It was equally hard to imagine Jack sallying forth without a coat and umbrella, his mobile phone, wallet, and a spare key to everything (even the windows) on a keyring. Jack could be autocratic, but he offered himself to be leant on. It was one of his many virtues as glamorous go-getter to her mild-mannered good egg. She'd always be better off with Jack.

But that didn't lessen the lacerating pain of Steve's card. Obviously, Flick was still in touch with him. How else would he know about her wedding? Perhaps she'd even invited him. Anything was possible.

She ran her finger along the chipped and peeling saddle pommel of the ancient rocking-horse. That bastard! The bitch!

She didn't see or hear Flick creep into the garage. 'I thought you'd be in here.' Katie whirled round.

Flick stood before her, Dan's jacket slung across her slim, gauzy shoulders. 'It had nothing to do with me, that card. I don't know how he found out about the wedding, but he has a way of popping up when you least expect it.'

'I don't give a fuck,' exploded Katie.

'You're giving a good impression of someone who very much gives a fuck. Surely not about Steve, though?'

Katie gritted her teeth.

'Look, I only came out to make it clear I had nothing to do with the card. Steve plays by his own rules. He's a shit-stirrer.'

'You were a match made in heaven, then.'

'Yeah, well, I can't be bothered pandering to your drama-queen hysterics,' shrugged Flick. She turned to go, then looked back at her sister, a smile hovering innocently on her rosebud lips. 'Maybe it would help to know a few home truths about the late-lamented Steve. Take that dress you wore to the restaurant, for example.'

Fear prickled Katie's spine. 'What about it?'

Flick continued to smile. Katie wanted to throttle her. As it was, she had to suppress the urge to yell, 'What about the dress, you scheming tart?'

'It's my dress,' said Flick. 'At least, it was. Steve must have nicked it on his way out of my flat for the last time, then used it to get in your good books or your knickers. I never knew the material was that stretchy.'

'Your dress?' Katie felt faint.

'I thought I'd lost it at the dry-cleaner's,' explained Flick calmly. 'Steve was crafty like that. He'd nick money from my purse – just the odd fiver – so if I did miss it, I'd think I'd spent it and forgotten where. I only rumbled him in retrospect. And he had a spiteful, petty streak. When I asked him to leave, he scrawled rude parting messages on the bathroom mirror with the toothpaste. I was sweating there for a while that he'd sewn dead fish into the curtain-rods or whatever it is revenge-seeking nutters do. Didn't take kindly to rejection, did Steve.'

The blood had drained from Katie's face. 'What are you saying?' she managed to croak.

'Isn't it obvious?' laughed Flick. 'I was seeing Steve before he ever met you! He even moved in with me for a while until I got sick of his sponging and kicked him back to Auntie. He tried to hang on by coming out with the usual stuff – that he loved me, couldn't live without me – all the predictable tosh.' She shook her sleek head thoughtfully. 'Odd, the way the male mind works. He was always asking, "Is your sister as good-looking as you?" And I'd play fair and say, "Go and see for yourself". Fancy him taking me up on it.'

Katie sat down on a packing-crate. 'But he was with me for over a year,' she whispered. 'If he didn't really want me, why didn't he leave me after a couple of weeks? Or engineer a meeting with you sooner, so he could taunt you with our relationship?'

'I admire that quality in you,' said Flick, putting her head on one side. 'The ability to think clearly in shock-mode. Who knows what shifty old Steve was up to? Maybe he was getting at both of us. You know, taking revenge on all the women of the house of Gibson, a curse on our first-born and all that jazz. It's a wonder he didn't try to get off with Mum.'

Katie flushed a dull red. 'You're enjoying telling me that the love of my life was no more than one of your hand-me-downs!' She clamped her lips angrily shut.

Oh fuck, now she'd gone and let Flick know what Steve had meant to her.

And all along, it had meant nothing. She owed his presence in her life – in the shop that afternoon – to Flick. He'd hooked up with her as a bizarre way of having Flick by proxy. Her confidence, her sense of being loved for herself – they had all been built on sand. And the moment it suited her to do so, Flick had plucked him back, toyed with him, and thrown him out of her pram again.

Katie stared at her sister. 'Why did you go off with him a second time? Just to spite me?'

'My, my, you do fancy yourself,' snorted Flick with a little toss of the head. 'I'd simply forgotten how toe-curlingly gorgeous the bastard was. He swans into Mum's for Sunday lunch like butter wouldn't melt, plays footsie with me under the table—'

'What!'

'I'm only human.' Flick studied her nails, looking slightly miffed. 'Maybe I should have sent him away with a flea in his ear. But let's face it, he was mine first. He was only yours on loan.'

'On loan?' echoed Katie.

'And before you ask, the second time was a short-lived disaster, because I'd forgotten all his bad points; the sponging, the pathetic excuses for not having his act together . . . At least this time, he went quietly. That card is the first I've heard from him since.' She gave Katie a mischievous smile. 'I'd kind of hoped you'd sorted him out on the pathetic sponger front, turned him into a model citizen.'

'Suppose it was the least I could've done,' hissed Katie. 'You're evil incarnate. I hate you!'

It was simple and direct, but childish. Tears spilling from her eyes, she knew she sounded like a foot-stamping child railing against a tolerant parent.

Flick actually laughed. 'The feeling's always been mutual, sweetie. You get what you deserve in this life, and you deserve to be kicked in the crotch because you set yourself up for it. God, I despised you when we were kids. You were as bouncy and eager-to-please as a bloody Labrador, lapping up all that tosh that virtue is its own reward and love makes the world go round. I was determined I'd never end up like you. As for Steve, I did you a massive favour. If it wasn't for me, you'd still be in that flat over the shop, washing his smalls and typing up his thesis. Instead, you went to university and met Jack.'

Katie looked up at her. 'So now you're Mother Teresa?'

'Actually, looking back, I think you deserved Steve. You're the sort who loves to martyr herself for a man. Here you are now, welcoming Jack's unhygienic father with open arms.'

'God, you're a fucking bitch.'

'From your perspective. You're just jealous of any woman who's able to cut through the crap and take what she wants.'

'Like Dan's trust fund?'

Flick's eyes glittered. 'You bad-mouth me to him and I'll see Jack suffers for it. Phil only has to make one phone call and he'd lose his job and never get another.'

Katie sprang up, her hands twitching beyond endurance.

She slapped her sister hard across the face. It felt

good. Satisfying. Years of pent-up rage flowed through her hand, followed by the pleasure of seeing Flick stumble backwards, gasping, clutching her burning cheek. But it wasn't enough. Murder wouldn't have been enough. 'Get out!' she spat. 'Go!'

Flick rubbed her cheek. 'Not a smart move. Last time we were alone together, I came a cropper on a flight of stairs. Now I emerge from my mercy-trip to the garage with a shiner. This time, it'll be official. You're a dangerous basket-case.'

'Go!' screamed Katie.

Flick turned surprisingly quickly, as if even she sensed that Katie had gone over the edge. She nearly bumped into the lawnmower as she turned – colliding with Jack as he hurried into the garage.

'Katie, I've been looking everyw— What's going on?' He peered at Flick, blocking her exit from the garage. 'You been having a go at Katie?'

'Oh, please.' Flick tried to edge past him.

He grabbed her by the wrist. 'You have, haven't you? What have you said now?'

Katie felt moved to intervene with the classic, 'Leave it, Jack, she's not worth it.'

But he wouldn't. 'The billet-doux from Sheridan was a nice touch. Write it yourself, did you?'

Flick twisted angrily out of his grasp. 'Calm down, Mr Knight on a White Charger. I had nothing to do with it.'

'Everyone knows you're a liar!' he exploded suddenly. 'What about the stairs incident at our place, you evil, twisted bag of bones?' He grabbed Flick again and shook her like a rag doll.

'Leave it, Jack!' begged Katie, alarmed by his raised

208

voice and white fury. She'd never seen him out of control before. It was much scarier than his angry brooding or even her own recent outburst.

'I will *not* leave it!' thundered Jack. 'This evil harpy spreads poison wherever she goes. It's a shame you didn't break your neck on the stairs that day, and do the world a favour. Can't see anyone missing you, and Danny boy would've been spared the miserable life that's coming to him.'

As Flick finally darted past him and out of the garage, Katie seized his arm. 'Thanks for the thought, but the fact is, you're angry with Freddy and taking it out on her.'

Jack sank down onto a packing-crate and put his head in his hands. 'Christ, he's made a right laughing-stock out of me.'

'Only if you let the likes of Phil put that spin on it.' Katie sat down next to him. She'd always dreamt of Jack riding to her defence against Flick, preferably before a large audience, but it all seemed irrelevant in the light of what Flick had just claimed.

Steve had never been hers to pine for. She'd shed buckets of tears over a true-love who had never existed.

Drained by her confrontation with Flick, she tried to focus on the bitch's threat to hurt Jack, using Phil as her conduit. That must never be allowed to happen. She really would commit murder before she let Flick screw up any more of her life. She felt solidarity with anyone doing life for a crime of passion. If their victims were anything like Flick, she reckoned they deserved a full pardon and a civic citation.

'I'm knackered,' she said in a small voice, leaning

her head on Jack's unyielding shoulder. 'Any chance we can go home in the near future?'

Back indoors, everything looked disconcertingly normal. The disgraced Freddy was chasing a choux puff round his plate. Flick, her face its usual pale oval, was showing off her engagement ring to Trish. Tess was deep in conversation with Dan. It was as if the altercation in the garage had never taken place.

'Katie!' Tess beckoned her over. 'You missed the cake-cutting, but I saved you a bit.'

'Don't want it,' said Katie rudely. She longed to force her mother to confront a few home truths. 'I lost my appetite around the time Steve Sheridan got a look-in.'

Dan blinked up from his seat. In her new, hard, cold mindset, Katie had never thought him more useless and wet-looking.

Tess said smoothly, 'It's much moister than the traditional fruit wedding cake. Wouldn't you say, Dan?'

Katie didn't wait to hear Dan's recommendation. 'Jack and I are thinking of going in a minute, Mum. Jack's got a migraine. That's if you can spare me.' She challenged her mother with a cold eye.

'Of course, dear.' Tess craned her neck towards the bar. 'It's winding down now and most people seem to be helping themselves. Don't worry about the clearing-up. Simon can pull his weight for once.'

'Thanks, Mum.' Katie knew that acts of kindness were her mother's substitute for diplomatic intervention. It was the best she could hope for.

'I'll just go and have a word with Freddy before he

leaves,' added Tess, peering round Katie. 'Don't want him feeling embarrassed about earlier.'

Katie tried to move away with her mother, but Dan clutched her arm. 'Katie, that bloody card. I'm sorry. It must have really upset you.'

'Not really. Excuse me.'

'Flick's promised it wasn't her doing.'

'Whew, that's a relief. See you, Dan.' Unable to be civil to the man who'd sworn to love, honour and protect her bitch of a sister, she gently removed his hand and walked away.

Jack drove home in silence. Katie knew this was only the calm before the storm. Jack hung over the steering-wheel, still pinched and pale, while Freddy fidgeted in the back seat. Katie suspected he longed – just like her – to be somewhere else.

Chapter Nine

Katie flung herself into the flat and onto the sofa. 'Right, let's get this over with. Jack, accuse Freddy of showing you up in public. Freddy, accuse Jack of over-reacting and being a social-climbing snob. Then we can all go to bed and get some shut-eye.'

Wrongfooted, both men stared down at her. Katie dared to hope the sting had been drawn from Jack's tail, until Freddy went and said, 'I could make us all cocoa.'

'Cocoa!' snarled Jack. 'Slightly more original than "a nice cup of tea".'

'I know I owe you an explanation,' said Freddy, clasping liver-spotted hands together. 'I acted shameful, brought the pair of you into disrepute back there. I didn't know I was doing it, that's the truth, until that fat little feller yelled at me.' He coughed discreetly. 'Whenever Suzette had a do, I'd clear up the afters. Not that I wasn't invited, but I preferred to be well away from women's chatter. Anyway—'

Jack held up a Caesar-like hand. 'I can see where you're going with this. Your eyes were bigger than your stomach today, because Suzette kept you on a diet of Spam and Fray Bentos sarnies, didn't she?'

Freddy looked pained. 'Suzette was wasteful, but she didn't like having it pointed out, so I'd spirit the grub away instead.' He looked appealingly at Katie.

She nodded wearily. 'I understand, Freddy.'

Jack turned and walked into the bedroom, slamming the door with such force that a candlestick fell off the mantelpiece. 'I'll see about that cocoa,' murmured Freddy, and shot into the kitchen.

Katie braved the bedroom. Jack, lying face down on the bed, sat up slowly, as scowly as Oliver Reed and as tousled as Heathcliff. Katie felt a frisson of dark sexual pleasure. This uncaged, menacing Jack was a worrying departure, but offered an exciting glimpse into his vulnerability. The remaining two-thirds of his iceberg were rising gradually to the surface, nudged above the waterline by Freddy's bumbling propensity to infuriate him.

'Think Shaggy will challenge me to pistols at dawn for insulting Flick?' he mumbled. 'Wouldn't do myself any favours with Phil either, if he knew.'

'Um . . .' Katie was seriously worried herself on that score. Oh God, why did they both have a go at Flick on the same day?

'Stuff the lot of them,' said Jack savagely. 'Phil's enjoying dangling me on a string. As for Flick, what a piece of work. I wish I'd stuck up for you more over the Stairs Incident when it happened.'

Katie waited for a thrill of self-justification that never came. 'I doubt Flick will tell Dan or Phil what you said,' she said, trying to reassure herself, too. 'It's not something she wants dragged up again, seeing as she doesn't come out of it well.' She sat down beside him and took his hand, hoping to draw comfort as much as give it.

Like a compliant child, he laid his head on her shoulder. 'I'm sorry for behaving like a tosser, Katie. But she followed you into the garage to wind you up about Sheridan's card, didn't she?'

'She came to deny all knowledge.' As far as Jack and everyone else was concerned, Steve Sheridan had once exclusively been hers. She would only humiliate herself by revealing Flick's claim. Flick had won again. 'Freddy's making cocoa,' she said bleakly, stroking Jack's dishevelled hair. 'Go easy on him, Jack. He's more fragile than Flick, likelier to break than bend.'

Jack sat up suddenly, almost chinning her, his face a thundercloud. 'You would stick up for him. You're just like him.'

Katie blanched. 'Much as I like Freddy, I take it that's not a compliment?'

'You think I don't love him? I do in my own way, useless as it is. But loving a parent should be the most natural thing in the world.'

'I don't know about that. If you don't like them, it's the hardest thing in the world.'

'I do like him. Sort of . . . Oh fuck. Mostly, I've felt sorry for Dad because I think he's weak and needy, that he'd be lost without me. It's hard to resist being needed. I started off thinking *you* were needy and I had to take you under my wing. That's how I used to see myself: Jack Gold, defender of insecure women and ageing fathers.' His dark face twisted into a self-mocking smile. 'Taken me ages to suss you're the strong one. You put up with my moods and now you're putting up with Dad. Not even finding it an effort, either. You're an effortlessly nice person. You don't judge him or moan about him or reduce him to a nervous wreck just by walking into a room and looking at him.'

Katie fiddled irritably with a duvet-edge. 'You make me sound about as three-dimensional as a TV evangelist. I can be as horrible as the next person. I slapped Flick's face in the garage.'

'You didn't!'

'I bloody well did. For all I know, she's down the cop-shop this minute filing a charge for GBH.'

'Oh Christ, K, you had to pick her wedding day.' Jack looked at her with the sort of sardonic admiration he'd once reserved for Flick.

'So that puts your row with her in perspective,' said Katie bravely. 'Don't worry about it. As for Freddy, it's easy for me to be nice to him because there's no history between us.'

'That's true,' said Jack gloomily. 'You've no idea what he put me and Mum through. Mostly Mum. One Christmas, when I was about six, we literally had nothing to eat. The Sally Army must've got wind of our plight, because they came round with a parcel of Christmas cheer – pudding, a turkey, the lot. Mum was mortified. "You have the wrong address," she sniffed, ramrod-straight, and sent them packing. I watched from the window, seeing them take away any chance of a half-decent Christmas, and cursed Mum. But deep down I knew it was *his* fault, snoring his head off in the corner after his latest booze and gambling session.'

'Oh, Jack. That breaks my heart.' Katie rested her head on his shoulder.

'How much do you think your mum's house is worth?'

'I don't know.'

'Guess,' he barked. 'Prime location in London, original features, good local amenities.'

'Well, easily over a hundred grand, I suppose.'

'More like two hundred in the current climate. Do you know what that old bastard did with our house? He sold it from under me, then *gambled* away the money. The one bit of collateral he had, the one bit of security to see him through old age, a house bought and paid for in London. Most parents think of leaving something to pass on to their kid. Not him, God rot the old bugger!'

'Jack, I'm sorry.'

'So's he. Always after the event. He's self-destructive, takes masochistic pleasure in it. Once he got rid of the house, I wasn't in a position to help him until I'd left uni and got a job. By then, he'd shacked up with Suzette. I knew it wasn't a match made in heaven, but I looked at him and thought, "You made your bed, sunshine. Now you ruddy well lie on it, Spam sarnies and all." Think I'm awful, do you?'

'No, Jack, I understand.'

'I don't want you to understand!' he shouted, crashing his fist into his palm. 'What the hell would you know about having a gambler for a father? A serious, inveterate gambler who'd never get help or acknowledge he had a problem, who was just biding his time to put himself out on the street and make himself *my* problem?'

'Ssh. I do know. Don't get upset.'

He shouldered her away and stared at her. 'What do you know?'

'Well . . .' She bit her lip, knowing she had to come clean. She'd already kept one secret too many from Jack. 'I know about him selling the house to go to Australia, then losing the money. He told me.'

'He had no right to tell you!'

'Why? What have the sins of the father got to do with the son?'

'A lot, as far as other people are concerned.'

'I'm not other people.'

'Cocoa's up,' declared a voice, and Freddy launched himself into the room, clutching a tremulous tray of mugs. From his mottled complexion and downward gaze, Katie reckoned he'd been eavesdropping behind the door.

Jack leapt up. 'You told her stuff behind my back.'

'Well, you were never going to tell her,' quavered Freddy. 'Girl had a right to know what you had to put up with, and it was my story to tell. So while we're on my life story, you might as well have the latest instalment.' Freddy took a deep breath. 'I wrote a while back to a mate of mine, owns a bar in Greece. Reply came the other day. He's invited me out for an indefinite stay, so I'll be out of your hair and you'll have no need to worry what I'm up to. Seb's as sensible as a registered baby-sitter.'

Jack gaped at him. 'Not Seb Hatcher?'

'The same.' Freddy handed Katie a mug of cocoa, attempting a wink to signal that the worst had passed.

Jack clutched his tousled hair. 'That raving poof from your army days?'

'Delicately featured, we called it,' coughed Freddy. 'Seb's what you might call hermaphrodite,' he informed a startled Katie.

'Dad, you've lost the last bit of the plot!' yelled Jack. 'Hermaphrodite? You'll be telling me next he's a eunuch! I met him twice when I was a kid and he used to look at you like a starving dog looks at a chop. You're not the fine figure of a man you were back then, admittedly, but he must be on his last legs, too, and grateful for what he can get.'

'Thanks, son.'

'If he's invited you out to some Greek island where men go around in leather hotpants after sundown, it's for one reason and one reason only.'

'Jack, get a grip,' sighed Katie, weary of policing his emotions with twittering imperatives. 'Freddy, you never told me Seb bats for the other side.'

'So he confided in you about *that* as well?' hollered Jack. 'A very cosy set-up you two have got going. Maybe I should move out and leave the pair of you to it.'

'What's his sexuality got to do with it?' Freddy asked her, coming over all PC.

'Nothing at all,' she spluttered. 'I suppose.'

'If anyone's interested,' growled Jack, 'I'm going to bed.'

He left Katie nursing a mug of cocoa, a king-sized headache and a whole lot of confusion.

Dan knocked on the bedroom door. 'Come in,' called Flick.

He opened the door. She was staring at herself in the dressing-table mirror, touching one side of her face. She'd changed out of her wedding dress into her going-away outfit. 'Ready for the off?' he asked, dizzy with wine and the responsibility of being Mr Flick Gibson.

'Ready as I'll ever be,' she said briskly, zipping up a small make-up bag. He hovered, reluctant to go downstairs and face the farewell throng, noticing she'd gone a bit heavy with the foundation. 'So this is the room you used to share with Katie?'

'Yep. Mum's papered over the bloodstains. Katie wouldn't even fucking believe me about that card from Steve. She prefers clinging to her handy little myth that I'm evil incarnate.'

'Oh Flick, I'm sorry.' He loped over and wrapped her in his arms. She didn't repel him, but she didn't encourage him either, staying obediently still.

'If I could find that Sheridan bloke, I'd wring his neck,' he said into her hair.

'On my account, or Katie's?'

'Both.'

She began gathering up her bits and pieces. 'She's actually got it into her head that I knew Steve first and he came sniffing after her on the rebound.'

'What a bizarre notion.'

'I know. I warned you what she's like. Rational thinking's not her forte.'

'She'd be one hell of a person if she could get past all that neurosis.'

'In other words, if she had half a brain, she'd be dangerous. Let's go, sweetheart. We want to reach Marsham before midnight.'

*

Several hours later, Dan switched off the engine of the hire-car. Flick was asleep beside him. Somewhere out there in the dark, beyond sick apple trees and cankered rose bushes, stood Cloverley, awaiting the kiss of care and money to resurrect its sleeping glories. He already had plans for the patch of boggy water that had once been a pond, well before Mrs Gibson's father's time. He could redefine its marshy edges by planting the Siberian flag iris, one of his favourites with its rich shades of blue and purple. And he was sure he'd spotted a barely-alive holly bush round the back of the house on a previous visit. Maybe a Golden Queen, but he'd have to take a closer look.

Flick stirred. Her going-away suit was thin red silk and she shivered. Dan grabbed her pashmina shawl from the back seat and tucked it tenderly round her. 'Keep warm, Mrs Avebury. You're very precious to me.'

Flick ran a thin, manicured hand over his leg, setting off pleasurable alarms. 'Dan, ever since we left my mum's, you've been talking in besotted-husband mode.'

His confidence wavered. 'That too soppy for you?'

'No. I like it, Mr Avebury.' She arched a delicately-sculpted brow at him, then noticed the darkness outside. 'What are we doing at Cloverley? The cottage back in Marsham is all ready and waiting. Sheets turned back and fire stoked, local biddies waiting to pounce on a bloodstained sheet in the morning and wave it to a cheering crowd.'

Dan was stumped and a little repelled by the obscure mention of bloodstained sheets. He clung on to his role as MC of events, the keeper of a secret that gave him delicious power over Flick. 'All will be revealed, Mrs A. Out you get.'

He sprang out of the car, landed mushily on terra non-firma and bounded round to open the door on her side. Flick launched a dainty-heeled shoe onto squelching dark countryside. Standing on uneven ground, she clutched her butter-yellow pashmina around her shoulders and pouted. 'Dan, I'm not dressed for— Argh! What are you doing?'

Impatient to reveal his secret, Dan swooped her up and carried her, light as a twig, towards the house.

'Dan, you'll trip.'

'I won't. I've come this way a fair bit.'

She peered at him. 'When? We've only been down here twice before.'

'I might've been here on my own as well. Organising a few things.'

'What things?'

He didn't reply. He knew he'd give the game away if he responded to her curiosity too soon. As he ducked under a Moroccan broom by the remains of the gate-post, a shriek greeted them from the rooftops. Flick clung to him. 'What the hell was that?'

'Owl, I think. I'll have to read up on the fauna as well as the flora.'

'Do you think there's a torch back in the glove compartment?'

'Nearly there.' Dan was enjoying this rare moment of Flick-dependency, her thin body wedged against his, greedy for protection. She was far too skinny, though he'd never dream of saying so. She'd had a fridge magnet back in Hampstead that declared,

'Never too rich, never too thin'. He didn't agree. His father was living proof of fat wealth. Once Cloverley was habitable, he'd feed her up with chutneys and stews and good old country food. She needed looking after.

He'd left the front door on the latch. All he had to do was push it open with one foot, and carry Flick over the threshold.

Once inside, he set her down gently, brushing flaky plasterwork off his shoulders. The house shed it constantly, like dandruff. He stood in the centre of the cold, musty hallway, patterned dimly with black-and-white tiles, and flung out his arms. 'Welcome to the honeymoon, phase one.'

Flick frowned. 'You're not suggesting we stay here?'

'Not overnight,' he smiled. 'I realise our toothbrushes are back in the car, and there's nowhere to have a wee. This way.' He led her down the dark, cobwebby hallway and pushed her gently through another doorway. 'Ta-da!'

He savoured the moment, watching her revolve slowly to take it in.

The largest downstairs room, complete with Dutch-tiled fireplace, glowed in the light of several candles stuck into bottle-necks and on waxy saucers.

A huge, tasselled rug, swagged across the cracked window, shut in the light and spun cosiness out of the shadows. The fireplace itself gleamed with soot-free cleanliness and a real applewood fire, extra logs piled nearby in a brass scuttle on the fender.

In the centre of the room stood the only furniture: a card table covered wonkily with a flowered paper tablecloth and a pair of spindly cane chairs facing each other intimately across two of everything – candles, crystal goblets, rose-embossed plates, and cutlery. Plus a bottle of recently uncorked wine.

Flick approached in wonder. She touched a plate. 'How did you . . . ?'

'Aunt Dorrie gave me the cutlery and plates,' he revealed shyly. 'And Dad felt generous enough to offload the goblets.' He looked at her anxiously. 'I wanted to make it dead special, our first night. I know you want to knock Cloverley into shape before we go on a proper honeymoon, but I thought, why can't we start our proper honeymoon here? Enjoy a taste of the good life to come.'

With her back to him, Flick walked towards the mantelpiece, her heels wobbling on the brick floor. At last, she turned and looked at him. For a second, he was disconcerted by the candlelight gleaming back from her eyes, giving her a glassy, green, basilisk stare.

Then he realised the light was picking up tears. He blinked rapidly, in danger of being borne away on a tide of emotion. Even today, even as they exchanged vows, she hadn't been moved to tears. This moment was the culmination of his carefully laid plans. With Flick's reaction, he felt he'd buried for ever his moment of madness with Katie.

She shook her hair over her face. 'This is the loveliest thing anyone's ever done for me,' she said, almost inaudibly. 'And I don't deserve it. If you only knew . . .'

She crumpled so suddenly that Dan was taken aback. For a split second, he didn't know what to do. At last, he forced his legs to cross over to the mantelpiece, where she stood, quietly weeping, and gathered her into his arms. 'Flick, don't cry, please.'

Something in her desolate sobs told him these weren't tears of happiness. He folded her into his large frame, running his blunt fingers through her hair. She wore her hair like a veil, shielding her tears.

At last, she fell quiet and pulled away from his chest. When she looked up at him, her face was only slightly damp and he saw a hanky vanish by sleight of hand up her sleeve. She'd been mopping up the worst of the ravages under her hair, repairing her image as best she could, even in front of her husband.

'What is it?' he asked tenderly. 'You can tell me anything. That's what I'm here for.'

She smiled wanly. 'I was just overcome by the lovely surprise. I'm more knackered than I thought.'

He touched her cheek silently, articulating his doubt. Then he led her back to the table. 'You plant your sweet tush on one of these chairs. I'll run back to the car and go get us a takeaway. Sorry, that's the best meal I can lay on.'

'That'll be fine.' She sat down and watched him pour wine into the goblet. 'How did you arrange this?'

'I got that old dear who cleaned the cottage to pop down here for an extra tenner and lay the fire and table. She did a great job.'

'I'll have to watch you. You're always claiming to lack imagination.' She narrowed her eyes in mock suspicion and peered at him through the distorted side of her goblet. His happiness returned, displacing the doubt that had surfaced over her strange, tearful outburst.

The only takeaway food he could find in Marsham was fish and chips, big portions leaking through greasy paper. But back at the house, Flick devoured hers eagerly, licking grease off her fingers as she told him about her childhood visits to Cloverley.

He hung on every word, greedy for her unsolicited memories.

It seemed Tess had sought refuge in the house the summer Don left, spending hours in conference with her father while Flick and Katie ran amok (separately), sliding down banisters, ransacking cupboards, collecting wormy apples and jars of tadpoles, then forgetting about them until the day they left.

'I loved it because I had my own room here,' Flick confided, swinging her foot. 'Katie said her room gave her the creeps at night. This from the girl who moaned non-stop about sharing a room with me back home. At least ghosts don't take up wardrobe space. Once, I found jackdaw eggs in the chimney-flue in my room.' Her face closed up for a second. 'The woman who did the cleaning said they were nasty, dirty things, and carted them off in her dustpan. They were lovely eggs, light blue and speckled.'

'Country folk are more ruthless than us sentimental townies,' observed Dan, lapping up every shared confidence. 'Go on. What else did you do here?'

'One day I went with Mum and Grandad and picked out new wallpaper for the kitchen, a yellow one dotted with tiny blue kingfishers. I papered my dolls' house with the remnants. It's still hanging in the kitchen, though the kingfishers have disappeared under grease from Grandad's fry-ups. Oh, there was a dead rat under the kitchen range once. Simon toddled in one day, noticed it and pulled it out by its tail. Mum poked it with a stick and it twitched – just an after-death spasm, but Katie and I screamed like banshees. Simon joined in out of solidarity.' She smiled and flicked her hair absently. 'Not what you'd call a treasure-trove of childhood memories, but better than nothing.'

'Better than mine.'

'Poor Dan.' She reached across the table and brushed his hand. Hers was icy-cold. He caught it and chafed it between his own. 'You're freezing, Flick. Come and warm up by the fire before it dies out.'

'You can't do enough for me, can you?' She smiled her strange, wan smile again.

'I wanted . . .' he paused, struggling for the right words. 'I always wanted to look after you, ever since I first saw you—'

'Poking divots in your lawn with my impractical shoes.'

'—but I thought that might be sexist. And when I met you properly, I knew you were way stronger than me, anyway. You had Dad wrapped round your little finger five seconds after meeting him.'

She looked away. Her green eyes had that watery film again. He pressed her hand and murmured, 'All this mush is upsetting you.'

'It's not that.' She slid her hand away, pushed back her chair and reclaimed the mantelpiece, mumbling something as she fiddled with a crack in a worn Dutch tile.

'What did you say?' he asked, a shade desperately. 'Flick, please tell me what's wrong.'

A sudden thought turned his blood to ice, and he

cursed himself for not thinking of it sooner. He could only pray to God that her strange mood and earlier tears were in no way connected to her argument in the garage with Katie. Had Katie lost her rag over the Steve Sheridan card, and told Flick about *that night*, after all? Not on his wedding day, surely to God.

She turned towards him, stiff-backed and abrupt. 'I said, I can't bear it, you bending over backwards to please me, when the fact is . . .' She took a deep breath. 'I'm up to my tonsils in debt and I need your lolly to bail me out.'

He stared at her, feeling punch-drunk. This was the last explanation he'd been expecting.

She gave a long, shaky sigh and refused to meet his shocked eye. 'So now, still besotted with your new wife after that little confession, Mr Avebury?'

Chapter Ten

The flat was empty without Freddy. Even though Katie was glad to have the bedroom back, she missed him. She and Jack had got used to tiptoeing and whispering, and now they seemed unable to break the habit.

Katie, however, kept her counsel as much as possible on the whole Freddy subject. Two weeks after Flick's wedding, Freddy and Jack, after a long stand-off of mutually stilted politeness, had parted on unhappy terms. Freddy had even sneaked off alone to the airport.

That had been a fortnight ago. His creeping departure had devastated Katie, who felt very hurt that he'd left them as he'd left Suzette, like a thief in the night with a battered suitcase. He'd simply vanished one morning before sun-up, tiptoeing past the sofa to a taxi he must have had waiting.

It was typical of him, professing to want to be no trouble at all while behaving selfishly. Until Jack found the note under the fruit-bowl confirming

Greece as his intended destination (no specific address given), they had entertained all sorts of nightmare scenarios. Katie had envisaged frogmen searching the Thames. Jack had kept his fears to himself, crushing them into the note as he lobbed it towards the bin. But Katie had rushed to rescue it. The note was their last point of contact with Freddy.

Thanks for everything, said the note. *I got my ticket with a bit of savings I had. I don't want any fuss so I'm going this way. You two have been good to me. I'll be in touch as soon as I'm settled in with Seb. He has a spare room.*

This sparse epistle did little to allay their fears. Jack was back on champion brooding form, his mood matching the sultry July weather.

Katie had begun to fear seriously for their marital prospects. Weddings (and diamond engagement rings) were the last thing on Jack's mind – and on hers, if she was brutally honest. With the newlyweds safely stashed away in deepest Kent, she'd been able to put the sordid Dan episode on the mental back-burner, but in the interim, Steve Sheridan had got a stranglehold on those parts of her psyche labelled doubt, anguish and self-esteem.

She and Jack weren't talking to each other much, post-Freddy. They sighed, pushed food around their plates and communicated by the telepathy of the long-acquainted. This particular Saturday morning was proving to be atypical, with Jack waxing lyrical on the topic of his errant father. 'What'll happen when old Seb realises Dad isn't going to play ball?' he fretted over the remains of an early lunch. 'I doubt Dad's had the foresight to buy a return ticket, meaning I'll have to ride to the rescue and bring him back here. Then we're back to square one.'

They'd tried international directory enquiries, but there was no listing on Halkidiki for a Sebastian Hatcher.

'Look,' reasoned Katie, 'Freddy knows Seb better than we do. He's one of the old school, so I very much doubt he's a promiscuous homosexual. When Freddy called him hermaphrodite, he might have meant Seb's one of those men with no apparent sex drive who are close to their mum and buy a lot of Bette Midler records. Asexual rather than gay.'

'I doubt Dad knows what he means. What's going to happen when Seb comes on to him? Dad will either hit him or have a stroke.'

Katie stood up and stacked the plates. 'Have you ever thought it might work out? That Seb might be a lonely old man who welcomes Freddy's company, no strings attached? Freddy's always wanted to see the world and a Greek summer will do wonders for that chesty cough.'

'Or kill him with sunstroke.'

'Think positive. To give me a break, if nothing else.' She stomped into the kitchen, followed by Jack, pulling sheepishly at his bottom lip. 'I don't blame *you* for Dad just taking off like that.'

'Could've fooled me.'

'It's him. He used the old divide and rule principle, luring you into his camp by convincing you I had to be kept in the dark. For my own protection, of course. Poor old Jack can't bear too much reality, that sort of thing.'

She sighed. 'It wasn't like that. He has his pride and

wanted to get the nod from Seb before he told you his plans. Look how he lost track of Alfie Barker when he emigrated to Oz.'

Jack snorted. 'If there ever was an Alfie Barker. That whole Australia whim after Mum died is typical of Dad. If he was so keen on Oz in the first place, why didn't he go years earlier as a young man, make something of his life?'

Katie bit her lip. She couldn't break her promise to Freddy to keep quiet about Janet's intervention on that front, so she'd said nothing about Alfie's job offer all those years before, or Freddy's readiness to follow it up. She was as keen as Freddy to protect Jack's memory of his mother. It was important to Jack, and to Freddy, she realised, that Jack cherish at least one parent with unambiguous love, even if it did cast Janet in the role of heroic failure for choosing Freddy in the first place.

She dropped the dishes in the sink and ran the hot tap.

'I'm worried sick about the old goat,' said Jack quietly.

'I know.' She turned and brushed his hair back from his forehead, trying to straighten his perpetual dark frown. 'But I reckon Freddy wants to prove he can go it alone. I know he's being thoughtless, but in his own mind he thinks he's doing you a favour, shouldering his burden and heading off. He'll get in touch when he's settled, not because he wants something off us.'

'He doesn't think like that. He's gone off in a huff, putting me in the wrong for all those things he heard eavesdropping.'

She sighed. It was a circular conversation at the best of times.

'I'm sorry,' he said again, annoying her with his out-of-character humility. Everything about him annoyed her these days. 'I know I've been hard to live with. It's just if Dad c—'

'Look!' She turned from the sink. 'Can you stop banging on about Freddy for one second? Is there the slightest chance of my problems getting a look-in?'

'What problems?' His gaze fell to her waistline. 'You're not—?'

'It's Steve Sheridan!' She bit her lip and rushed on. 'Flick followed me into the garage on the wedding day to tell me they were an item before he met me. She chucked him, and he tracked me down at the health-food shop and asked me out to get back at her.'

There was a short silence.

'You didn't fall for that?' asked Jack.

Her hopes rose. 'Why wouldn't it be true?'

Jack laughed dryly. 'It's not true because it's the perfect way to ruin your happy pre-Flick memories of Steve. It's way too perfect.'

So she took a deep breath and told him about the dress, watching a spark of doubt appear in his eyes. 'Again, you've got to give Flick credit for spinning a watertight tall story,' he said carefully. 'She knows how to pull your strings. She's had years of practice.'

'Yes, but when Steve gave me that dress, I remember thinking it was just like something Flick would go for. The clues were there. I just didn't add them up properly.'

There was another short pause. 'I still reckon she's lying,' said Jack, sounding less certain.

'We'll never know, will we?' shrugged Katie. 'If she retracted it, I'd think *that* was a lie. I'll just have to forget about it.' She turned back to the sink and fiddled with a tap.

'I'm off to squash,' Jack mumbled. 'Sure Simon's coming to give you a lift to Nikki's?'

'He promised faithfully.' While Jack got ready, Katie washed the dishes, filing away her Freddy, Steve and Dan worries (in roughly that order), to worry about her relationship with Nikki.

She was in the doghouse with Nikki, who had failed to get the job at the shop and laid the blame at Katie's door. Katie had clean forgotten to put in a good word for her with Frank, but Nikki was taking her grudge too far. Today was Sarah's second birthday, and Nikki hadn't phoned to invite Katie to drop by.

Katie wasn't Sarah's godmother (as she'd secretly hoped to be) but, even so, Nikki knew how fond she was of Sarah and Max. And why should Sarah be deprived of a present? Katie had it carefully wrapped on the coffee table, a Fisher-Price talking alphabet, both a gift for Sarah and a peace offering to Nikki.

So now Katie was girding her loins to gatecrash a two-year-old's party. Never having sunk this low in Nikki's opinion, she had no idea what reception she'd get. She'd already primed Simon to wait when he dropped her off, just in case Nikki wouldn't let her in. He'd urged her to seize the initiative and gatecrash the party, throwing in the offer of a lift to make up her wavering mind.

Given all that was already going on inside his head, she hadn't bothered to tell Jack about her fall-out with Nikki.

Simon arrived an hour after Jack had left. When Katie opened the front passenger door, she was surprised to see Tess in the back seat. 'Hi, Mum. Si dropping you off at the shops?'

'I'm going to Nikki's with you. Simon said you might need moral support.'

'Did he?' Katie glared murderously at her brother, who started whistling as he pulled into traffic. She knew she shouldn't have blabbed to him about Nikki when he'd answered the phone on her weekly catch-up call to Tess.

Hands folded on her lap, Tess leant back without allowing her sausagy curls, tinted a pale magenta with a home-colouring kit since dinosaurs roamed the earth, to touch the scarred vinyl of the seat. Her papery eyelids drooped. 'Simon is going to America in a couple of months,' she announced.

'Is he?' Katie dutifully feigned ignorance, although the loose-lipped rat didn't deserve it.

'For a year. He's staying with your father,' Tess revealed.

'Blimey!' Katie felt astonishment was called for. 'And, er, how do you feel about that, Mum?'

'As I said to Si, it's his life. His father's in a position to help him get on over there, so we mustn't be small-minded and look a gift horse in the mouth.'

'No,' mumbled Katie, wondering if the 'we' was a royal one, practised with gritted teeth in front of a mirror as Tess rehearsed her official reaction.

'I'm more interested in your row with Nikki,' said Tess. 'I've come to knock your heads together.'

'Mum, there's no need.' She tried a light laugh. 'You know me and Nikki, a tiff here, a kiss and make up there. It's the usual storm in a D-cup.'

'The horse's head on your pillow is just a rumour?' asked Simon.

Tess cocked an eyebrow. 'I want to interfere in your life, Katie. I have to cultivate interests, now Simon's leaving the nest.'

Katie was stumped. She'd never heard her mother attempt irony. 'Look, I'm persona non grata with Nikki. She might not even open the front door.'

'Just what I'm looking for, a bit of excitement.'

Katie sighed. 'Heard from the newlyweds yet?' Though actually, the last people she wanted to talk about were Mr and Mrs Avebury.

'Not a peep,' Simon replied. 'Is it true Shaggy's old man is stinking rich?'

'Apparently. Jack got wind of it just before the wedding.'

'Trish told me and I couldn't believe it. I mean, look at the state of Shaggy's clothes. They kept that quiet, didn't they? The old man could've stumped up for a big do instead of Mum doing all the donkey-work.'

'Now Simon, Dan and Flick bought all the food, and Jack and Katie provided the booze. So I'm hardly out of pocket. I don't see how Phil could have muscled in without causing offence. The wedding is always the bride's shout, and Flick wanted an intimate family do at her family home. It reflects well on her set of values.'

'If you say so, Ma,' said Simon, unconvinced.

'I do,' said Tess firmly. 'How's Freddy getting on in Greece, Katie?'

'Arrived safely and having a good time with his pal,' reported Katie, lying on Jack's behalf (anyway, it was true, as far as they knew. There had been no reversed-charge calls requesting bail money/return air fare/a troubleshooter from the Foreign Office).

'As soon as she gets the nod, Mum's off to Marsham to take a butcher's at Rome being built in a day, now there's money like water to chuck at it. I'm banking on you to make her go, Katie. Don't let her be put off by changing trains. Hey, maybe you could go with her.'

'Thank you, Simon,' said Tess. 'Your conscience need not be troubled about leaving me to fend for myself and change trains unaided. I knew you'd be flying the nest sometime.' Her fingers tapped her handbag clasp. 'A funny thing about a nest. It's supposed to be the last word in domestic cosiness, but it's actually a hollow structure. And birds abandon them regularly, don't they, and start all over again. I've only just thought of that.'

'Now, Ma, don't go all philosophical on me,' warned Simon, glancing uneasily at Katie. 'You'll have me cancelling my plane ticket.'

'I doubt that.' Tess exchanged a knowing look with Katie.

Twenty minutes later, Simon parked haphazardly outside the Bissett residence. The front door opened cautiously. 'Wait here,' Katie instructed her brother. Clutching her present, she marched up to the front door, Tess bustling behind her. A barefoot Nikki stood in the doorway, wearing piratically bright trousers and a stained T-shirt emblazoned with a rainbow. Sarah clung to her hip in a festive bib declaring 'I am 2 today!', covered in chocolate. Sarah was also covered in chocolate. She smiled a chocolatey greeting at Katie and waved her fingers like busy starfish.

'Hello there, cootchy coo.' Side-stepping Nikki for the moment, Katie grabbed the starfish fingers and rubbed her nose against Sarah's. She didn't mind the chocolate.

'Hello, Mrs Gibson,' said Nikki stiffly, flinging back hanks of dreadlocked hair.

'Afternoon, Nikki. What a bonny baby she is.'

'Chocolate buttons from the top of the cake,' said Nikki defensively, wiping Sarah's smeary bib across her face. 'They melted in the candle heat.'

'I've missed the candle-blowing?' asked Katie, hiding her dismay in an over-bright smile to Sarah. 'Did you make a wish, sweetheart?'

'Katie and I are the cavalry, come to relieve you and Doug,' announced Tess. 'Just point us towards sandwiches that need making or dishes that need washing.'

A series of shrieks from inside were followed by Doug's raised voice. 'Come in, then,' said Nikki ungratefully. 'Look before you park your bum is my advice.' Katie brought up the rear, turning to give Simon a thumbs-up, his signal to depart. He tooted the horn and drove off, due to return and collect them at four.

The dining-room table looked like a scene from the *Titanic*; upturned chairs, tablecloth nearly on the floor, crockery and half-masticated jammy food sliding slowly in its wake.

Katie traced the shrieks to the kitchen window. Out in the garden, about five older children (including Max) were playing a frenetic game of tag, marshalled ineffectually by a terrified-looking Doug. A plump little girl staggered over to the swing with the cat in her arms and lowered the portly ginger tom between the child-safety bars. Another little girl awaited the signal to start swinging.

Katie decided to leave Doug to it, and retreated to the dining-room. She righted a chair to sit on. 'The guests seem to be Max's age.'

Nikki had flopped onto the settee, Katie's gift on her lap. 'Sarah's best friend at the moment is her bath duck. We thought Max would benefit more from a blow-out with his horrible little chums, while still having the cake and nosh in Sarah's honour.'

'What a good idea,' said Tess, peeling off her coat, rolling up her sleeves and advancing on the table. 'I'll get cracking on this lot while you girls talk. You must have been on your feet all day, Nikki.'

'You don't have to do that, Mrs Gibson. Not in your nice jumper.'

'But I want to.' Tess carried plates into the kitchen and came straight back, looking concerned. 'Your cat's in distress. I'll sort that out first.' She disappeared again, and seconds later the shrieking in the garden levelled off to a bearable hum.

Nikki fiddled with the wrapping on Katie's present. 'Your mum's imposed order within two seconds of arriving. Which makes me feel *so* adequate.'

'Mum's a one-woman Panzer division. She's also had loads of experience.'

Nikki slid Katie's present over to Sarah, who ignored it and continued making chocolate hand-prints on the cushions, a look of concentrated effort on her face.

'Believe it or not, I think Mum might be enjoying herself. She just turned up with Simon when he came to give me a lift.' Katie chucked Sarah under the chin. 'Does she talk yet?'

'She's not a flamin' parrot. You don't chuck her a sunflower seed every time she says "pieces of eight".' Nikki gave Katie a deeply offended look, then sniffed and curled a ringlet round her finger. 'She talks when she's in the mood. "Da-da", "biskwit", that sort of thing. You implying she's slow?'

'Oh get real. What do I know about kids? And by the way, the purchase of this is entirely coincidental.' Katie leant over impatiently and tore the wrapping off her own present. Then she hunkered down beside Sarah and demonstrated pressing a lettered button to elicit an American voice warbling, 'B is for bee. A bee goes "buzz".'

'Whoo!' crowed Sarah delightedly. Encouraged, Katie pressed a for aeroplane.

'Want a drink?' muttered Nikki. 'A proper drink, though don't be picky. I may be down to bog-cleaner at this stage.'

'Bog-cleaner is fine,' replied Katie, relieved but still cautious.

Nikki padded away and returned with two mugs of cheap red wine. 'Nice of your mum to pitch in. I've just seen her in the garden, directing things like the scourge of the Women's Institute. Not that I'm complaining. Doug's decided he's surplus to requirements and sloped off to read the paper in the loo.'

'Things any better between you two?'

'Not really. I took it out on him when I didn't get the job.'

'I'm so sorry. Phoning Frank went right out of my head.'

'Didn't take much to shove me down the priority list,' grunted Nikki. 'A poxy wedding you wanted to boycott.' She rolled her eyes tragically. 'I never thought you'd let me down, Katie. Husbands, parents, children – I'd expect it of them. But you're closer than any blood sister.'

'Enough, already.' Katie knew Nikki was pulling her strings, but she couldn't help feeling terrible all the same. She shoved her hands through her fringe. 'I had more on my mind than the wedding,' she admitted. She took a deep breath, casting a furtive look around the room before she spoke again. 'This is top-secret, never to be spoken of outside this room.'

'Oh my God, what, what?' Nikki almost bounced on the sofa with excitement.

'That night we went out for a meal at L'Etoile, I kind of slept with Dan.'

'You what!' shrieked Nikki, making Sarah look up in alarm.

'Shush.' Katie gulped down some wine. There, she'd said it, started that ripple in the pond Dan was worried about. Though Nikki was the one human being she'd trust with this secret. 'We were left on our tod for a bit while Flick and Jack trailed around Avebury Towers with Phil. We were both out of our skulls, so details are mercifully sketchy, but we can remember enough. Unfortunately.'

'I assume you did a pregnancy test to be on the safe side?'

'I've had my period since,' mumbled Katie, deeply ashamed.

'Right. So it's over, finito. You are not – repeat not

– to go dredging up your Catholic guilt complex and telling Jack. What would be the point?'

'It would be honest.'

'Overrated virtue,' said Nikki crisply. 'White lies oil the wheels of social interaction. There's no difference between diplomacy and skilful lying.'

'But Jack and I are supposed to be getting married.'

'So? Believe you me, there are a hundred and one little indiscretions Jack's kept to himself. Oh, not necessarily sexual. Maybe he pulls a few scams for his clients, helps dodgy old Germans run their offshore accounts from South America. Wouldn't tell you, would he?'

'Infidelity's different.' She blanched at the word. It made her feel dirty.

'You were too drunk to know what you did,' insisted Nikki. 'Your defences were down. If Jack had made a similar mistake at an office party, do you think he'd waste five minutes agonising over it? He'd chalk it up to experience and stay on orange juice at the next shindig. No way would it cross his mind that it had anything to do with you and him.'

Katie looked shocked. 'Not my Jack. He's too principled. He once took the rap for a trainee's mistake, so the trainee wouldn't get the sack.'

Nikki folded her arms. 'I bet Dan's not telling Attila the Hen.'

'He's not keen to, no.'

'Because she'd skewer him and have him on toast.'

'Actually, she'd skewer me. Ironically, I'm the one benefitting from Dan's silence. I don't think she'd want Dan dead unless she was certain of automatically inheriting his worldly goods.'

'Well, there you go. You've been losing sleep over nothing.'

'You know me too well to say that.'

'OK,' sighed Nikki. 'You've been losing sleep because, when you reached puberty, your pituitary gland over-stimulated your conscience, mistaking it for a secondary sexual characteristic or something. That's the only theory that makes sense to me.'

'Don't be daft. And don't give me that "drunken flings are meaningless" line. You'd do your nut if Doug had a drunken fumble.'

'Point is, I'd never find out, would I? Now you've got me thinking,' she muttered darkly, and flashed Katie a bleak smile. 'How's the old sex life since you started thrashing with this moral dilemma?'

'It's OK.' Katie's cheeks burnt. In fact, their love life had been on a gradual downward trajectory since the giddy heights of tenderness reached on Rhodes. Her abject guilt and their restless nights on the sofa hadn't helped.

But there was something else.

She no longer saw Jack as a brooding, invincible Mr Rochester. Since his Freddy outburst after the wedding, she'd come to regard him more as a brother than a lover, almost as matey as a true sibling.

She couldn't stop thinking of him as that six year old with his nose pressed to the window, watching a Christmas hamper being carried away. She'd taken to touching him a lot non-sexually, trying to stroke away the aches and pains of his past. He didn't seem to mind.

'How's it going, girls?' A rosy-cheeked Tess came in, clutching the hand of a hot and breathless Max with a thin line of blood oozing from his nose. 'This little man's been in the wars, so we're going to get him cleaned up. Have you got Savlon, Nikki?'

'Under the sink, Mrs Gibson. It's the other kid I'm worried about.'

Tess smiled. 'That's what I like to see. A sensible, non-fussy parent. I was sorry you didn't get that job, dear.'

'Wasn't my scene,' muttered Nikki.

'I'd have to agree with you there,' said Tess, leading Max away. 'I'll be back in a tick. I've had an idea.'

Nikki's black brows shot up to her hairline. 'The mind boggles.'

They heard Max complaining about Tess's ferocity with a moist-wipe. She returned alone. 'He's gone back into the garden for round two. I've been thinking, Nikki. There's a flexi-time thing advertised at my supermarket, aimed at getting mothers back to work. Oh, and it's not just shelf-filling – I know that would bore you rigid. They want more women in middle management, the ad says, and seem keen on what they call "multi-tasking mums". Women who juggle. I thought of you straight away.'

Nikki plucked a cushion-fringe. 'Don't get my hopes up, Mrs Gibson. That other job was all pie in the sky, anyway. I can't afford a childminder.'

'Look no further,' declared Tess regally. The two younger women gaped at her.

'Is it such a surprising offer?' asked Tess stiffly. 'I've raised three of my own, more or less single-handedly, and I love the innocence of these little ones.' She thrust her face down to Sarah, who gawped up solemnly, then reached out for the whiskery hairs dotting Tess's chin.

'Young minds are so malleable,' said Katie in a mock-sinister Simon voice.

'You serious, Mrs Gibson?'

'Never more so. To be honest, I'm bored. Organising Flick's reception was the highlight of my year, which doesn't say a lot, does it? All I did was heat a few things under the grill and put pineapple chunks on Ritz crackers.'

'You did a lot more than that, Mum.'

Tess shrugged slightly. 'Soon Simon won't be around to tease me, and the pot's too big for one, so I'll have to use tea bags.'

'What's that got to do with the price of fish? A baby's a lot to take on to alleviate boredom.'

'Shut up, Katie. You're on, Mrs G,' said Nikki excitedly. 'I only want to work part-time, so you wouldn't have Sarah more than a couple of days a week. Well, at first. And I'd be home most days, or Doug would, to collect Max from school. Oh, this is brill. Only I feel I have to make you sign a contract in blood in case you get to the door and change your mind.'

'I don't change my mind,' said Tess, with a steely dignity that carried, to Katie's ears, a refrain from possible final exchanges with Don. 'Well, that's sorted, then. Find a job, Nikki, and I'll help all I can. Katie, remind me to pick up one of those flexi-time application forms next time I'm going shopping.'

As her mother bustled off to prevent a fresh outbreak of suburban warfare in the back garden, Katie rounded on Nikki. 'You're taking advantage of her! She's lonely and bored and wants to feel wanted. She's forgetting about the sheer hard work.'

'Poppycock. She's a strong-minded, independent woman. And I've got to get a job first. I'll ring that supermarket and see if they can send out a form, save your ma the trouble. Don't look at me like that. I'll pay the going rate, though I assume she'll do a discount for friends. Do you think she'd come here if I asked her? It's not far on the bus. Or would she want me to drop Sarah off at her house?'

Katie was at a loss. Her mother's offer had caught her on the hop. Because Tess usually gave so little away, her revelation of boredom and loneliness had come as a shock. But it was all too sudden. Tess was having a rush of blood to the head, and Katie reckoned it was her way of dealing with Simon's act of betrayal, an act she'd trained herself to come to terms with on the surface, while incubating its effect in secret grief.

'Remember what I said,' said Nikki wisely, breaking into her thoughts. 'On the probably-slept-with-Dan front. Cut yourself some slack.'

Katie looked at her bleakly. She wished she hadn't been quite so frank with her mother's future employer.

She said nothing to Tess as Simon drove them home.

Tess turned to her. 'I'm looking forward to it, you know. Sarah is no trouble at all.'

'Not for a younger woman, maybe,' said Katie, then bit her tongue and looked anxiously at her mother. Afternoon sunlight strobed into the car every few yards, washing each crease and fold on Tess's face with garish light. 'I'm sorry, Ma. I didn't mean to imply you're past it.'

'In an ideal world, little Sarah wouldn't have to be farmed out to a stranger. But better me than some other stranger. And I'm in no position to claim that the traditional set-up is the best way: father out at work, mother keeping the home fire burning. I decided I'd rather go it alone than give you children the full complement of parents you had a right to expect. He asked to stay and try again, and I said no.' Time stood still in the car. Katie looked at Simon, who looked doggedly at the road. Never, in their joint experience, had Tess passed comment on her past.

'He asked to stay?' Katie risked at last.

'Oh yes. He said that Tanya woman was a fling. They call it a mid-life crisis nowadays, although he was only thirty-one.' She clicked her teeth speculatively. 'Sometimes, I can't think why I made such a fuss when you see husbands getting up to all sorts and wives having them back. Those politicians, for a start.'

'It was a year-long fling,' murmured Katie daringly.

'Oh, at least. You know, very few men want to end up with the mistress full-time. It defeats the object if she becomes another wife, tying him down to responsibilities. I'm afraid I was feeling spiteful and wanted to punish him. Of course, you always end up punishing yourself when you give in to spite.' Her gaze shifted between her children. 'And other people.'

'We've managed fine without him,' said Katie defensively.

'So have I. But I'm not the one with the possible chip on my shoulder because my father didn't want me. Or at least, didn't want to keep in touch.'

'I don't feel like that,' protested Katie. 'Do you, Si?'

'My chips are perfectly balanced,' replied Si, flexing his shoulders.

'I said "possible" chip. Just because damage isn't obvious, it doesn't mean it's not there.'

'All families are damaged,' said Katie, thinking of Jack and Freddy. 'Goes with the territory. He did us a favour by clearing off. He might have had more affairs if you'd let him stay, and then you'd have ended up chucking pots and pans at him, with us kids hiding under the stairs, waiting for Childline to be invented.'

Tess patted Katie's hand. 'You're probably right, dear.'

Katie sensed her mother slipping back behind her mask. 'Are we nearly home yet, Si?' Tess asked briskly, checking her hair in the rear-view mirror, then folding her hands on her lap. 'I can't wait to soak my feet. That Max is a naughty little monkey, but bright with it. He's going to take after Nikki.'

Katie tore up the stairs to the flat. She couldn't wait to get Jack's opinion of Tess's behaviour. It would make a change from discussing Freddy.

She threw herself into the flat, to find Jack standing by the coffee table, frowning down at a letter in his hand. He looked up at her, his brow taking a moment to clear. Katie couldn't speak until she got her breath back. She was so unfit.

'I've reached a decision,' announced Jack, dropping the letter on the coffee table, next to his parents' wedding photo. 'I'm going out to Halkidiki next week. Milo will see I get time off, and a week should be long enough to track down Seb's bar, save Dad from Freddy Mercury lookalikes and drag him back here. Then we can look at options. No, hear me out!' he commanded, though she'd merely opened her mouth to suck in more oxygen. 'Option number one: get married, buy a house and give him the spare room. Possibly put a telly in it. Option number two—'

'Hold your horses.' Katie realised he'd been rehearsing this speech before she came in. 'Let's start at the beginning. What does that letter from Freddy say?'

'This?' He picked up the letter again. 'This is from Shaggy. Must've come in the late post, and insists we go down and visit them in their pastoral idyll. Of course *Pops* hasn't written. He'd only write if all was well. It's obviously gone pear-shaped and he's clinging to his last scrap of pride before he calls for help. Fact is . . .' He took a deep breath and declared savagely, 'I can't afford to wait until he's snuffed it in some foreign field and I've got him on my conscience for the rest of my natural.'

Katie sank down onto the sofa. 'I suppose it's only right you want to go after him. It'd be more worrying if you didn't care.'

'He's been gone over a fortnight and not a dicky bird.'

'I know.' Much to her own surprise, she held out a hand to him, just as he'd offered himself to be leant on in the past.

He came eagerly and rested his head on her shoulder. 'Do you think he could be all right, all this time, on his own, in a foreign country?'

'He's not on his own. Seb's an old friend.'

'He wouldn't have gone if I hadn't said those horrible things in his earshot.'

She kissed a lapwing of hair. 'Don't torture yourself. He went to Greece because he wanted to, first and foremost. I don't think Freddy does anything unless he wants to. He was also very sensitive about outstaying his welcome.'

Jack winced. 'Thanks to my lukewarm welcome, you mean.' He burrowed deeper into her shoulder. 'I'll leave him out there if it's all going OK. I'll be back no later than Saturday week, promise. I'm going Monday morning, so you won't be able to come to the airport. Anyway, I don't like airport farewells, and I'll ring every evening.' She sighed. It would have to do. Jack would never rest otherwise.

Chapter Eleven

Jack was on a stake-out. From the café across the street, screened by an awning pole, he had a clear view of the bar of iniquity. Like the café, Seb Hatcher's bar boasted pavement tables. Every so often, a familiar white-haired figure in shorts and T-shirt pottered outside and wiped the tables, collecting the empties. So far, Jack noted, Freddy hadn't been trusted with collecting money. He was probably still getting to grips with drachmas.

Jack tensed beside his empty coffee-cup as Freddy shuffled out again, clutching a yellow Vileda sponge. Between that and the stripy apron he wore, Seb's dandifying influence was clear. But Jack still paused to ask himself the 64,000-dollar question – the one Katie's voice kept asking in his head – 'Does he look happy?'

'How should I know?' his psyche was prompted to reply. Freddy had spent so long pottering around Suzette's in a semi-servile role, it was impossible to tell at a spy's distance if Seb was a whip-cracker or a liberator.

Jack peered up at the relentless sun and shifted slightly into the shade. The beautiful weather left him unaffected, because he was a man with a mission: to make Freddy see sense and come home. Trouble was, he still didn't know how to – or indeed whether to – confront or appease him.

The answer suggested itself a few minutes later, when Freddy re-emerged from the bar, clutching a string shopping-bag. Aha! Jack straightened his sun-glasses. He was probably off to buy lemons for the ice-and-a-slice crowd. That might be for the best. Why confront Freddy at all until he'd had a chance to suss out Seb? Plus, Freddy would be half expecting him to turn up, while Seb would be caught out cold and confess what was really going on.

His mind made up, Jack waited until Freddy was out of sight down the street. Then he rose, crossed the street, and entered the bar.

It took him a few seconds to adjust to the indoor gloom. The bar was almost empty. Perfect. A portly bloke stood behind the wooden counter, polishing a glass with a queenly over-fussiness. Jack marched up to him.

'Yes, squire,' beamed Seb (for it was he), in that 'terribly terribly' voice Jack vaguely remembered. 'What can I do you for?'

'You can tell me what you're doing, corrupting my poor old father.' Despite his intention to play things cool, the accusation leapt off his tongue.

Seb peered at him. 'Jack? Freddy said you might turn up. He'll be back in a jiffy.'

'It's you I want to talk to, Mr Hatcher.'

'Can't think why, old boy. Gosh, talk of the devil.

That was a quick shop, Fred.'

Jack turned. Freddy stood there, clutching the string bag. 'Forgot the money.' He ignored his son, a high colour mottling his neck, liver-spotted hands twisting the bag into a cat's cradle of meshed strings.

Seb looked from one to the other. 'Go and sit outside in the sun, the pair of you. I'll bring out a couple of coffees.'

Father and son, silenced by the sudden apparition of each other, moved slowly to a pavement table. Seb came bustling in their wake with a pot of coffee and two pastries, glazed stickily in honey. 'They're pecan and maple,' he explained, only his fixed gaze at the table betraying his embarrassment. 'I've given them a quick zap in the microwave. Now you boys take your time. You've a lot to discuss.'

'Who the hell does he think he is?' demanded Jack ungraciously, watching Seb dart back into the bar. He looked down at a treacly substance oozing from his pastry. 'Is this a local delicacy? Looks like ear-wax.'

'No point picking on Seb when you're cross with me.'

'Cross? Try furious for size. Why did you go skulking off to the airport, bracketing me and Katie with Suzette? We even got the note-under-the-fruit-bowl treatment. For all we knew, you'd actually gone to Beachy Head and chucked yourself off.'

'Not my style, is it? You knew I was coming out to see Seb.'

'Oh yes, *Seb*. Well known on the local dating scene, is he?'

'You've stayed narrow in your views, Portillo, despite Katie's influence.'

'You know you've caused a rift between us? You had to go spilling all our nasty little family secrets, without checking with me first.'

'You're planning to marry her, aren't you? Shouldn't be any secrets.'

'That's not for you to decide. And yes, I'm hoping to marry her, if she'll still have me. She's had a pretty low opinion of me since you – you forced me to lose my rag with you after the wedding. And when you gave her your side of the great house-money fiasco, I bet you made me the villain of the piece, rolling up at the B and B full of righteous wrath.'

Freddy looked pained. 'It wasn't like that, son.'

'Oh?' Jack, enjoying putting Freddy on the defensive, refused to be mollified. 'I can't see you giving Katie your life story without appealing to her compassionate side. At the expense of me and Mum, of course.'

Freddy inhaled wheezily. 'Be so kind as to leave Mum out of it.'

'Why should I? You turned her into a nagging drudge and then made your gambling buddies feel sorry for you because you'd married a sharp-tongued old shrew. Neatly forgetting cause and effect.'

Freddy paled. 'Just leave it be.'

'There could've been a lot more to her than a shrill-voiced harpy forever turning out your pockets. But she had to make you and your vice her full-time career. You loved it, didn't you, being the centre of attention in your marriage, keeping her on a knife-edge of worry and distraction twenty-four hours a day? You're the most selfish human being I've ever met. OK, so Mum got cancer, but they say stress brings it on, don't they? And she got nothing but a lifetime of stress from you. Ergo, you shoved her into an early grave.'

Jack snapped his mouth shut as Freddy drew in his breath with a sharp whistle. Almost immediately, Jack's heart plummeted. He'd hidden his theory about Janet's ultimate demise all his adult life, even from himself. He wasn't sure it even counted as a theory. Just a few malevolent observations tossed into the pot, dressed up as righteous indignation on his mother's behalf.

Jack raised his sunglasses slowly. Freddy's face had gone grey. 'I didn't mean that, Pops,' he mumbled hastily.

'You did so, son. We always say what we really mean when we're not watching our words.'

'Pops, I—'

'I'm proud you're not a waste of space like me. You'll never put Katie through the wringer.'

'Katie . . .' Jack cleared his throat. 'I don't know if I should marry Katie after all. I didn't know I had such a vicious tongue.'

'You're just not used to speaking without thinking, lad. Don't be too hard on yourself. 'Course you'll marry Katie, you'd be mad not to. Don't want some other bloke nipping in through the back door, do you?'

Jack stared, wondering if Freddy was taunting him. But Freddy cast his eyes downwards. 'Not that she'd ever do the dirty on you, like. She hasn't got a low opinion of you, lad. No one could have. A strong one, maybe. I'm dead proud of you and I know I should've said it more often—'

'Don't, Dad.' Glad of his sunglasses, Jack looked across the street.

Freddy nodded towards the bar. 'It's all going to plan here. I've got free food and board, and Seb pays me for the bit of work I do around the place. Even if he kicks me out in a few weeks, I'll have enough saved to rent a room for months to come. He's all right, you know, once you get to know him.' Freddy looked at him appealingly. 'Come out to dinner with us one night. What have you got to lose? I won't run off anywhere again without giving you all the details. I'm sorry for that, son.'

Jack wanted to apologise as well, for what he'd said about his mother and the cancer. But the words stuck in his throat and his eyes began to smart. He couldn't do it! He couldn't bring himself to say a few simple words without fearing a scene of dreadful mawkishness where he'd burst into tears. He was an emotional coward. But Freddy – Freddy was big enough to take his insults on the chin, repay him with compliments, and invite him out to dinner. He realised why it was easy to dislike people who were good at heart.

'I still want you to come back home with me, Dad.'

'I thought we'd just had this out.'

'You're my responsibility,' Jack almost shouted. 'And where will you go when Seb gets sick of you, like everyone does in the end?' The sight of Freddy flinching drove him on, spurred by self-loathing. 'Don't give me that rented room stuff. You wouldn't last five minutes on your own. I have a duty to look out for you and no one else is going to do it.'

'You don't owe me anything,' said Freddy, quietly stubborn. 'You never did.'

Jack glared, relieved to be back on the familiar ground of tit-for-tat bickering. 'What's that supposed to mean?'

'Nothing.' Freddy stood up suddenly, his pastry and coffee untouched. 'I'm going for a walk on the beach.'

'In this heat?' Jack glanced at the sweltering sun. 'It's nearly midday.'

But Freddy turned away without further explanation and stepped, apparently blindly, into the street's steady flow of traffic. 'Dad, wait!' Jack leapt up and lunged after him.

Katie snatched up the phone on the second ring, but all she heard was a burst of static. 'Jack, are you there? This is a crap line.'

A warning beep was followed by what sounded like the frantic rattle of coins, and then the line went dead.

Katie stared at the phone in frustration. Why couldn't he simply reverse the charges? He'd done so at the beginning of the week, when, as promised, he'd filed regular reports on his progress.

But as the scent grew stronger and the leads firmer, his calls had grown more fractured and tantalising. Had he found Freddy and persuaded him to return? It looked like she'd have to wait until Jack's own return the following night. She had decided to go to the airport to meet him off the plane, as a surprise. She liked airport hellos.

After waiting in vain for Jack to call back, she padded self-consciously round the flat. It was half-eleven on a Friday night. A TV thrubbed in Mrs Domenica's flat below. Katie had never stayed alone in the flat before. It had been odd – dislocating – returning from work on Monday evening to find the place dark and silent. Usually, Jack was home from work before her, with the oven warming and the news humming on the telly.

She straightened a few things on the coffee table. The letter from Dan fell out of the TV guide, and she picked it up reluctantly and scanned its familiar contents. It was a stilted letter, written in the knowledge that Jack would read it, but aimed at her. She got the impression he'd never liked Jack much. Jack was too outwardly self-assured, too much the son Phil Avebury would happily have settled for.

We hope you can come down to Marsham in the near future, Dan had written. Who was he kidding with that 'We'? *Our cottage is nice and the one next door is free, so if you came to visit, I'd book it up for the weekend. It has everything – power shower, air-conditioning . . .* She shook her head. In his desperation to entice, he'd listed a power shower. *There are lots of great walks near here and that ye oldy parish pump is right outside our front door, Katie.*

No mention of wedded bliss or work progressing at Cloverley. Had things turned sour so quickly? Katie felt sorry for him, but anything deeper was a luxury she couldn't afford. Look where feeling sorry for Dan had got her before.

She turned off the lights and padded into the bedroom.

She found it difficult to sleep at night, although part of her luxuriated guiltily in Jack's absence. The whole Dan episode seemed light years away, as if unwittingly carried by Jack to a distant shore. She was having time to think clearly for the first time since their return from Rhodes, and she had formed a most disconcerting notion, one that didn't expiate her guilt, but complemented it.

She had begun to wonder if Jack now saw marriage as a way of sharing the Freddy-load. It was the way he'd talked about getting married, buying a house, and shoving Freddy in the spare room all in the same breath, as if one couldn't be achieved without the other.

Back in Rhodes, it wouldn't have mattered. She had wanted to marry Jack, whatever the circumstances of his proposal, but now she felt strong enough to be unsure. Ironically, her guilt had led her to evaluate Jack's fitness for marriage as well as her own. Could she really spend the years ahead playing peacemaker between father and son? Should she be expected to?

She climbed into bed and drew the duvet up to her chin. Outside, a steamy July rain pattered on the window pane. July in Greece would be baking. She hoped Jack had enough sun cream and was making Freddy wear a hat.

Having failed to get through to Katie, Jack was feeling philosophical. Perhaps it was for the best. He might have blurted out his news on the phone, when he needed time to digest it for himself before he decided when – if – to share it with her.

Slowly, he went up to his hotel room. Did he feel any different?

He looked carefully in the bathroom mirror. Did he look any different? Was the old Jack with the old certainties gone for ever, or had he, without knowing it, been true to himself all along?

He lay down on the bed, arms crossed behind his head, and echoed back to himself what he'd said to Freddy on the beach earlier today.

'I can't believe it. I just can't.'

He had grown hot and bothered shadowing Freddy on his midday walk along the beach. Sun-worshippers had long retreated to umbrellaed bars for lunch and even the sea flopped tiredly on the shoreline like a dog's hot tongue. Only mad Englishmen – two of them – were striding along the sand as if son-evading and father-following were Olympic sports meriting the testing furnace of noon heat. Jack couldn't remember seeing Freddy stride before. Come to think of it, he hadn't coughed or wheezed once while they were talking in the café.

Just as his younger and fitter body was developing a stitch, he saw Freddy clamber inelegantly over a few scrubby rocks and sit down on a small ledge, his sandalled feet dangling above the sea. Spray pounded the rocks and spat cooling foam over Freddy's shins. Jack fancied some of that. He scrambled onto the rocks and sat down beside his father.

The ledge was narrow. They had to sit close together, elbows touching, legs dangling side by side.

'Look, I'm sorry about all that Mum stuff,' began Jack breathlessly, soothed by spray on his hot legs. 'You were great the way you shielded me when she was ill. You made life normal for me and I never told you how grateful I was.'

Freddy turned to look at him. 'I thought you always

resented me for keeping you at arm's length. You weren't even in the room when she died.'

'Listen, Dad,' grimaced Jack, 'I'm a hopeless coward about stuff like that. If you want to know the truth, I hated my sick-room visits, having to pretend I wasn't appalled at how yellow and shrivelled she looked, nails rasping away on top of the duvet like someone trying to get out of a coffin. She gave me the creeps.' He shrugged. 'I was a selfish little sod.'

'You were only a lad,' said Freddy gruffly. 'No need to apologise for anything. Your mother understood.'

'You were a saint, though,' said Jack. 'I never heard you complain.'

'What did I have to complain about?' asked Freddy with sudden sharpness. 'I wasn't the one dying a painful, lingering death.'

Jack stared out to sea. 'Can I ask you something I've always wondered?'

'Go on.'

Jack sensed every muscle stiffen in the aged body next to him.

'I know Mum was in a bad way with the pain. Did you – help her on her way? Give her a few pills too many one day, to put her out of her misery?' He swallowed. 'I mean, I came home from school one day and she was gone. Vanished. And you wouldn't meet my eye, I remember that very clearly. There's no way I'd blame you, Dad. I just want to know.'

Freddy was silent for so long that Jack braced himself for a confessional outpouring. But eventually, all he said was, 'You've been watching too many films, lad. I didn't know enough about your mother's medication to go taking liberties with it.'

'I wasn't implying anything.'

'You already implied back at Seb's I brought on her cancer, so I suppose it were only natural you'd think I'd finish the job.'

'I didn't mean that back at Seb's.'

'The funny thing is, I had everyone thinking I was a regular Florence Nightingale, when, in actual fact, I ended up hating your mum. And she hated me, every day I nursed her. I found her once, when she was high on morphine, trying to gas herself in the kitchen. She'd forgotten we had an electric oven. Even though she was doped up to the eyeballs, she was looking for a way out before the next pain attack struck. We made a regular fight of it on the kitchen floor before I got her back into bed. She hated me for stopping her and for needing me at all, and I hated her for – well, I had my reasons.'

Jack's mouth had gone dry. He'd been protected from images that now flashed unpleasantly into his mind. 'It wasn't fair to hate her. You weren't dying of cancer.'

'No, it wasn't fair, right enough.'

'Why did you hate her, then?' Jack was getting worked up again on Janet's behalf. 'For lumbering you with a terrible insight into death? I suppose I can see how you'd end up recoiling from someone who'd forced that on you. Not just you, anyone.'

'It wasn't that.' Freddy's voice was dull. 'I don't want to talk about it. She was a good woman and a good mum to you. We had our differences, let's leave it there.'

'If you say so.' Jack stifled his curiosity. 'I mean it about wanting you to come back with me, Dad. Katie wants you to as well.'

'And I mean it about not coming back. You don't owe me anything.'

'Oh, come off it.'

'I mean it, Jack. Stop treating me like a burden when I'm not your burden in the first place. I'm nothing to do with you!' Freddy clamped his mouth shut.

'Dad, if you think I'm going to let that cryptic little remark fall by the wayside, think again. How can you be nothing to do with me?'

Even as he asked, a terrible suspicion took dark shape in the back of his mind. He suddenly knew what Freddy half-wanted him to guess. The grey pallor was back in Freddy's face, signalling his realisation that he'd gone too far – or not been cryptic enough.

'Christ Almighty, Dad!'

'I'm sorry, Jack,' Freddy half-gasped, half-whispered, his whole face sagging like a battle-weary punchbag. 'I never meant to let that slip. Bloody hell, can't I be trusted to keep my big trap shut over anything?'

Jack stared into the foam at his feet. 'You'd better tell me the grizzly details.'

Freddy sighed. 'It's not fair on your mother.'

'Oh – and leaving me thinking all sorts is?'

'All right, then, all right! Here goes.' Freddy paused, coughed, played for time. Jack felt he would scream with the tension if he didn't get on with it.

Finally, wearily, Freddy spoke. 'After I'd accepted an offer on the house for my move to Oz, I started a clearout and found some of your mother's things in a box at the back of the wardrobe. They'd been there for years. There was a letter, scorched in places, like she'd tried to burn it and thought better of it—'

'Who is he?' Jack butted in, voice hoarse. 'Who's my real father?'

'Bloke called Alfie Barker,' muttered Freddy. 'When you were a little lad, he offered me a job Down Under. I thought he was doing an old mate a favour, but Janet had kept this letter from him. He must have wrote to her after she'd persuaded me to turn down the job. He said if only he could be near you, that would be enough. He'd never go making waves for her, spark a scandal, he just wanted to see his son growing up—'

'Jesus Christ!' The sun dazzled Jack in a road-to-Damascus blinding conversion to the truth. He had dedicated his life to not turning out like Freddy. He had guarded against the emergence of traits such as addictive behaviour and backsliding as vigilantly as any eugenics enthusiast of the Third Reich when, all along, he wasn't even the fruit of Freddy Gold's loins! Instead, he was the son of a distant, perhaps long-dead emigrant who had flitted in out of Freddy's conversation down the years as surely as he'd flitted in and out of Janet Gold's life.

'How?' he began, the sun turning to a pinwheel of light above him. 'When? How did—?'

'I don't know any more than was in the letter,' said Freddy thickly. 'Which I burnt. I don't know if it was an affair or a one-night thing and I never wanted to know. Janet was pregnant when Alfie emigrated – with his wife in tow, mind. I don't know if he went knowing about you, or somehow found out after. I'd lost touch with Alfie by the time your mother died, but after I read that letter, I was damn sure I wasn't going near Australia, no matter how big the bloody place was. As it was, I was terrible scared he'd read your mum's death notice somewhere and come galloping over to throw fat on the fire, telling all and sundry you were his son. So with Oz not an option and you not my son, I exchanged contracts on the house and went on a bender with the money. I didn't give a stuff what happened to me, and that's the truth. Apart from you, the only person I felt anything for was Janet – and I hated her. You were the only thing I could be proud of, the one thing I'd ever got right. And she took you away from me.' A familiar wheezing noise bubbled up from his chest.

'But how can you be sure?' asked Jack numbly.

'I'm sure all right. The letter from Alfie showed clear as day it was common knowledge between him and Janet. And when we never had more kids, I wanted Janet to get checked out and she got mad and said she knew there was nothing wrong on her side. That made all the sense in the world after I found the letter. There were other things in the box – a photo of me and Alfie as kids. I burnt that as well. The likeness to you was so obvious, I knew I'd been blind.'

A tear dripped unnoticed on Freddy's T-shirt. Jack reached a shaking hand up to his own face and discovered, with a sense of detachment, that it was wet. 'You have to look at it this way, Pops,' he said, and they both started at his Freudian slip. 'Mum didn't want to go to Australia for all the right reasons. She believed in her vows. Morally, she was as upright as they came, and she didn't want anyone coming between us as a family. You're my dad. She knew it and I know it.'

'You don't have to say that,' muttered Freddy. 'If I was you, it'd be a big weight off my shoulders, knowing I wasn't responsible for you. Literally, like. And now, that means you're not responsible for me.'

Compassion welled up in Jack, so suddenly and forcefully he wanted to shout out his love, like an evangelical Christian. 'I want to be responsible for you, you troublesome old git! I love you. I've hated you sometimes, been driven bonkers by you most of the time. That sort of passion is the habit of a lifetime and it's a hard habit to break.'

Freddy blinked up at him. 'I love you too – son. I never stopped just because I found that letter. It didn't change what I've always taken for granted, being prepared to lie down and die for my kid. Are you saying it's a bit like that for you, too?'

His cautiously optimistic tone tugged at Jack's newly-unfurled heartstrings. 'I'm saying exactly that, Dad! It was clearly Mum's wish to take her secret to the grave. We should honour that wish.'

'I don't know . . .' Freddy hunched his shoulders. 'I feel funny calling you "son".'

'Portillo will do,' said Jack, shading his eyes from the glare on the sea.

When he looked round, Freddy was staring at him with the dazed intensity of a father introduced to his first-born – and perhaps it *was* that moment for him, all over again. Jack imagined what it must have been like when those first introductions were made – Freddy awestruck by the responsibility and wonder of fatherhood, perhaps counting fingers and toes, resolving solemnly to do his best by his child and never dreaming how weak the flesh would prove to be.

'I never want to hear Alfie Barker's name again,' declared Jack, his tugged heartstrings tightening to form an unusual umbilical cord, one linking father and son. 'I've no interest in him, no plans to ever look him up. As far as I'm concerned, that letter was never written.'

Freddy looked out to sea for what seemed an age. Then he nodded – just the once. They sat side by side in the sun, warming their backs on the rocks. It was a moment of true serenity, touched by the deepest truth of all. Jack had chosen Freddy, and he could be magnanimous because the choice had been offered. It was Freddy who'd given the greatest gift of all. He had given Jack his freedom. There were no mistakes waiting to be made because a long line of male Golds had made them in the past and incorporated the DNA for failure into a genetic blueprint for the future. Jack Gold, son of an unknown quantity, was now a free agent, a blank template – and he couldn't wait to see how he turned out.

Saturday started for Katie as a listless, rain-filled day, with Jack waiting at the end of it. She had loads of chores, but little will to do them. She was excited and nervous at Jack's imminent return. It wasn't just that he'd be bringing news of Freddy. They had things to discuss, heavy things.

How would he react when she wondered aloud if marriage was the right step after all? She didn't love him any less, but all this Freddy stuff had got in the way and clouded the issue. Then there was her very unmatrimonial feeling of brotherly tenderness for him recently. And lastly, of course, her own capacity for drunken infidelity. It was all a million miles away from a boyish marriage proposal and a giggling acceptance in a hotel bar just a few months earlier.

She loaded the washing-machine and made a mug of coffee. As she carried it from the kitchen, the intercom buzzed loudly. She set down the mug quickly, slopping coffee, and flew to answer the summons. 'Yes?'

'It's me,' mumbled Dan's disembodied voice. 'Can I come up? I'm getting soaked and it's really public here.'

Galvanised by pure shock, her finger buzzed him in. Then she waited, listening to his big feet make their hesitant ascent. When the doorbell rang, she took a deep breath before she opened the front door. 'Dan!' Her smile felt tight. 'To say this is a surprise is an understatement.'

He came in, shaking droplets from his shagginess, wearing a light twill suit, the summer garb of a country gent. She detected the hand of Flick.

'I know. I'm sorry to just turn up,' he murmured, flushed face averted. 'Did you get my letter?'

'Hang on.' She ran to the airing cupboard and returned with a towel. 'Take off that jacket and anything else that's wet through.' She paused. 'Well, maybe leave it at the jacket.'

'You're always so thoughtful.' He rubbed his silvery mop of hair.

'I'm nothing special. Um, would you like a hot drink?' She thrust her mug of unsipped coffee at him. 'Get this down you. It's unsugared. Do you take sugar?'

'I knew Jack would be off playing squash for a

couple of hours,' he said, stubbornly suggestive, sinking damply on to the sofa and accepting the coffee. 'I had to come when you didn't answer my letter.'

'You didn't give me a chance.' She perched on a nearby armrest. 'Where's Flick?'

His face closed up. 'I invented a reason to come up to London to see a non-existent old friend from the garden centre. She dropped me off near a tube station and drove on to your mum's in our new car.' He said the last bit gloomily. 'We're meeting up later at your mum's. I knew I'd see you at Simon's send-off in a couple of weeks, but I couldn't wait that long.'

Katie gazed at him, horribly intrigued. In a few short weeks of marriage, Dan had been driven to uncharacteristic subterfuge. 'What's all this about, Dan?'

'You were right,' he blurted, grey eyes downcast. 'She told me on our wedding night, would you believe. She married me for the money, like you warned. She's got loads of debts.'

Suddenly comprehending the whole aim of her sister's masterplan, Katie slid down next to him on the sofa. 'But she earned a fortune in her job.'

'Apparently not. I mean, she earned a good wage by our standards, but she took out credit and store cards right, left and centre to keep up with the spending habits of her swanky mates. That's what she told me, anyway. For all I know, she's run up a big tab with a drug dealer. I can't believe anything your sister says any more.'

Katie's mind whirred. 'How much does she owe?'

'Thirty grand, give or take,' he muttered. 'It's sorted. I got a quarter of a mill from the trust fund for starting work on Cloverley and bunged the necessaries her way. But you were right all along. She went on about loving me after she told me, but she must think I'm a complete, flamin' mug. I can't bear to be near her, yet I can't bear the thought of *not* being with her, either.' He sifted his hair through his hands, while Katie tried to take in the news. 'We're in separate bedrooms now. Well, I moved into the spare room, and she's never said anything about it, just acted the same as normal, only really, really polite, so I can't find an excuse to get mad like I want to. Only, I don't want to as well, if you see what I mean. I don't want a big showdown that could drive her away, until I work out how I really feel. So I go out all day, pretending to keep an eye on the builders at Cloverley. I dunno what she does. I go home late and I don't ask. I don't know what to do.' Very quietly, he began to cry. 'Tell me what to do. Please.'

Katie put an awkward arm round him. She patted his shoulder as the rain swished against the window, and she wondered what on earth she could do or say. She couldn't take away the pain of betrayal or make it any easier to stop loving her sister.

'I had plans,' he muttered thickly. 'I told you about them. Do up Cloverley's garden and wait for the commissions to flood in. Everyone would live happily ever after.' He sighed. 'I can still follow some of it through. I'm deffo going to see Auntie Dorrie all right on the money front, to make up for Dad using her and Uncle Sid over the years.'

Feeling helpless and hopeless, all Katie could do

was murmur, 'It might still come all right, Dan. Maybe—'

The intercom buzzed again, like an angry blue-bottle. They jumped apart.

'Hasn't Jack got a key?'

'Jack's in Greece,' she told him, moving slowly towards the intercom. 'Gone out to visit his father. Hello,' she finished up breathlessly, speaking into the intercom.

'It's me,' announced the reedy voice of Flick. 'If Jack's out, I'd like to come up for a few minutes.'

Chapter Twelve

Katie took her finger off the intercom. 'Flick!' she mouthed, and Dan sprang clumsily into action, swooping up the coffee mug and lunging towards the kitchen, nearly falling over his feet. 'The bedroom, quick!' hissed Katie. 'There's no way out without meeting her on the way up.'

He flew past her in the opposite direction and slammed the bedroom door shut. Katie turned back to the intercom, her stomach churning. She mustn't sound guilty. Why should she? Her brother-in-law was entitled to drop in and see her on a Saturday morning – although the fact he was now lurking in her bedroom did add to the clandestine overtones.

She pressed the intercom. 'Come up if you must,' she said coolly.

This wait was worse than the wait for Dan, as she heard her sister's heels clip-clopping up the concrete steps.

Just in time, she noticed the damp, man-sized towel on the sofa and ran into the bathroom, shoving it into the linen hamper. Then she ran to open the door, seriously out of breath, and stood back to let her sister in. 'Look what the cat sicked up. Where's Dan?' she puffed.

Flick took in her sister's dishevelled state with a delicate feline smile. 'Off meeting an old friend. I gave him a cock and bull story about going straight round to Mum's, but came to see you instead.'

'Should I be honoured?' asked Katie, heart pounding.

'Not particularly.' Flick sashayed into the room, but without her usual confidence. She, too, was dripping wet. A purple shift dress clung to her, as did her hair, snaking down her back in a sleek question mark. She wore her trademark kitten-heeled stilettos and carried a tiny purple lozenge of a shoulder-bag into which she shoved her car keys. Katie felt duty-bound to offer her a clean towel from the airing cupboard.

'I'm fine.' Flick waved the towel aside and sat on the sofa recently vacated by Dan. Katie prayed there wasn't a damp patch exuding the twiggy, earthy, not unpleasant smell of Dan when wet.

'Where's Jack?' asked Flick.

'Out. But you knew that, or you wouldn't be here,' frowned Katie, trying to keep one step ahead. 'You probably even know he's in Greece, so cut the crap and get to the point.'

Flick crossed her legs and twitched her foot. 'Mum might have mentioned Jack was Greece-bound, checking up on the pork-pie rustler.'

'Get on with it.'

'You'll get a kick out of what I've come to tell you.'

'Will I?' Katie glanced at the closed bedroom door. If Dan was behind it, he couldn't help but overhear all this, unless he had too many scruples to eavesdrop and was lying on the bed with a pillow over his ears.

'Don't look so worried,' said Flick, with a brittle laugh. 'I haven't come to tell you Jack's about to be handed his P45. I knew you'd be anxious after our set-to in the garage.'

'Well, I'm not!' snapped Katie, nerves stretched to breaking-point. Flick was playing one of her little games, and she wasn't in the mood. She felt like cutting to the chase herself by admitting she knew Flick's marriage was already in trouble. And why.

Flick twirled her wedding band round a damp-reddened finger. The gold circlet shone dully beneath the whopping Avebury diamond engagement ring. 'I've come to you as a wise older sister for much-needed advice. The problem is, I told Dan I had a few debts that needed clearing, and now he thinks I only married him for his money.'

'Oh, er, blimey,' said Katie, dragging her eyes away from the bedroom door. 'Debts how big exactly?'

'A few grand, same as most people.' Flick waved a regal hand. 'It all crept up on me when I wasn't looking, lenders showering me with credit because I had a half-decent job. They're the ones to really blame, suckering you into a deal they know you can't keep before the ink's even dry on the dotted line.' She smoothed a slightly shaky hand across the sheer material hugging her thighs. 'Even you must have wondered how I managed to pay for clothes like this.'

'I thought that was a perk of being a fashion buyer for a big store. Lots of in-house discounts.'

'You don't think I'd wear Stempson's old rags?' The green eyes flashed contemptuous fire. 'The plebs shop in Stempson's. It's a British institution, too affordable to too many people. My stuff's from ready-to-wear collections straight off the catwalk. This little number, for example, cost over five hundred.'

Katie gasped. 'But even with flash tastes, how did you get into trouble when you earn loads?'

'How much would be loads in your scheme of things?'

The taunting tone made Katie bristle. 'The rumour was, you were clearing around eighty grand a year.'

Flick laughed without humour. 'Just as well I didn't come to you and Jack looking for a loan. Try twenty-five grand. Before tax.'

Katie's eyes widened. She glanced again at the bedroom door. 'So Dan's got you down as a gold-digger. It's all a bit coincidental, you've got to admit, revealing the sorry state of your finances five minutes after the wedding ceremony. Maybe he wouldn't be doubting your motives if you'd come clean earlier.'

'He was so happy, I couldn't bear to burst his bubble. There I was, playing the happy bride-to-be and I had people threatening me from all sides, credit companies putting on the squeeze, a court summons for unpaid council tax. I was in arrears with the flat, too, so that was looking nasty.' She played with her wedding ring again. 'If I'd told Dan before the wedding, he *would* have have seen me as a gold-digger, to say nothing of Phil's reaction. Even if Dan had still loved and trusted me enough to marry me, Phil would've tried to convince him I was a bad financial risk – maybe imposed big financial penalties on Dan for persisting with me. As it was, I had to hurry the wedding along in case Phil took it into his head to run a credit check on me. You never know with that wily old bastard. So I did the most honest thing possible, telling Dan on the wedding day itself.'

'Yeah, when you were home and dry without having signed a pre-nup. More to the point, why are you telling me?'

Flick looked up at her. 'Because you and Dan are alike, straight-as-a-dye muckers. He'd listen if you put in a good word for me. If you told him I do love him, that I didn't just use him for his money.'

'Why the hell would I tell him that?'

'To stop him making the biggest mistake of his life. You could come down to Cloverley for a weekend, find a pretext to take Dan aside and let him pour out his heart. It wouldn't take much prompting. He's itching to diss me to someone who'd be happy to confirm his suspicions. When he's finished slagging me off, you could say it kills you to admit it, but you think I do love him, from what you've observed and so on. He'd trust your judgment. You're not an impartial observer, you hate my guts. But you're also honest. If you thought I did love Dan for himself, you'd want him to know.'

'I'll be honest now. I think you're a scheming, gold-digging slut and I'd tell him he was well out of it.'

'Would you really say it, if you knew it wasn't true? For his sake, more than anything. Why should he have his heart broken and think I've used him, when it isn't true?'

'Of course it's true. Better he has his heart broken

early and soon, so he can move on before you break his spirit as well.'

Flick sat back, a playful smile on her face. For someone asking a favour, Katie detected a less than humble attitude. 'My, my, aren't you a right little judge and jury?' taunted Flick. 'Look, I'll be totally straight with you. Maybe that way you will believe me.'

'Like you were totally straight with me about Steve?'

Flick shrugged. 'I knew you were too happy with Jack to care about the whys and wherefores of Steve. I should have left him in the past where he belongs, I'll admit that much.'

'Good boggling God, that was almost an apology.'

'Listen, I'll crawl over broken glass for your favourite charity if you help me get Dan back.'

'Not a chance!'

'Hear me out. I didn't love Dan at first. I'll admit it, because there's no point in denying it. Someone at work passed me an article in the paper about dear old Phil and the name struck a chord. I saw no harm in checking any connection between Phil and sweet old Dan at the garden centre.'

'Which came up trumps.'

'Yes, it did. I already knew he was caring, gentle, decent-looking. They're all bonuses when you set out to marry for money.'

'So who would you draw the line at – Hannibal Lecter?'

Flick smiled sweetly. 'Hold on to that hate. That's good. If you liked me, Dan would be wary of you singing my praises, so it's fitting I get the one person who really loathes me to put my case. What else have I got to gain by coming here and spilling my guts, humiliating myself like this? If you can convince Dan I love him, this visit will have been worth it.'

Katie snorted her doubt. 'So when did the love thing kick in? Come on, convince me.'

'The wedding night, actually. Nothing to do with sex. You should've seen what he did.' She leant forward, eyes bright. 'Candles everywhere, a little table set for dinner, all in Cloverley's front room. It took so much forethought. I hadn't expected that, not from Dan. He seemed too straightforward for imaginative romantic gestures.'

'How would you know? You rushed into marrying him.'

'Needs must when the devil vomits in your kettle. It shocked me to my marrow, looking across the table that night and feeling responsible for him. That's what happens when you fall in love, isn't it?' She glanced curiously at Katie. 'It's never happened to me before. Do you feel responsible for Jack? Kind of panicked he'll get knocked down crossing the road and you'll never see him again?'

'It's like that at first,' admitted Katie, in spite of herself. 'It's almost like sending a child off to school for the first time, I imagine. Every time Jack went out of my sight at the beginning, I thought he'd be snatched away by an act of God, just because nothing that made me so happy could possibly last. Fate was bound to step in and muck things up.'

Flick nodded vigorously, then her face fell. 'Only it's ten times worse for me, because Dan's turned his back on me. I always planned to marry for money, and if I could get Mr Moneybags to be nicer to me than his point-to-point hounds, that would be a bonus. I've never wanted or expected emotional intimacy, but that's what I got with Dan at Cloverley on our first night together. It hit me like a ten-ton truck that I actually loved this man – and it pissed me off no end, because I knew I had to come clean about my debts. The timing couldn't have been worse.'

Katie glanced surreptitiously at the bedroom door. Now was Dan's chance to burst forth, declare he'd heard every word and interpret it as he saw fit. 'So this is where I come in – acting as go-between?'

'If he gave away his dosh to a cats' home tomorrow, I wouldn't give a toss.'

'Really?' Katie's tone was scathing. 'Tell him that. I hope he calls your bluff.'

'I'm determined to show I can live within my means. My real means, if I was still working at Stempson's.'

'Until, of course, convinced of your love, he insists on buying you the Kohinoor diamond.' Katie's tone dripped acid. She was so busy concentrating, searching for the cracks in this particular story, that she didn't hear the bedroom door open.

It was Flick who glanced up first. 'Dan! What the hell . . . ?' Her wide-eyed gaze flew to Katie. 'You two? My God, you're not, you haven't been . . . ?'

'Of course not!' shouted Katie, guilt making her angry. 'He just came round and I— Hang on a minute.' Because Flick was halfway to the door.

'Flick, wait.' Dan outpaced Katie to the door and followed Flick out to the stairwell.

He caught up with her at the top of the stairs. 'I

heard everything you said and I love you too.' He grabbed her arm.

She shook him off. 'Looks like it, fraternising with her behind my back.'

'We were just talking. You said yourself just now I needed someone to confide in.'

'Not like this, all cosy in her flat, with Jack out of the country.'

'Flick, please.' He reached out again and tried to draw her towards him.

She struggled against him. 'Just get off! I don't want anyt—' Her protests died on a grunt of surprise. No theatrical scream now.

Katie and Dan watched in horror as Flick, almost in slow-motion, lost her balance on the top step of the stairwell and fell backwards.

Katie returned from the hospital coffee machine with acrid drinks for herself, Simon and Tess. Dan refused to drink. He hadn't moved since sinking down into a hard little plastic chair in the relatives' waiting-room.

Tess, grey-faced but stalwart, looked at Dan with concern. 'The X-rays will be back soon. The doctors seemed quite positive.'

'What about the brain scan?' mumbled Dan.

'She's got a thing about falling down those stairs,' observed Simon unnecessarily, shredding the polystyrene from his two previous cups of coffee. Katie couldn't help thinking him surplus to requirements in a crisis. His laconic charm had no channel to run into.

'But I still don't understand,' sighed Tess. 'She

slipped *again* on those stairs? I didn't even know you two were in this neck of the woods, Dan.'

Katie had an unseemly urge to digress selfishly and point out, 'You said it! She slipped *again*. So you admit I didn't push her the first time?' Instead, she kept her cool and threw Dan a worried look. She had no influence over what he might say.

Dan studied his toe-caps for what seemed like an age. 'We popped into Garden Close on our way to visit you, Mrs Gibson. I know we should've said we were coming. We only decided to come up to London on the spur of the moment.'

'Please call me Tess.'

Dan blushed furiously.

Katie looked at the wall-clock. Half-two. Jack was due to land just after six, and probably return to an empty flat. She'd left the front-door key with Mrs Domenica, explaining she didn't know what time she'd be back, and that Jack hadn't brought his own key with him.

Katie couldn't leave the hospital until she knew Flick was safe. She had to stay and offer Tess moral support. But her instinct was to run, get away, never see Flick or Dan again, let them sort out their own problems.

She'd had a lot of time to analyse the morning's events, cooped up in this room with her twitching, bored, worried family, drinking cup after cup of horrible coffee. She'd felt her brain throw switch after switch to illuminate a mystery that her mind kept playing with. She'd reached a startling conclusion about Flick's real reason for calling on her with an outlandish appeal to intervene in her marriage. A conclusion that made more sense than Flick's discovery of true love amid convenient riches.

The door opened and they leapt up as one. The doctor's pleasant smile was a giveaway, noted Katie subliminally. Medics used a range of expressions that were as textbook as their diagnoses. In tragic cases, they didn't smile at relatives and flap the X-ray charts.

'She's lucky, no fractures. She's concussed but conscious, with a badly bruised hip. We'll keep her in overnight.'

'Can we see her?' asked Tess, her blanched knuckles finally releasing their grip on Simon's sleeve.

'She's a bit groggy – can't bear the light and she's high on painkillers, so don't know how much sense she'll make.' He scanned the group. 'Mother and husband have first claims, but only one at a time, so I'll leave it up to her to choose. All right?'

They nodded mutely.

After he'd gone, Katie remained standing. Now was the time to make good her escape. She could sidle out, promising to phone later for an update, leaving husband and mother at the bedside, with Simon in a supportive role.

A nurse wearing a plastic apron crackled into the room. 'Katie Gibson? Your sister wants to see you.'

She stood at the foot of the bed, knowing she was supposed to feel compassion. But even in extremis there was something theatrically beautiful about Flick. Her hair was fanned across the pillow just so, its splayed strands as symmetrical as a six-pointed star. Had someone arranged it like that?

The blinds were drawn in the private room. Katie

should have known that Mrs Dan Avebury would be going private. The green eyes opened gingerly, pupils looking dilated.

Katie approached. 'How are you?' she whispered foolishly.

'Just one question,' croaked Flick. 'What was he doing there?'

Katie wasn't nonplussed. She'd been expecting this question, though not quite so soon. She smiled enigmatically (she hoped), the aggravatingly self-satisfied smile that Flick had perfected over the years. 'What do you think he was doing there?'

Flick's eyes registered confusion and she winced in pain.

Katie's confidence in her private diagnosis grew. 'Don't worry, Dan and I are just friends. Like you said, I'm just the sort he'd turn to for sisterly advice.' She heard herself from a distance, sounding coolly self-assured, never allowing a hint of shame to creep in that she was hiding a sordid secret about herself and Dan. Flick had taught her well.

'You *knew* Dan was at my flat,' she went on, circling the bed. 'After you dropped him off, you drove straight to my place and waited to see if he'd turn up. You'd never fall for that feeble line about him visiting an old friend. That's when I first got suspicious. Things haven't been hunky-dory between you and Dan for the last few weeks. You'd suspect his motives as soon as he wanted to come up to London, because he doesn't get on with his dad or have any close friends. You realised he was coming straight to the horse's mouth for sympathetic, highly prejudiced advice.'

Pacing the room like Poirot poised to unfrock the murderer, Katie paused dramatically and looked searchingly at her sister, whose green eyes gazed back impassively. 'Oh, you had me going there for a bit, that only I could get Dan back onside. But sitting out there in the relatives' room, I've finally worked it out. You knew Dan was listening avidly behind the bedroom door. Oh, it was perfect. The only way you *could* convince him was making sure he overheard you telling a third party. Especially *me*. The more I poured scorn on your declaration of love, the more pathetically sincere you'd sound as you struggled to convince me. Why would Dan doubt you were telling the truth about loving him when you told the truth about less flattering things, like setting out to snare him? All that guff about the wedding night at Cloverley.' Katie's admiration upped a notch to awe.

'Even I briefly entertained the notion you might be human after all, until I had all this time to think about it. You never do anything without an ulterior motive. I feel like giving you a slow hand-clap, but better not. The nurses might think me an unfeeling bitch.'

Katie sat down on the chair next to the bed, almost out of breath with the brilliance of her pinpoint analysis. 'Obviously, hurtling down the stairs wasn't part of the masterplan. Dan was supposed to come flying out of the room, profess undying love, and then have to explain what he was doing at my place. You'd have ended up taking *him* back. The prosecution rests.' Katie folded her arms. 'Have you come up with another load of self-justifying lies while you've been listening to me?'

'Maybe you're right,' said Flick wearily. 'You go

right ahead and think what you want. As long as I've got Dan back, I don't care. Has Mum gone to pieces with worry since they brought me in?'

'No,' admitted Katie, taken aback by Flick's change of direction. 'She's not the type. You know that.' She hesitated. 'But she was worried sick underneath, you could tell.'

'Could you?' Flick gave a ghostly smile. 'That would be a first. Mumsy's so nice, isn't she? Good. Decent. Appropriate.' She licked cracked lips. 'The right face for every occasion. A drawerful of faces.'

Katie leant closer to the bed. Then she simply waited. She knew Flick had something to tell her, something that had nothing to do with Dan or debts or avarice versus true love. Flick was gearing up for another performance, but this time Katie really was her sole audience.

'I broke them up,' said Flick. 'Mum and Dad. After he took me out one day to the park.' She winced in pain and sweat broke out on her brow.

Instinctively, Katie touched her sister's hand, willing her to draw support. This new claim intrigued her. How could Flick have split up their parents? She'd been six when Don left. Was this another story, an airy confection of lies and half-truths, to win the sympathy vote? Or was it just possible that beneath the pain and sweat might lie the real Flick, when the layers were finally peeled away? She could concede her that much by listening to what she had to say. 'Can I pour you some water?' she mumbled.

Flick shook her head slightly. 'Park,' she repeated. 'He took me one Saturday, just me. I was six, so excited. He never took much notice.'

'Of any of us,' conceded Katie sadly.

'You were lying down with tummy ache, Mum in garden with the baby. It was just him and me.'

She paused. Katie pressed her hand.

Flick continued. 'Soon after we got to the park, a woman came along and sat down on our bench. She and Dad got talking, like they'd just met. Then he sent me off for an ice-cream. There was a long queue and it was too hot to stand in it, so I started walking back, and that's when I saw them on the bench, kissing.'

Katie gasped. 'Was it Legs Up To Her Armpits Tanya?'

Flick nodded. 'They didn't see me. I didn't know what to do, so I went back for the ice-cream. When I got back the second time, she was gone and he was acting normal. They must have arranged to meet there.'

'Jesus, how low can you get?' said Katie thoughtfully. 'Him, I mean,' she added hastily.

'I said nothing to Mum or anyone,' murmured Flick. 'Not even when we got home. Not for ages. I didn't know what to make of it. Then, one day, I wanted Mum to show me how to cut cookie shapes out of pastry. She said she was too busy, so I got angry and I told her about the kissing. I wanted *her* to be angry and drop that perpetual bloody mask.'

'Did she?' asked Katie, fascinated.

'Nothing. Just a pat on the head and "You must have imagined it, dear". I knew I hadn't, but even then Mum was an ostrich. She'd rather suffocate with her head in the sand than call a spade a spade.'

'She was trying to protect you,' frowned Katie. 'She was hardly going to chuck pastry round the kitchen and call him a good-for-nothing adulterer in front of an impressionable six year old. Especially not without checking the facts.'

'Oh, she checked. A week later, he left. All their rows must have been behind closed doors, like she talked to Grandad for hours behind closed doors. She took me aside and said I wasn't to worry about what I'd told her. Couldn't have me growing up damaged by guilt, could she? Good old Mum. He made a big fuss of signing my autograph book to show there were no hard feelings. He didn't let on he knew that I'd snitched, and neither did I.' She squeezed Katie's hand with urgent force, crushing the bones. She let go just as suddenly.

'After he went, I'd slip on to the landing when you were asleep, listening to her cry in her room. Imagine if I'd said, "Mum, why were you crying last night?" What would she have said?'

Katie knew straight away. '"Oh no, Flick, that must've been the wind". And she'd have made you feel embarrassed for suggesting loss of emotional control like that.'

'She hides everything. It all goes under the carpet. I've tried it – the drawerful of faces, never letting the guard down. You're the total opposite.' She peered at Katie almost pityingly. 'You and Dan are so easy to control, wearing everything you feel loud and proud on your sleeves.'

'Maybe.' Katie stroked the thin hand almost absently. 'You had nothing to do with him leaving, though. It wasn't because you spilt the beans. *He's* the one who messed things up.'

'You think that worries me?'

'Yes,' said Katie, looking directly at her. 'I think what happened when you were six is the reason you're an actress and a total poser now, not 'cos you copied it off Mum. You were only a little kid, but you dropped a few well-chosen words with devastating consequences, and it made you realise how vulnerable everything is. Anything we build up is just a house of cards to be knocked down again, so, as you say, never let your guard down, stay alert, invent yourself to fit the occasion. But you didn't break up their marriage. He did. And Mum said recently he wanted to stay and make a go of things, but she wouldn't let him. *They* took the decisions. And let's face it, anyone who uses their kid as a pawn in a park assignation with their mistress – well – he has to be a bastard. Excuse me for wearing my heart on my sleeve.'

Flick turned on her pillow to gaze at her. 'Nice speech. Are you going to tell Dan your interesting little theory that I manipulated today's scene at the flat?'

Katie had been thinking about that, too. 'You know I can't. He'd think it was all in my anti-Flick mind. He's sitting out there now, ready to apologise for ever doubting you. The poor sod.'

'You're an arrogant piece of work, Katie. How do you know your theory is right?'

Katie's inner certainty wavered briefly, but she recovered enough to reply calmly, 'Because I know you, Flick. I know how you operate – even more so since this little chat. Just be careful. If you live your life behind a mask, you can't afford to let it slip. The shock of what's behind might be too much for some people.'

Flick gazed at her levelly. 'Fuck off now and send him in to me.'

'In a sec. I have a question.'

Flick sighed. 'I'll allow the one.'

Katie hesitated. This could be her one chance to find out the truth before the old, brittle Flick reasserted herself, or it could be an open invitation for Flick to humiliate her. She decided to go for it.

'Look, tell me straight. Did you make up all that stuff about Steve? Or did you really know him first?'

Flick's gaze held hers for what seemed like an age. Then she crooked her little finger, beckoning Katie down to whisper in her ear.

'It's all true. Sorry.'

A dull sense of inevitability flooded Katie's soul. She straightened up and walked away from the bed without looking back, choosing to be philosophical. At least the cow had apologised. It also convinced her that Flick had been telling the truth about her part in Don's downfall. She'd been afforded a rare glimpse into Flickworld before the gates clanged shut again, guarding its secrets from the outside world. By the time the bruises faded, Flick would be once more immersed in her life of role-play; Dan's loving wife, the world's witty and sophisticated friend. And a sister to approach with extreme caution.

At the door, she took a belated peek over her shoulder. Flick's eyes were shut. She looked as peaceful and beautiful as Ophelia floating down the river. Possibly, every bit as barmy.

Dan, hovering outside the room, gripped Katie's arm. 'How is she?'

'Compos mentis. She'll be up and about in no time.' She squeezed his hand. 'It was an accident, Dan. She doesn't blame you for the fall.'

'God, I love her so much,' he said shakily. 'At least I know she really loves me. But what does she think—?'

'—About you being at the flat? I've told her you came round for a heart-to-heart. She knows you needed a friend and she doesn't hold it against you that you chose me.'

'But you didn't tell her . . . ?'

'No, Dan,' she sighed. 'Our secret is safe with me.'

He looked relieved, grateful, haggard – and uncomfortable about what he had to say next. 'Don't take this amiss, Katie, but we should try and avoid each other for a while. I think we'll go abroad when Flick's up to it. A change of scene – a good, long honeymoon – should kickstart everything again. We could put the last few weeks behind us.'

Kate looked at him, thinking sadly of the excitement she'd detected in his plans to make a home at Cloverley. How long would he stay in sunny exile just to avoid her and reclaim Flick? How long before Flick, living the high life with the means to sustain it, made serious inroads into his inheritance? She had got into debt in the first place spending wildly to maintain an image, ensure the gilded mask never slipped. Now, Katie suspected, there would be no stopping her.

'A long honeymoon is a good idea, Dan. For both of you.'

His face suffused with happiness and relief, he hurried in to see his wife.

*

It wasn't strictly true that she'd keep their secret safe, she admitted to herself, travelling to Heathrow on the tube. She'd made up her mind to tell Jack about her drunken encounter with Dan. She was sick of duplicity and masks.

Flick was wrong. Even Nikki, with her theory about lies and diplomacy, was wrong. Nothing healthy or lasting could grow from a bedrock of deceit, and lies of omission were as deceitful as any others.

She'd decided to go straight to the airport without returning to the flat, arriving with half an hour to kill. Her head ached from the day's drama and her empty stomach heaved at the prospect of drama yet to come. Maybe she wouldn't tell him tonight . . . In fact, it would be daft. He'd just be back from a draining week away. He needed time to unwind before she hit him for six with her confession.

As soon as she saw him coming towards her in that ridiculous Hawaiian shirt, she felt a rush of tenderness that had nothing sisterly about it. Tears filled her eyes. She loved him too much to tell him, and surely lose him.

He ran the last few yards, lifted her up in a bear-hug and spun her round. 'Christ almighty, thank God you're safe. Oh Jesus, I've been in agonies all the way home!'

'Jack, what are you talking about?'

'I rang the flat this morning and got Mrs Domenica, who gave me a garbled message in pidgin English that you'd come a cropper on those bloody stairs and been carted off to hospital. She couldn't be *sure* the medics hadn't covered your face with the blanket.' He clung to her and kissed her hungrily in a very public display of lustful affection. 'Then I rang your mum's, but no one answered. I wanted to ring every hospital in London, but I'd have missed my flight. Seb and Pops were unbelievable, though. Said straight off they were coming back with me. Must've paid a fortune in late-availability tickets.'

'Jack.' She laughed, in spite of everything. 'Hold on. You know what Mrs D's like for making a drama out of a crisis. It was Flick who fell, but I'll fill you in later. Did you say Freddy and Seb are here?'

'Offered to stay at the carousel while I got cracking on emergency phone calls. Forgot my mobile, didn't I? Not that they'd have let me use it on the plane. Christ, I'm gabbling, but I'm just so relieved. When I saw you standing here waiting, it was the sweetest sight I'd ever seen.' He ran his fingers over her face like a blind man committing her to memory. 'I love you so much. I missed you so much!'

Katie blinked, a little overwhelmed by this openly emoting Jack.

'That's enough of that,' said a familiar voice, and Freddy appeared at his son's elbow.

'Freddy!' Katie embraced him, feeling him stiffen briefly with embarrassment, then return the hug with tentative interest.

She stood back to look at him. He was deeply brown, with a fresh network of crow's feet radiating from his watery eyes, resplendent in a turquoise T-shirt and cream chinos – no sign of the dreaded cardigan. 'Don't know how I can look you in the eye,' he grunted. 'Running off the way I did like a scalded cat.'

'That's all behind us now, Pops,' said Jack – a little impatiently, thought Katie – and turned to include a third member of the party. 'Katie, this is Seb, Dad's partner in crime in the sun.'

Katie shook hands shyly with the elderly man wheeling a loaded trolley. Seb was portly, balding, his summery clothes immaculate but too tight, as if he was chasing the summer of a slimmer past that stayed just out of reach. It was clear from his confident handshake and friendly smile that he was more socially skilled than Freddy, but a certain sad something lurked behind his cheerful brown eyes. The love that dared not speak its name, she presumed. Perhaps Seb had lived his whole life suppressing an instinct that his upbringing had convinced him was degenerate. The poor guy.

'Great to meet you at last, m'dear,' he said in ringing tones. 'And in one piece. Always a bonus.'

'I'm sorry you've had a wasted journey,' blushed Katie, feeling irrationally guilty that she'd been the cause of a stressful flight. 'It was really nice of you both to come back with Jack in his apparent hour of need.'

'Especially as I've been a bastard to them,' grimaced Jack. 'I don't want to go into that now. The boys are booked into a hotel, but I said we'd stand them dinner first.'

'Don't be daft,' snorted Seb in his fruity vowels. 'You're dropping with tiredness, dear Jack, and want to be alone with Katie. Freddy and I also need our quality time together.' He glanced at Katie, then laughed. Freddy winked at her.

Jack sighed. 'They both think it's hilarious that I

went rushing off to save Dad from a fate worse than death.'

'I love Freddy,' chortled Seb, linking arms with his old National Service buddy, 'but I couldn't eat a whole one.'

'And Seb's not my type,' added Freddy, with a dash of experimental humour.

Katie grinned at him. 'Abroad's done you a power of good, Freddy.'

'And will continue to do so,' predicted Seb. 'Couldn't run the bar without him. Don't know how I managed without his cocktail-making skills.'

'You can make cocktails, Freddy?' asked Katie in surprise.

He looked bashful. 'Shifty old gambler taught it me, down the lock-in we used to frequent.'

'He's a man of many parts,' said Seb crisply. 'Now, you two be off. We'll get an airport bus to the hotel, but we'll be calling round to Crystal Palace tomorrow, mind, to take you up on that dinner offer.'

'OK, Seb.' Jack shouldered his holdall, hesitated briefly, then clasped Freddy in a swift and untidy hug. They separated and looked off in opposite directions. Katie realised that a fair bit of male bonding had taken place, but Rome wasn't built in a day. She kissed Seb and Freddy goodbye, and followed Jack to the Underground.

'It's good to be back!' Jack bounced into the flat and tossed his holdall on to the sofa. 'So what was this latest drama with Flick? Come on, spill. There was no chance to talk in that crush on the tube.'

'Well, she's out of danger, you know that much.

Hang on.' Katie hurried past him into the kitchen. She reached into the fridge for a half-bottle of extremely flat wine. She'd decided to tell him the Dan stuff after all (God, all this mind-changing was draining every molecule of energy out of her), and finally, utterly, get it over with – whatever *it* was. Her relationship with Jack, probably.

Which was why, first and foremost, she needed a hefty shot of Dutch courage.

'I'm starving,' announced Jack from the doorway, making her whirl round. 'Any chance of a toasted cheese sarnie while I have a quick wash?'

'Yes, of course. I'm hungry, too.' While he whistled in the bathroom, still riding the crest of a wave of relief that she hadn't fallen down the stairs, she got busy rooting around in the bottom of the fridge for spring onions and cheese that wasn't past its sell-by. Every stalling measure was a reprieve – and a fresh prelude to agony. Oh God!

At last she brought the tray of toasties, plus mugs of wine, into the living-room. Jack was reclining on the sofa, relaxed and refreshed-looking. Belatedly, she remembered the mission he'd set out on. 'So how did you find Freddy in the end? Was he intending to fly home with you before you all thought I was a goner?'

He hesitated before replying. 'Freddy's as happy as Larry out there, and Seb seems happy enough to put up with him. You were right all along. He didn't need saving by me.'

'I thought, at the airport, you'd both reached a new understanding.'

'Mmm.' He pushed back a wave of damp hair. Clearly, it wasn't up for discussion. He was back to his old, guarded ways when it came to Freddy. 'Never mind Pops. Tell me what happened with the dastardly Flick.'

'Where do I start?' So she started from the beginning. With Dan's arrival at the flat, followed by Flick's, the accident on the stairs . . . Then her theory of Flick knowing all along that Dan was behind the bedroom door. And finally, Flick's revelation of her key role in exposing Don's adultery.

Jack gave a low whistle when she got to that bit and said unexpectedly, 'Poor, screwed-up kid. Remember what I said when I first met her? That she's not happy, deep down, with who she is. Some people drink to forget. Flick goes out and buys a pair of handmade Italian shoes. And all because your dad screwed around, more or less in front of her, burdening her with the horrible responsibility of having sussed him. Why do people who should know better do things like that?'

'Screw around, you mean?' Katie's hand shook, pouring more wine into her mug. She felt Flick was getting off a bit too lightly for a life of calculated extravagance.

'Maybe there are some things a person's better off not knowing,' he mused, looking at her with an expression in his eyes that made her heart beat fast with fear. 'Flick would have been better off not knowing what your dad was up to – maybe your mum would have, too.'

She recalled her own homily to Flick about the impact of a few words dropped with devastating consequences. An irrational fear sprang to mind as Jack looked straight at her. *He knows about me and*

Dan already! Is he saying he doesn't want me to spell it out? Or is he calling my bluff, to see if I plan to carry on keeping him in the dark?

'What sort of things is it better not to know?' she mumbled, looking back at him with all the courage she could muster. The wine bottle felt greasy with sweat in her hand.

Jack shifted uneasily. Her look seemed to be going right through him, probing for a secret he didn't want to share with anyone, only take out of its hiding-place every now and then to look at, and remind himself that life was full of plot twists; that parents weren't always who they said they were; that glimpsing a stranger kissing your father on a park bench could alter a family's future. 'Not everything has to be dragged out of the shadows and into the light, does it?' he asked tetchily. 'Especially if it makes no difference to anything in the long-run.'

He took the bottle from her nerveless hand before it fell. 'I love you, kiddo,' he said solemnly. 'I had to go all the way to bloody Greece to discover I really loved the old codger, which was a pretty blinding revelation for a cold fish like me. Taking care of Dad and being with you is all that matters to me, but don't ask me to elaborate on my feelings because I'm a two-dimensional bloke, a stuffed shirt. That little outburst at the airport isn't the sign of a new Jack, I'm afraid.' He gave her a wry smile. 'I'm hoping the old Jack is good enough to be getting on with.'

She gulped. He didn't know about her and Dan, but he knew something – enough, by instinct, to want sleeping dogs left to lie out their days in the sun.

And she saw he was right. Not everyone benefited

all the time by the revelation of every petty weakness and mistake. She had long accepted that both she and Jack were entitled to an inner life, sailing their dreamboats and policing their fears in complete privacy.

And was she really so virtuous in wanting to confess all, when he was the one who'd bear the ultimate punishment?

I'm a coward, she thought. Perhaps that means I'm still making excuses, finding false virtue in accepting what I cannot change – my stupid fumble with Dan. But if I am a coward, it's only because I love Jack Gold so much.

'I was hoping you'd say you loved me, too,' he said, to break her continuing silence, his face splitting into its slow, spontaneous smile. 'If you don't say something soon, I'm going to be thinking all sorts.'

'Maybe I should show you instead,' she said softly, and inched her way slowly towards his surprised but receptive mouth.

Taking the initiative in love-making – another first for Katie Gibson. She felt as if she was finally growing up.